BACCANO!

1931 The Grand Punk Railroad: Local

FORTY-SEVEN

RYOHGO NARITA
ILLUSTRATION BY KATSUMI ENAMI

A first-class passenger compartment, embellished with dazzling ornamentation.

In contrast to its elegant décor, the room's atmosphere felt endlessly heavy.

"Death is by no means an equal thing."

A stone-faced group in severe black suits. The man who seemed to be their leader was addressing them with a gravelly voice.

"Life certainly has value. The fact that it has value means, namely, that disparity also exists."

It wasn't clear who the words were directed at. They simply melted into the air

though they precipitated something even darker.

Here, where everything seemed to have stopped, only the vivid scenery that rolled past the train window illuminated the passage of time.

The black suits' eyes held dark enthusiasm, and on every face was eager anticipation for the execution of their operation—all except one: that of a woman with an imposing knife in her hand.

The woman in the black dress made no attempt to meet anyone's eyes. As if all the

suits around her were equally worthless, she gazed only at her own eyes, reflected in the blade she held—sealing fierce, murderous intent into the sharp and gleaming knife as she did so.

Except for her sense of sight, all her nerves were focused on the men around her; her countenance marked her as the group's overseer.

Although they were aware of this, the black suits showed no dissatisfaction.

The men simply continued to wait intently for their leader's words. As if responding to their expectations, the corners of the man's mouth twisted very slightly in a smile.

"There is no need for hesitation or pity. After all, the lives of these passengers were destined to end cheaply. However, in our hands, their value will increase to the greatest possible worth. In the service of necessity, there is no need to show mercy. Put an end to their worthless past—"

As he spoke, the man's calm tone actually held a hint of pleasure.

"—and give them a proud death."

In a relatively luxurious room, Ladd shouted. He was wired.

"Man oh man oh man oh man, I can't wait, can't wait! I'm way looking forward to this, yeah? What am I looking forward to? I'm looking forward to looking forward to it while we wait to do this thing. You fellas feel the same, right?"

That bastard Ladd has really gone off the rails.

Does he seriously think we'll get money this way? The other guys don't have a shred of doubt; there's something wrong with them, too. Everyone in this room is a damn

idiot. ...Including me, since I didn't stop him.

"Hey, Lua. Are you looking forward to it, too?"

As he spoke, he put a hand to the face of the woman in front of him. "Not at all," she said in a very soft voice, turning her eyes demurely toward Ladd.

"Hya-ha-ha-ha! Ha-ha-ha-ha! I see, I see. You're not looking forward to it at all, huh? Well then, let's talk about something fun, all right? All the mugs on this train are gonna die, and then we'll kill all the mugs in New York, and then once we've killed off all the people in this country and in all the other

ountries, let's you and me get married in a hurch in the forest, just the two of us. Then, hile we pledge our love, I'll kill you in style. ou'll be the very last person in the world to et killed by me, and I'll do it big, carefully. eautifully, brutally—and I'll have as much n as possible while I'm at it."

Saying something absolutely psycho, he miled gently at his fiancée.

craziest of the bunch.

Maybe I've known Ladd since we were kids, but still: Why did I sign up for this? All the other guys are carnage addicts, too, same as Ladd.

Without a thought for my nerves, Ladd's eyes sparkled like a little kid's.

"Now then, now then, now-now-now. Let's teach the fat cats in first class and the

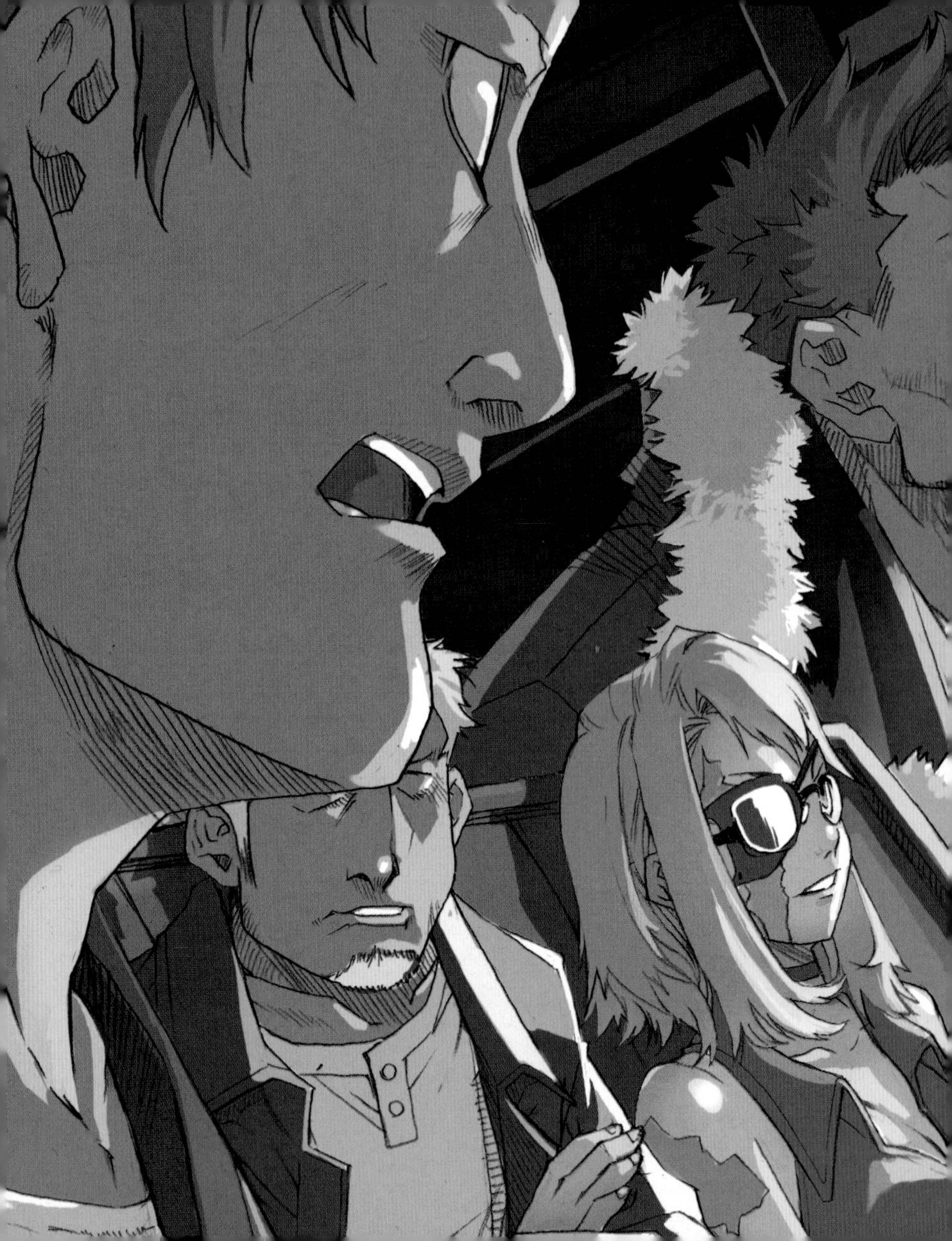

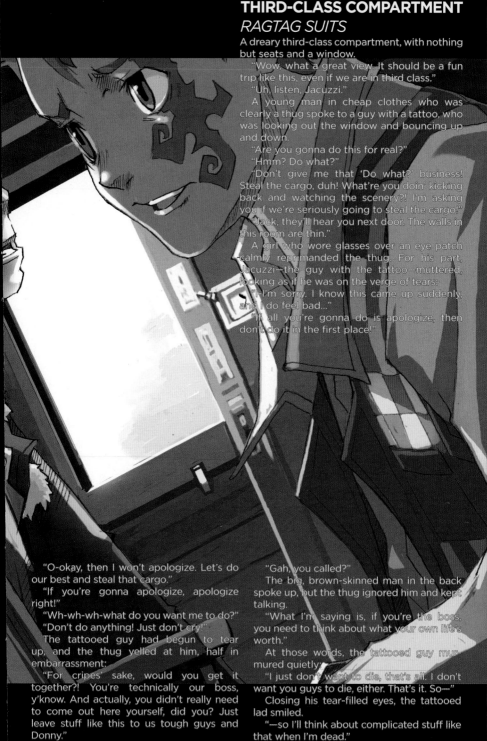

THIRD-CLASS COMPARTMENT
RAGTAG SUITS

A dreary third-class compartment, with nothing but seats and a window.

"Wow, what a great view. It should be a fun trip like this, even if we are in third class."

"Uh, listen, Jacuzzi."

A young man in cheap clothes who was clearly a thug spoke to a guy with a tattoo, who was looking out the window and bouncing up and down.

"Are you gonna do this for real?"

"Hmm? Do what?"

"Don't give me that 'Do what?' business! Steal the cargo, duh! What're you doin' kicking back and watching the scenery?! I'm asking you if we're seriously going to steal the cargo!"

"Jack, they'll hear you next door. The walls in this room are thin."

A girl who wore glasses over an eye patch calmly reprimanded the thug. For his part, Jacuzzi—the guy with the tattoo—muttered, looking as if he was on the verge of tears:

"I-I'm sorry. I know this came up suddenly, and I do feel bad..."

"If all you're gonna do is apologize, then don't do it in the first place!"

"O-okay, then I won't apologize. Let's do our best and steal that cargo."

"If you're gonna apologize, apologize right!"

"Wh-wh-wh-what do you want me to do?"

"Don't do anything! Just don't cry!"

The tattooed guy had begun to tear up, and the thug yelled at him, half in embarrassment:

"For cripes' sake, would you get it together?! You're technically our boss, y'know. And actually, you didn't really need to come out here yourself, did you? Just leave stuff like this to us tough guys and Donny."

"Gah, you called?"

The big, brown-skinned man in the back spoke up, but the thug ignored him and kept talking.

"What I'm saying is, if you're the boss, you need to think about what your own life's worth."

At those words, the tattooed guy murmured quietly:

"I just don't want to die, that's all. I don't want you guys to die, either. That's it. So—"

Closing his tear-filled eyes, the tattooed lad smiled.

"—so I'll think about complicated stuff like that when I'm dead."

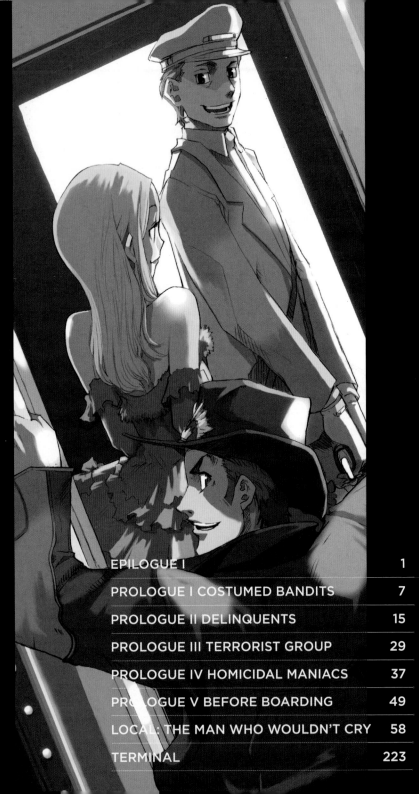

BACCANO!

1931 The Grand Punk Railroad: Local

VOLUME 2

RYOHGO NARITA
ILLUSTRATION BY KATSUMI ENAMI

YEN ON

NEW YORK

BACCANO!, Volume 2: 1931 THE GRAND PUNK RAILROAD: LOCAL
RYOHGO NARITA

Translation by Taylor Engel
Cover art by Katsumi Enami

This book is a work of fiction. Names, characters, places, and incidents
are the product of the author's imagination or are used fictitiously. Any
resemblance to actual events, locales, or persons, living or dead, is coincidental.

BACCANO!, Volume 2
©RYOHGO NARITA 2003
All rights reserved.
Edited by ASCII MEDIA WORKS
First published in Japan in 2003 by KADOKAWA CORPORATION, Tokyo.
English translation rights arranged with KADOKAWA CORPORATION, Tokyo,
through Tuttle-Mori Agency, Inc., Tokyo.

English translation © 2016 by Yen Press, LLC

Yen On
1290 Avenue of the Americas
New York, NY 10104

Visit us at yenpress.com
facebook.com/yenpress
twitter.com/yenpress
yenpress.tumblr.com

First Yen On Edition: August 2016

Yen On is an imprint of Yen Press, LLC.
The Yen On name and logo are trademarks of Yen Press, LLC.

The publisher is not responsible for websites (or their content) that are not owned by the publisher.

Library of Congress Cataloging-in-Publication Data

Names: Narita, Ryōgo, 1980– author. | Enami, Katsumi, illustrator. | Engel, Taylor, translator.
Title: Baccano!. Vol. 2 : the grand punk railroad: local / Ryohgo Narita ; illustration by
    Katsumi Enami ; translation by Taylor Engel.
Other titles: Grand punk railroad: local
Description: First Yen On edition. | New York : Yen On, 2016. | Series: Baccano! ; 2
Identifiers: LCCN 2016013676 | ISBN 9780316270397 (hardback)
Subjects: | CYAC: Science fiction. | Criminals—Fiction. | Railroad trains—Fiction. |
    Nineteen thirties—Fiction. | BISAC: FICTION / Science Fiction / Adventure.
Classification: LCC PZ7.1.N37 Bad 2016 | DDC [Fic]—dc23 LC record available at
    http://lccn.loc.gov/2016013676

ISBNs: 978-0-316-27039-7 (hardcover)
       978-0-316-27040-3 (ebook)

10 9 8 7 6 5 4 3 2 1

RRD-C

Printed in the United States of America

EPILOGUE I

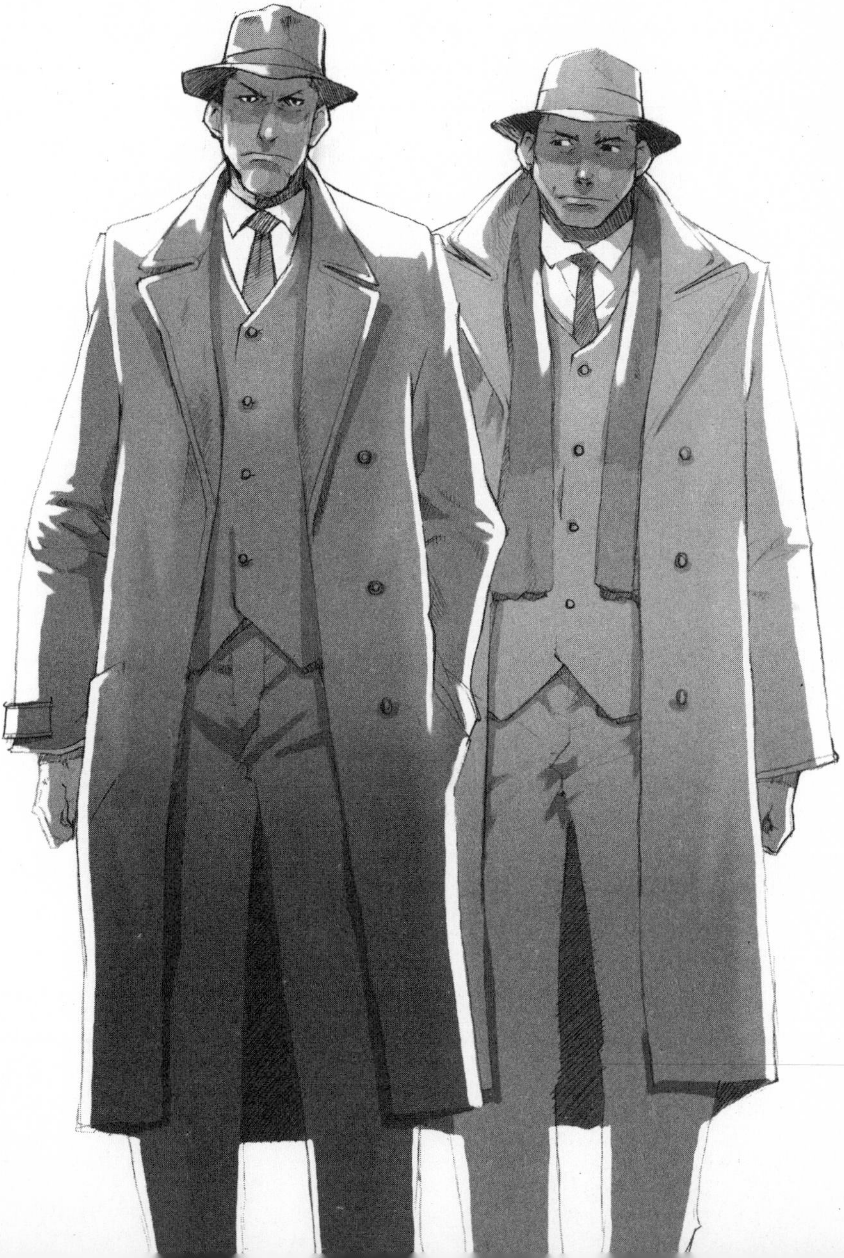

December 31, 1931   Evening

As he gazed at the corpse that lay beside the tracks, a man muttered, sounding as if he couldn't be bothered:

"Aah… If they'd at least left 'em all in one place for us, this would've been easier."

"That's disrespectful."

In the midst of a light snowfall, two men conversed.

Bill Sullivan and Edward Noah: agents employed by the United States Bureau of Investigation. The two men were cleaning up after a certain strange incident that had occurred at the end of the year.

Although it was clean-up work, they were naturally investigating as well. Many police officers were separately carrying out their duties in front of the corpses that lay scattered along the tracks. While they'd used the term *scattered*, the intervals between the remains ranged from several hundred yards to several dozen miles. However, there was no doubt that all the bodies were all from the same incident.

The corpses all seemed to belong to people who had been on the same train.

"Nn… Don't be so stuffy."

"Never mind that. There's something I want to ask you."

Bill scratched his head. Edward, his face serious, put forward his question:

"Why did they summon us here together? This would generally be a job for men from another post, wouldn't it?"

Edward and Bill worked for a rather unique branch within the Bureau of Investigation. Although it wasn't independent as far as structure was concerned, there was a tacit understanding at the Bureau that it held several men who were to be given special jobs intermittantly with their regular work. Bill and Edward were among those who took these special missions.

"Uh... Well, to be frank... *They* were on the passenger list. They spotted it at Chicago Station."

"'They'... You mean immortals?"

Immortals. Here, as they were collecting corpses from the tracks, it was the most unsuitable word imaginable. If the medical examiners working beside them had overheard, it wouldn't have been at all strange for them to bust out laughing.

No, it wasn't just the medical examiners: It would have been normal for any ordinary person to laugh after hearing that. After all, big, important agents were talking, straight-faced, about fairy tales like "immortals."

However, these two knew it wasn't make-believe.

More than two hundred years ago, alchemists who'd crossed to this continent had summoned a demon during their voyage and had managed to acquire indestructible bodies. Stories that clichéd were rare, even among fairy tales, but it was the truth, so there was no help for it. The greatest proof was that their direct superior was one of them.

In other words, they were in charge of monitoring—and guarding—the immortals who were scattered across America. Of course, the existence of immortals wasn't officially acknowledged. Moreover, they absolutely could not *allow* it to be acknowledged.

"Erm... Do you remember the characteristics of immortals?"

"Yes. One: 'They don't age, and no matter how badly their bodies are injured, they will completely regenerate, with a focus on their heads.' Two: 'The single exception occurs when immortals fight to the death. In this case, if one puts his right hand on his opponent's head and wishes to eat them, the other will be absorbed into that right hand and die.' Three: 'The one who absorbed the other is able to make all the other's knowledge his own.' Four: 'Immortals are unable to give false names to each other or to register them publicly.' End list."

"Aah… You don't have to recite the document verbatim like that. Well, so, that means they're forced to give their real names on passenger lists… You see?"

Mildly disgusted, Bill continued speaking. Edward peppered him with even more questions.

"And? What about those immortals? Were they involved in this mess?"

"Nn… Donald's currently checking to see whether they arrived intact. Since detection was delayed, we lost the initiative."

Even as they continued their conversation, another body bag joined the ones behind them.

Seeing this, Edward clenched his fists.

What in the world had happened here?

The *Flying Pussyfoot*, a transcontinental limited express bound for New York via Chicago.

Just what sort of tragedy had transpired on that train…?

PROLOGUE I
COSTUMED BANDITS

December 1931   California

The curtain rose on this crazy ruckus with one dumb sentence from a moron:

"Let's do a train robbery! I hear those pay well!"

Another moron agreed with that moron's moronic remark.

"Wow, that's terrific! We'll be rich!"

In darkness so deep they couldn't even see each other's face, a man and a woman—Isaac Dian and Miria Harvent—were getting all excited over a subject that fell halfway between dangerous and absurd.

Deep in a certain mining gallery in California... The couple who, up until a year ago, had been famous among a (very) select few as "the costumed bandits" stood in front of a rock wall, illuminated by the light of a lantern.

The pair's modus operandi had been to conduct robberies in flashy costumes and then, once they'd fled a certain distance, to change into different costumes and make their escape. Of course, since all the things they'd stolen had been incomprehensible articles like clocks, chocolate, and the doors of a museum, they'd never managed to make the national newspapers.

The job they'd pulled in New York in November of the previous year had been their last one, and they hadn't dirtied their hands with a robbery since. Currently, they spent every day excavating gold, saying, "We'll steal treasure from the earth." They'd arrived too late, more than eighty years after the Gold Rush, and the only work left for them was endlessly swinging pickaxes in an abandoned mine.

One day, more than a year later, Miria—dressed in women's coveralls—spoke:

"By the way, Isaac, people usually take gold from rivers, right? Why are we digging a hole?"

Isaac answered that tragically late question with absolutely zero hesitation.

"Ha-ha-ha, the people around here don't know where to find gold, that's all! Actually, when I tried to pan for gold dust down at the river, some guys bawled me out; something about 'claims' or some such. And I didn't even know them!"

"How humiliating!"

"But! I saw a centipede in front of this abandoned mine! It was a monster of a centipede, too, with hundreds and hundreds of legs!"

"Eeeek, how creepy!"

At Isaac's very specific yell, Miria shivered in spite of herself.

"Heh-heh-heh! Well, you see, Miria, in the Far East, they say centipedes are the gods of gold mines! At that, I was convinced! I knew we'd find tons of gold here!"

"We haven't found any at all, but that's *amazing*!"

Applause from one lone person echoed vainly inside the mine.

"Oh, but, but, if centipedes are gods in the Far East, what do you suppose their crosses look like?"

"Let's see. They probably have a centipede twined around a cross, don't you think?"

"How Catholic!"

They had conversations like this every day, but today, one thing was different.

"Oh, that's right, Isaac! A letter came from Ennis and Firo!"

Smiling innocently in the light from the candle, she took a letter from inside her coveralls.

Ennis and Firo. Friends they'd met in New York a year ago.

Firo was an executive in a small criminal organization, while Ennis was a homunculus who'd been created by a certain alchemist, but Isaac and Miria didn't know a thing about the pair's circumstances.

In addition to this, during the trouble over the "liquor of immortality" that had broken out at the time, these two had also become immortals. However, they didn't have the slightest inkling of the changes that had taken place in their own bodies.

That's right: They weren't human, but immortals, monsters that would ordinarily have traveled back and forth between fear and envy.

That said, either way, they were living happily now, and it was a topic that had absolutely nothing to do with them.

Miria read the letter from Ennis and Firo aloud by the light of the candle.

Most of the content consisted of suggesting that they come to New York City for a visit for the first time in a year.

However, there was a part of Ennis's letter that concerned them.

> **Isaac and Miria, the two of you feel just**
> **like a brother and sister to me. I never**
> **got to meet my real brothers, the ones who**
> **existed before I was made. Thinking of them**
> **makes me very sad, but thanks to you, I'm**
> **able to overcome it—**

As she read that passage, Miria asked Isaac a question, sadly:

"Say, Isaac? Does that mean Ennis's big brothers are already dead...?"

For his part, since Miria suddenly looked as if she was about to cry, Isaac hastily contradicted the idea.

"No, no, no, that's not it, that isn't it, uh... Made...? Never got to meet...? Erm, this is, you see—"

He worried for a bit, but before long, he smacked his hands together.

"Ah, that's it! She means she wants a little brother!"

On hearing this, Miria's expression brightened cheerfully, and she cried out:

"Like when a happy-looking little kid pesters its mommy!"

"Yes, that's the one! I see. So Ennis is happy, then."

"She's happy!"

After satisfying themselves with this for a short while, the two of them noticed a different problem.

"But we're not Ennis's mother, so we can't do anything about it, can we?"

"Hmmm. Well, that's a pity, but let's bring her some sort of incredible souvenir instead!"

At that point, for the first time, the two began discussing plans to head to New York.

However, they currently had one massive problem: a lack of money. Over the past year, they'd been able to sell the blue stones they'd dug up instead of gold for high prices—for some reason—and they'd managed to keep themselves fed that way, but at this point in time, they really didn't have the extra to buy a souvenir.

Then Isaac smacked his hands together in realization again, calling out in a loud voice that echoed through the mine:

"Let's do a train robbery! I hear those pay well!"

"Wow, that's terrific! We'll be rich!"

"By the way, train robberies are when you take the train to your destination, do the robbery, then get on a train and escape, right?"

"That has to be it!"

"All right, then, just like last time, let's steal money from the evildoers in the mafia!"

"Yaaaay, Isaac, you're an ally of justice!"

"Now then, which mafia outfit should we train-rob...?"

Just then, abruptly, the flame of the lamp went out.

Their surroundings were plunged into pitch-black darkness.

"Eeeeeek, scary!"

"Wa-wa-wa-wait, Miria, don't worry! At times like this, you mustn't move around! Just hold still and wait right here until help comes!"

"Wow, Isaac, you're so reliable!"

The next evening... In a mine near where Isaac and Miria had been, men in coveralls were enthusiastically shooting the breeze as they swung pickaxes.

"Say, remember the folks that were digging up the abandoned mine over yonder?"

"Yup, the ones that dug up lapis lazuli sometimes?"

"They took 'em away on stretchers this morning. Suffocation, they said. They were doin' just fine by afternoon, though."

"How 'bout that. They must've found 'em real fast. Normally, they'd be dead."

With no idea that Isaac and Miria were immortal, the miners honestly admired their good luck.

"The guy said something about seeing a centipede with several hundred legs, and that's why they were digging for gold, didn't he?"

"What's all that about?"

"Damn if I know. He spouted off something about eastern religion or some such. They knew so much about the Far East it was weird."

An elderly miner who'd been listening to their conversation from the side jumped in, disbelief in his eyes.

"Y'mean the boss of that mine? The thing that's got several hundred legs?"

"You know about it, Gramps?"

"Do I _know_ about it...? That ain't no centipede. That's a millipede."

By then, Isaac and Miria were on a train.

First, they were headed to Chicago, that mafia hotbed. After they'd done a job there, they'd get on the train and make their escape.

They'd already settled on a getaway train.

A limited express bound for New York: the _Flying Pussyfoot_.

PROLOGUE II
DELINQUENTS

December 29, 1931   The Dead of Night

"No, uh, so, um, um, how do I put this, let's—*you* know, peacefully, let's settle this peacefully, okay? We're, all of us, we're adults, so, all right? Okay? It's fine, we can do it, see? So, so listen, let's just calm down and think about this."

Near a factory on the outskirts of Chicago. There were no streetlamps or neon signs to be seen in this alley, and a hushed darkness had settled in. Here, in a place that silence would normally have suited well, a voice echoed, clearly out of place.

Of course, conversely, when you considered that it was the shrieks and pleas of a man being held at gunpoint, there might have been no more appropriate place for it. In the moonlight, several men with guns—most likely members of an urban mafia family, given their clothes and demeanor—surrounded one young man.

If there was one odd thing, it was the black tattoo in the shape of a sword that was inked on the blubbering lad's face.

"So, so, those guns! Put them dooown! Okay, okay? Please, I'm so scared I think I'm gonna go crazy, I mean it! Please, I'm begging you, only I don't have one red cent on me at the moment, so for now I'll just apologize, so please put down the guns, *put down the guuuuuuns!*"

Meanwhile, the men with said guns looked at each other

dubiously. They all wore dark-colored trench coats, and as they stood, surrounding the crybaby of a young man, they blended into the darkness.

"Hey, are you sure this is the guy?"

"Should be. 'Has a sword tattoo on his face.' It's gotta be him."

"Yeah, but he's completely pathetic. It's really him?"

"Well, let's just ask 'im."

The man who seemed to be the leader of the group grabbed the boy's collar. He'd already started crying anew.

"Hey, cut the waterworks. I'm about to ask you a real easy question. Depending on your answer, we may send you back home to your mommy, safe and sound. You get me?"

"Wah, wah, I-I don't have a mommyyy..."

The next instant, the butt of a gun slammed into the wailer's face, just below his eye.

"Yegyaaah!"

"Nobody asked about your situation! Huhn? What did I just say? I asked you, 'Do you hear what I'm saying,' you rotten little maggot."

The mafioso hauled the boy—who was on the point of falling over—back into place by force, shoved the gun right under his nose, and began speaking slowly.

"—Listen up, you lousy blubberer. If you don't want me to combine your nostrils by drilling a new hole in the top of your skull, say your name, slowly and clearly."

Trembling, the boy nodded vigorously, swallowed his tears, and said his name:

"Hic...hic... Ja-Jacuzzi. Jacuzzi Splot."

On hearing those words, the mafiosi exchanged looks and snickered, their expressions deflated.

"Bwa-ha, you gotta be kidding me... We catch the boss of the scum that's been causing all this grief for the Russo Family, and he's a sniveling coward? Truth is, we were only planning to scope out your hideout today. Then there you were, with a dumb mug that matched your description, out strolling around without guards, see? Kind of a letdown, ain't it? Ha-ha, it's hilarious, right? Right?"

When his laugh, which was almost a sigh, ended, the suit knocked the lad who'd called himself Jacuzzi to the ground.

"Yeah, it ain't funny at all, ya damn brat. What's *with* you, huh? You tore up our turf, so I was wondering what sort of tough guy you were, and this is *it*?"

With veins standing out on his face, the ringleader slammed a kick into the boy.

"T-tore up your turf? We—*hic*—we were just..."

"Just what? You made liquor and sold it without permission, you teamed up and obstructed Russo Family business like it was goin' out of style, and then you robbed businesses under our protection—what about that *ain't* tearing up our turf?"

Jacuzzi had just been enduring the kicks, but he abruptly stopped whimpering and loudly objected.

"Y-y-yes, we're punks, but, but, the first—the first time we sold liquor, *you're* the ones who killed eight of us! And so, and so, we made up our minds to, to fight the Russo Family for all we were worth!"

That tearful accusation seemed to really get under the mafiosi's skins; their faces went bright red, and they clenched their fists.

"To hell with that! Don't think we're gonna let you die easy. We'll take lots of money and time and turn you and all your friends into—"

"Wah, wah...*hic*, never mind that, please, hurry and put down the g-g-guns, i-i-if possible, I don't want to—k-k-kill you."

Jacuzzi's voice clearly interrupted the mafioso's.

"You little runt! Do you understand the situation you're—?"

"No, *no*, NO, I hate it, it's really scary! I hate seeing blood, and hearing bones break really scares meeee!"

Realizing that the conversation was weirdly failing to mesh, the mafiosi quietly stopped the fists they'd raised.

"So, please, Donny, not yet, please wait, wait for them, I'm begging you, please, I know these guys are gonna put down their guns for u-hu-huuus!"

"Donny? Huh? Whozzat?"

The leader stared hard at Jacuzzi's face—— And then he noticed.

The guy's eyes weren't focused on him. They were looking at something *behind* him, over his shoulder.

In the instant the air went tense, he heard it.

Grunch.

The second Jacuzzi heard that sound, he screamed and covered his ears. He was trembling hard.

The leader let go of Jacuzzi, violently sharpening all five of his senses. During the moment it took him to turn around:

His eyes took in his subordinates, who had spotted something and were standing stock-still.

His ears picked up the sound that came on the heels of the unpleasant noise from a moment ago: a sound like something hard being scraped together.

His nose caught the scent and the chill of the freezing air.

His tongue tasted the bitterness and acidity of the gastric juices that were working their way up his throat.

And the instant he'd completed his turn, his arm took a direct hit from the worst pain he'd ever experienced.

"Ghakh... Aaaaaaaaaugh!"

A sudden impact. When he looked at the affected area, giant fingers that seemed several times the size of a normal person's were wrapped around his fist, the one that held his gun. His wrist was twisted at an unnatural angle; the flesh had split in places, and dark red liquid was spurting out in time with his heartbeat. Somehow managing to hold his pain-dazed head together with logic, the leader looked at the *something* in front of him.

It was a giant shadow with the moon at its back.

It was about six feet tall. The huge man, who was cloaked in shadows, had twisted and broken one of the leader's hands with his own right one. Meanwhile, his left hand was high in the air, violently choking the throat of one of the other mafiosi. The big man's grip had warped the man's neck, and his head and body hung, unnaturally limp, from either side.

The moon was directly behind the monster's head, and he couldn't see his expression in the shadows. In the place where his face would ordinarily have been, there was nothing but deep, still darkness.

"Muh, muh, monsteeer!"

His terror was greater than his pain. Desperately, he flung his hand up into the air; its nerves had already shorted out. Without any particular resistance, the big man released his right hand from its restraint.

Set free, the leader took aim at the giant in front of him and attempted to pull the trigger. However, naturally, the muscles in his fingers were in no condition to take orders.

"Wh-wh-wh-what are you doing, men?! Hurry, fill this guy with lead!"

He fired off an order to his subordinates, but nobody moved. Not only that, their eyes weren't even focused on the giant. They were wandering through the surrounding darkness, moving this way and that.

At that point, the poor leader finally noticed them: the many shapes in the darkness around them, picked out by the light of the moon. He and his men stood around Jacuzzi, and their group was surrounded by kids about twenty years old with glaring eyes. Each of them wore clothes that had nothing in common with the others, but the made men immediately realized what they had to be. It was the group of punks they had to wipe out—the foot soldiers of the crybaby in front of them.

On both sides of the alley, in the shadows of the telegraph poles, at the edge of the fence that surrounded the road, they easily numbered more than fifty. They had the area surrounded, and with extraordinary slowness, they were closing in on the criminals.

"What…What are you?!"

When he turned to look at his men a second time, in an attempt to break out of the situation somehow, the leader lost his voice yet again.

What he saw was the faces of his subordinates. They were still standing frozen.

However, two things were different from what they had been a moment ago.

One was that they'd tried to fire at the big man or the surrounding human wall, or at Jacuzzi.

The other was that their eyes were no longer moving, and the life had completely drained from their faces.

Before the leader even had time to blink, his men fell to the ground, one after another. A sharp silver knife towered from the back of each head, dully reflecting the moonlight.

As the leader stared dazedly at the corpses of his men, he realized that several men and women were standing beside him.

"How are you feeling, sir?"

Abruptly, the woman who stood in the center spoke to him. She was young, probably about the same age as Jacuzzi. The woman was distinguished by the large scar on her face and the rough eye patch that covered her right eye. The fact that she wore a pair of glasses over the eye patch made her abnormal appearance all the more striking.

Even though it was winter, she wore clothes that exposed her arms, and both arms had countless scars on them as well.

Struck by the illusion that he'd heard a human voice for the first time in years, the leader—or no, the man who had been a leader, and who had now lost all of his subordinates—gradually regained his presence of mind at the sound of the woman's voice. At the same time, the violent pain in his right wrist returned. In rhythm with his pulse, the heat of the blood and the pain assailed his brain.

"What is this?! What the hell are you people?! When did you get this—?"

He broke off in midsentence. A man who'd been beside the woman had struck him in the cheek with an iron pipe.

"Ah, ah, ga-ga, gwaah!"

"No one inquired about your circumstances! Well? What was it I just said to you? I inquired how you were feeling, you minuscule, putrefied maggot—— Wasn't that it?"

A polite version of the words he'd barked at Jacuzzi a moment ago came right back at him. *Dammit, were these guys here the whole time?! This rotten bitch led me—us—into a trap.* He tried to say the words and cuss her out, but the blood that streamed from his mouth wouldn't let him.

When he looked around, a human wall had formed around him, unnoticed. As they watched the bloody show that was unfolding here, some showed no change of expression, others jeered, and still others looked at him with pity in their eyes. He hadn't managed to grasp the true nature of this group, but one thing was clear:

There was really and truly no escape.

The mafioso had been reduced to a mere thug; his back was against the wall. Remembering the words Jacuzzi had sobbed earlier, he immediately took action.

Shaking the gun free from the mangled right hand that had been wrapped around it, he shouted a plea at Jacuzzi at the top of his lungs.

"I put down the gun! I put down the gun, I swear! I don't have a weapon anymore! Tell your friends not to kill me! Okay?! You don't want to hear bones breaking or see blood, right? So…"

When he'd screamed that much, he realized that Jacuzzi wasn't moving.

With both hands still over his ears, his eyes had rolled back, and he was frothing at the mouth.

"He seems to have fainted. How unfortunate for you."

The woman with the eye patch spoke coolly.

He was completely out of ideas. All that was left was to try to force his way through. On that thought, using his left hand, the mafioso reached for the gun he'd just thrown down—but failed to pick it up. The giant's foot, clad in a thick leather boot, stomped down on his hand, gun and all.

"Dammit, dammit, dammit, dammit, dammit! Little punks like you— Dammit, dammit, dammit, as if we'd let you punks make fools out of us, damn yooooooooou!"

Completely cornered, he dragged his left hand and the gun out from under the boot by force. He felt the pain of skin peeling off, and of divots of flesh being dug out here and there.

Even so, he paid it no attention. He turned the gun on the

weakest-looking part of the human fence: the woman with the eye patch. Entrusting all his remaining chances to the index finger of his left hand, he loaded all his hopes into the bullet.

However, in the end, the bullet was never fired, and his chips ran out right there.

He saw the woman throw something. Something small and round that hissed and smoked.

Then, with an abrupt noise, the thing burst.

"——A bomb?!"

By the time he caught on, it was too late. In terms of force, it wasn't much more than a firecracker with chest hair, but at the roar, he involuntarily covered his eyes.

Through the space between his arms, which dripped with blood, the last thing he saw…was countless silver flashes flying from the men who stood on either side of the woman. The knives reflected the moonlight, and their trajectories were all converging on him. Ahh, how lovely and terrifying and hideous.

It was the most—and the last—emotionally moving thing in his life.

Gazing at the man, whose body had sprouted countless knives, the woman heaved a deep sigh and muttered:

"You should have just begged us for your life directly."

Then, as if she'd lost interest, she turned to look at Jacuzzi, who had been woken up by the giant.

"Wah, *hic*, they're dead, they're all *dead*, and the blood's red, and their faces are white, and it's creepy…"

Ignoring his whimpers about the mafiosi's corpses, the woman directed words of appreciation at her boss. In a complete change from what she'd used with her enemies, her tone was casual and friendly.

"Great work, Jacuzzi. It happened just like you said it would: They walked right into our trap."

"Wah, but, but, but, you didn't have to kill them all!"

"There was no help for it. From where we were, it looked like they were going to kill you any second. Besides, all the survivors said these were the exact same men who killed Kenny and the others. That, and I couldn't forgive them for hitting you."

"Isn't that just a personal grudge...? I'm a little happy, though. Thanks, Nice."

Jacuzzi smiled quietly at the woman he'd called Nice, creating a mood that seemed to ignore the corpses. However, as if he'd remembered, he turned back to the bodies, and tears spilled from his eyes yet again.

"What's the matter? What are you afraid of now?" Nice asked. She sounded worried.

Jacuzzi circled around behind her; he was shaking like a leaf.

"No, it's just, well, I felt sort of like, you know, like the corpses might get up and come to kill me. I-I mean, a little while ago, I read about it in a book. It said corpses get up and drink the blood of the living and kill them..."

"You've got to learn to tell reality from fiction, Jacuzzi. That could never happen."

Just then, suddenly, a roar went up behind them.

"Rrraaaaarrgh... Corpses, get up, drink blood, trouble, scary."

"Oh, you think so, too, Donny? I'm glad it's not just me..."

"Luh, leave it to me."

The big guy he'd called Donny thumped his chest. His brown skin and halting English marked him as an immigrant who'd just come up from Mexico.

"I-I'll, kill 'em, real good."

No sooner had he spoken than the big man's foot stomped down on the pile of bodies. Dull sounds and sharp sounds formed a weird ensemble that echoed across the area. At the impact, the corpses bounded up almost as if they'd been alive, and the knives that had been stuck in them all fell out at once. In time with the impact of the next few stomps, blood geysered out from the holes left by the knives.

"Waaaaaaaaugh! D-Donny, stop it! You've got to treat dead people politely!"

Jacuzzi hastily checked his subordinate. As if trading places with him, Nice walked up to the pile of corpses. Then she took several long, thin cylinders from inside her shirt and began to dress the strings that sprouted from their tips.

"Um, Nice? What are you doing?"

He had a truly awful premonition. The unease was clearly audible in Jacuzzi's question. In response, Nice—smiling—took out a Zippo lighter.

"No, don't tell me, you wouldn't really, would you? Nice. ...Nice? Niiiiiiice!"

Before he could stop her, Nice had set fire to the fuses. They began to spark vigorously.

Gazing raptly at those fireworks, as though they were a lover she hadn't seen in a hundred years, Nice quietly laid the metal shells attached to the other end of those fuses atop the mountain of corpses.

Then, with a smile so pleasant it was startling, she turned to address her companions.

"Now, then. If you don't run fast, you'll be in danger!"

A roar echoed through the alley. Red flares repelled the moonlight, and then the alley was enveloped in a violent flash.

Even after that had died down, smaller lights burned here and there throughout the corridor. Fragments of something that had been sent flying by the exploding dynamite had turned into kindling, and they cast a dim glow over Jacuzzi and the others, who'd taken cover at a distance.

As she got up slowly, Nice comforted the shaking boy.

"There, there, don't cry. You see? The corpses are all in pieces now, so you don't have to worry. They won't be able to come back, so don't cry. I did it for you, Jacuzzi."

As he calmed his rough breathing, the boy glared at Nice with tear-filled eyes.

"Th-th-that's a lie. Y-y-you just wanted to use explosives, didn't you, Nice? You just wanted to see an explosion, right?"

"Actually, yes."

She answered without compunction, giving her very best smile with the only eye she had.

"Nuh, N-N-N-Niiiice, I'm going to hit you later!"

"You couldn't. You never could. You couldn't do anything that barbaric, could you, Jacuzzi?"

"Wah…"

"There, you see?!"

Watching the triumphant Nice out of the corner of his eye, Jacuzzi spoke to the one man who hadn't taken cover during the explosion.

"Then, Donny, you hit her instead."

"Mm, got it. I hit Nice, Jacuzzi happy, then I happy, too."

The brown-skinned giant swung his arms around happily.

"I'm-sorry-I-won't-do-it-again-I'll-never-go-against-you-again-so-forgive-meee!"

Holding her head with both hands, the one-eyed woman ran around among the flames.

As they watched this exchange—which happened once every three days or so—their other companions laughed: "Hee-hya-ha-hee-hee!"

"O-o-okay, guys, let's hurry and, um, get away from here. I mean, we've g-g-g-got to run!" Jacuzzi panicked, his steps unsteady.

Mystified, his friends inquired: "Huh? Why?"

Giving up on fleeing, Jacuzzi ran in place and raised his voice:

"L-l-listen, do you know why I told you not to use g-g-guns today?"

His friends said whatever they wanted: "Wasn't it 'cos you're scared of gunfire, too?" "Because it was a waste of bullets, right?" "Hya-haah!"

Weeping and raging at the same time, Jacuzzi stamped his feet even more furiously.

"Because if we made too much noise, the police or the other Russo Family members would catch on! A-a-a-and you went and detonated a bomb… Hurry, *hurry*, we gotta get out of here! Everybody hurry!"

No sooner had he spoken than he took off into the depths of the alley, running for dear life.

"Ooooooooooohh——"

A general cry of admiration went up.

"Huh! Was *that* why!"

"Jacuzzi's awesome! What a smart guy!"

"That's our boss for ya!"

Praising Jacuzzi, they all took off after what was probably the worst crybaby delinquent boss in Chicago.

Illuminated by the flames, he looked for all the world like a poor little lamb being pursued by a horde of demons.

"B-b-by the way, Nice. About the train tomorrow…Jon says there's only room for about five people in the cheap compartments. So that's me, you, and Donny, and then you pick out two more likely-looking guys."

"Will that be enough?"

"Y-yeah. It's not as if we're going to do anything with the train itself; we're just helping ourselves to the treasure in its freight room, so it would be more unnatural to have a lot of people, wouldn't it? Besides, Fang and Jon will be on board already."

"Okay. Tomorrow afternoon at four o'clock, then, at Chicago Union Station."

After saying good-bye to Nice and the others, who were going to get ready, Jacuzzi felt great unease and anticipation about the following day's plan.

"I wonder if it'll go all right. I wonder if it'll be okay. Still, to think we get to ride the transcontinental limited express, the *Flying Pussyfoot*… I'm already looking forward to that. I haven't seen Fang and Jon in a while, either; I hope they're doing well."

As he looked up at the starry sky, Jacuzzi thought about the friends who'd be on the same train with him, and the plan they'd be forcing through the next evening.

The plan for their first-ever train robbery.

PROLOGUE III
TERRORIST GROUP

December 29, 1931   Noon

In a wasteland a few dozen miles south of Chicago, an abandoned factory stood quietly.

Inside, in one of its larger halls, a group of more than fifty people stood in well-ordered rows. Each of them had an appearance that was completely different from ordinary people, and their bold, cunning eyes produced a tone halfway between the military and the mafia. Surrounded by the ash gray of the floor and the dull gray of the walls, their ranks were enveloped in abnormal silence.

Breaking that silence, one man spoke. He stood in front of the assembled, his sharp gaze holding a dark, quiet flame.

The man—Goose Perkins—delivered a line that was truly popular in that era, the golden age of the mafia—or at least, that would seem so, given the portrayals that would arrive from the movie industry in later years:

"Gentlemen, I regret to inform you——that there is a traitor in our midst."

The silence of the ranks was unbroken. Paying no particular heed to this, Goose loudly continued his speech.

"A short while ago, our great leader, Master Huey Laforet, was apprehended by the government's swine. Our great master is about to be judged by the benighted masses' chaotic law!"

His tone was gradually growing stronger, but there was no change in the dark light in his eyes.

"However, that is an issue of no consequence! Through the maneuver which will be executed tomorrow evening, we will retake Master Huey without fail! The problem lies in the existence of the traitor who has made our master crawl through the land of humiliation!"

Even after he'd said that much, there was no change. Not in the light in Goose's eyes, nor in the expressions of the fifty men who listened attentively.

"I investigated the existence of the traitor personally. However, even so, Master Huey is merciful. It is my intent to emulate him."

Clasping his hands behind him and turning his back on the ranks, Goose asked a question. A quiet, simple question.

"Let me ask the traitor. If he has realized his error, let him take one step forward, without saying a word. If he does not have that courage, know that neither sophistry nor lament will reach me any longer."

At that, for the first time, expressions appeared on the faces of the ranks of men.

The face of one man who had been standing at the head of a line twisted into a smirk, and he took a step forward.

Then, the instant they saw that gesture, every remaining member of the ranks *smirked*, and *all fifty men stepped forward together*.

"Well, Goose? How does it feel to be betrayed by everybody?"

With an ironic smirk, the young man who'd taken the first step drew his gun.

"After you tried to trick us with that painfully obvious bluff, too. My apologies. Still, you couldn't have anticipated this outcome, could you?"

However, Goose was unruffled. The dark glint in his eyes merely writhed, understated.

"Let me ask you one final question, foolish Nader."

Possibly, he'd taken those words as surrender. Nader's face twisted into happiness.

"What might that be, Goose? Just so you know, if it's about how you can be saved, I'll tell you—there's no way."

"So you dislike Master Huey and myself. Very well. However, on what sort of ideals do you intend to base your revolution? How will you bring it about?"

As he posed his question, Goose's expression was solemn. The traitors sneered at him with truly relaxed attitudes. Not even bothering to speak politely anymore, they answered him in tones mixed of pity and scorn.

"Ha-ha, revolution? You're well aware of the answer to that… It's not even possible! Listen, we're not gonna follow either you or Huey. We're going to go sign on with Chicago's Russo Family. With this many of us, all skilled fighters, we just might be able to take over the whole outfit one of these days. Actually, now that the feds have pinched Scarface, we could grab all of Chicago! From now on, the times belong to power, Goose, not ideals! At the very least, I'm more fit to use this group's strength than you, who got booted out of the army, *or* Huey, who's a total enigma."

Giving a faint sigh at that reply, Goose shook his head and told Nader:

"Your answer is one I'd anticipated, but to think you'd try to join the mafia's movement at this late date… What utter foolishness. Capone's fall is an opportunity, you say? On the contrary. It's robbed the Chicago mafia of any opportunities for the time being. Besides, without instructions from Master Huey or myself, do you imagine that greenhorns such as yourselves could last a single day in the shadows of Chicago?"

"…Thanks for the warning. Is that all you had to say?"

"No, there's more. You called my words a bluff, but I wasn't lying."

As he spoke, Goose lightly raised a hand.

"Hmm?"

"I told you, I'd investigated all the traitors. …As well as the friendly members who'd had enough of you."

As he brought his hand down, a ferocious roar rang out. It was the sound of several dozen guns firing at once, and after the roar had repeated several times, silence returned to the factory.

"Wha…?"

When Nader turned around, fearfully, the ash-gray floor had been stained a murky red.

The men at the front of the ranks had acquired ventilation holes here and there on their bodies and lost their lives and were lying in the sea of red.

The thirty or so men who were still standing had smoke-wreathed gun muzzles trained on the stunned Nader.

"Y-you!"

"What did I tell you, Nader? I said, 'There is a traitor in our midst.' However, I meant that *you* had been betrayed."

As Goose spoke, he was expressionless. In contrast, possibly because he hadn't been able to process the sudden turn of events, Nader said nothing, but he was visibly bathed in cold sweat.

"Each of these thirty men brought me reports that you intended to betray us. It seems they were unable to follow you. What a pity."

Maybe because he'd finally managed to get a handle on his situation, with his jaw chattering, Nader suddenly reached into his jacket and pulled out a glossy black handgun.

A sharp, hot pain ran through his right hand.

Thunk.

The piece he'd just pulled fell quietly to the floor. It wasn't until he saw the woman who'd appeared in front of him, unnoticed, that he realized his hand had gone with it, from the wrist down.

"Cha...Chané..."

Chané the Fanatic. The woman, who wore a military uniform, always followed Huey's orders to the letter and was the best assassin in the organization. They said the assassins of Asia paralyzed their senses with drugs; she had paralyzed her entire body with ideas, to the extent that one wondered if she'd forgotten she was a woman, or even a human being.

As Nader fought the pain in his arm, he desperately scanned the woman in front of him.

"I-I thought you were dead. Didn't you die when they caught Huey?!"

Even at Nader's scream, Chané stayed silent from beginning to end. Goose answered the question in her place.

"She lived. She regrets it more than anything. I expect that's precisely why she feels she must remove anything that threatens to obstruct the operation tomorrow evening."

Still silent, without even nodding in agreement, Chané quietly raised her weapon, which was dripping with blood. It was a thick, sharp military knife. The one that had just severed Nader's hand.

"Wait, Chané."

At Goose's voice, they turned; Chané's face looked questioning, while Nader seemed to be clinging to hope.

And then Nader learned: Hope was something he should never have expected in the first place.

"It would be boring to kill him easily."

"You sure about this, Goose? If you settle him like that, he might come back alive."

From the covered bed of a military truck, a subordinate spoke to Goose, who was in the driver's seat.

After the failed coup, Goose had tied Nader up, welded shut all the doors that led to the outside, and left the factory behind him. They'd stopped the bleeding from his wrist, but they'd destroyed all the vehicles except the ones they were using. This meant that, in order for Nader to be saved, he'd have to get out of the factory, then reach a town that lay several dozen miles away.

"That isn't an impossible distance to travel on foot, and it's not as if he doesn't have food."

"That's true. You're right. Right about now, he's probably worn through his ropes by scraping them against a post and is trying to break down an exterior door."

"In that case…"

"By the way, Spike. I trust your sniping skills haven't deteriorated?"

Stopping the truck when they were about three hundred yards from the factory, he interrupted his subordinate with a question.

"Uh…"

"Shoot the white box beside the building entrance."

"…Ah. Roger that, Goose."

Responding with understanding, the man named Spike unfolded a bundle that had been in the back of the truck.

Inside was a jet-black sniper rifle. It had been specially manufactured, and its barrel was longer than normal. Cheerfully, the man set it up in the back of the truck, took careful aim, and—

"Annnd kaboom."

With those anticlimactic words, Spike pulled the trigger.

A few seconds after the shot rang out, they saw the white box beside the entrance burst into flames. After Goose gained visual confirmation, he wordlessly set the truck in motion again.

After another minute had passed, the factory exploded from the inside, shooting ferocious flames and pitch-black smoke into the sky. Seen from a distance, it looked almost like a miniature, but the delayed roar that followed echoed in their stomachs, eloquently telling of the scale of the explosion.

"'I might be saved.' Dying in an instant while harboring that hope is a truly happy thing, wouldn't you say?"

"That's just like you, Goose. How benevolent."

At Spike's ironic comment, Goose smiled, though it didn't reach his eyes. Joining in, the terrorists riding in the truck bed burst out laughing.

All except one: Chané, who was in the passenger seat.

"All right: Tomorrow evening's plan must not fail. Once you've finished your preparations, make for Chicago Union Station."

Goose went over the next day's plan with his group of more than thirty elites.

"This country needs a rest. In order for that to happen, Master Huey is indispensible."

With the dark light in his eyes at maximum brightness, Goose made a quiet declaration:

"To that end, let us make the passengers on the *Flying Pussyfoot* the valuable foundation…under our grave marker, the headstone of the Lemures."

PROLOGUE IV
HOMICIDAL MANIACS

December 30   Afternoon

Today is the worst day of my life.

In a certain mansion in Chicago, Placido Russo, the boss of the
Russo Family, was sure of this.

The first trouble to occur had been that the month's takings—a
vast amount—had been stolen down to the last red cent while they
were being transported.

The criminals had been a man and a woman. Apparently, they'd
been wearing Babe Ruth and Ty Cobb uniforms. Someone had suddenly yelled, "Keee-*rack!*" at the transporters from behind, and
when they turned around, baseball bats had been swung at them.
They'd managed to dodge the first attack but had then been hit in
their faces with fistfuls of pepper and lime. While they writhed in
pain, the bag had been lifted and the getaway made.

Ridiculous. At first he'd thought it was a joke and had tortured the
couriers, but apparently, it had been true.

If that had been all, it wouldn't have been so bad. But after that, a
rumor had come in that one of his executives and several subordinates had been turned into pulverized cinders outside the city.

He hadn't confirmed it yet, but considering that a group had gone
out to that district the previous evening to spy on some delinquents

and hadn't yet returned, it was probably safe to assume that it was fact.

On top of that, the terrorist wannabes who should have joined up with them today hadn't made contact, either. According to his subordinates' reports, all that was left of the factory they'd been using as their hideout was a mountain of rubble and corpses.

It would have been a nuisance to have people making noise about the Russo Family in connection with that conflagration, so he had the majority of his men out dismantling the factory and hiding the bodies.

"Dammit! That lowlife Nader must've messed up. I guess he was just a two-bit punk. Which makes me an idiot to have expected anything from him."

However, the problem was serious. If Nader had sung about his relationship with the Russos, they might find themselves the target of unnecessary malice. After all, the other guys were terrorists. Not only that, but he really couldn't tell what they were thinking.

The gang of delinquents was a nuisance, too. They should have been able to ice the boss and his lieutenants at a stroke and end the whole thing; he'd never imagined they'd get killed by their targets instead.

"For now, I'll start with those weird robbers. Damn them. Starting tomorrow, I'll throttle every blasted couple in this town…!"

"Yeaaaah, I wouldn't, Uncle. Do it, and you'll have people thinking you're a jealous old geezer who can't get a date."

Someone suddenly spoke up from behind. When he hastily turned, his nephew, Ladd Russo, was standing there.

Hair that was neither long nor short, and the dark suit that was standard among the mafia. He was a bit on the tall side, but none of his features particularly stood out. He was a genial-looking young man, and the word *normal* seemed to fit him like a glove. In contrast, the way he spoke was incredibly flippant, and he had no concept of manners.

"Oh, it's you, Ladd. I don't have time to deal with you today. Scram!"

"Hmm? What's this, what's this, what's this? That's pretty cold, ain't it, Uncle? What makes you think you've got that kind of leeway, hmm? It's money, you know, money, *money*, the almighty money that you value right next to your almighty life, and some almighty somebody else took off with it. So this is what you really want to say, ain't it, Uncle? Leave no stone unturned— Nah, burn the jungles to ash if you have to, find the criminals, and choke 'em, choke 'em, choke 'em until they foam at the mouth and keep choking 'em until their eyes pop out and then keep right on choking 'em—"

As his nephew kept talking, his derisive tone never wavered. Placido shouted at him, his face bright red.

"Don't put me on your level, you murdering hedonist! Do you have any idea how much money and manpower I've spent cleaning up the guys you kill for fun?!"

Murdering hedonist. There was really no better way to describe Ladd.

His true nature wasn't his appearance or his words. It lay in the pleasure he sought, and in his greed for it.

He lived purely to kill. What distinguished him from hitmen, who killed for a living, was that he killed for fun.

Even so, Ladd had been kept in the family because he was incredibly skilled at finishing off enemies during disputes. It certainly wasn't his job, but it was true that as a result, he was known as the best killer in the Russo Family.

That's right: He was a crazed, murdering hedonist who lived to follow his desires. Placido was sure of it.

At least he had been, up until this moment.

"Hey, there's no problem. I brought you some good news, Uncle."

"Say your piece. Then get out."

His uncle brushed him off coldly, and Ladd gave an exaggerated shrug. Then he said something far too abrupt.

"See, I hear you've got money problems, Uncle, so I'm gonna go cause a little trouble tonight. If I pull it off, I'll lend you some of mine. My dough."

Because the way he'd phrased it had been unnatural, for a moment,

Placido didn't understand what his nephew was saying. Anticipating this, Ladd kept speaking.

"It's that, that thing—the limited express leaving from Union Station tonight. The *Flying Pussyfoot*, I think it was. The nonstop that goes straight to New York. I'm gonna hijack that a little and run it right into the middle of Manhattan."

At those words, the inside of Placido's head went pure white for a while.

"...And that bit's a bluff. First, I threaten 'em with that, see? Then, if they don't pay up, I turn it into a passenger kidnapping on the spot. Well, then, see, if I kill off about half the passengers, I bet the railway company will probably cough up for me. I get to kill people, I get money... Sounds like a plan, right, Uncle?"

"Get out."

That was all Placido could say. His reason had finally begun to work again. Whether the guy was joking or serious, he couldn't waste any more time on him. Where were the guards, where had the servants gone to?

"Hey, somebody toss this idiot out."

As Placido called for someone, the half-open door slowly opened farther, and several men and a woman came in.

They were all strangers to Placido. Disturbingly, all of them were dressed in white. The men wore white suits or sweaters, and the woman wore a pure-white dress. Their outfits were too much for a wedding; it looked as if they were headed to a costume party.

At that point, for the first time, a trace of impatience appeared in Placido's expression, and an alarm bell began to sound in his head.

Even then, holding onto all the dignity he could muster, he questioned the intruders:

"Who are you?"

However, Ladd was the one who answered the question.

"My men-and-friends who share my hobby. Oh, and the doll's Lua. She's my lover-and-girlfriend-and-fiancée, so treat her nice, Uncle."

"Um......uh, delighted..."

Even the woman's face was white, and she gave a greeting that wasn't a greeting in a scarcely audible voice.

"She's, whaddaya call it, kinda timid? See, though, I'm always wired, and it neutralizes that, so we go round 'n' round 'n' round, see? I guess you'd say we're a good couple?"

"Silence!"

Placido's angry roar echoed through the room. Lua flinched and shrank into herself; Ladd gave an especially exaggerated shrug.

"You come in here and spout complete hogwash— Dammit, what are the guards doing?!"

Placido stood up, striking the desk with his fist as he did so. He grabbed Ladd's collar and hauled him up.

"Listen to me, you blasted lunatic brat! Go right ahead: Kidnap or murder or whatever you want, but you are not allowed to use our outfit's name. Kill however you want and die however you want, but do it as a nameless nobody, a guy who doesn't exist!"

He spit the words at him, loaded with menace, but they seemed to have no effect whatsoever on Ladd; he talked back to his furious patriarch.

"Yeah, yeah. Killing's fun because I do it just for kicks, see? Using the outfit's name would make it boring, Uncle."

"Don't talk as if you know! If you want to kill people so badly, become a mercenary or something and go to the death fields of South America!"

"Isn't that real rude to mercenaries?"

"Shut that filthy mouth! If you go to a battlefield, as long as you don't get killed, you can kill all you want! That's what you want, isn't it?! Satisfy yourself by sneaking around and hiding and imagining the pleasure of killing tough guys!"

At that point, abruptly, the strength went out of Placido's hands. In response, Ladd's own hands went to the arms that had grabbed his collar and caught them firmly about the middle.

It felt as if something were being shoved into the spaces between the old man's muscles. As he felt the strength drain away, in the blink of an eye, his hands had released the collar.

Taking advantage of the opening, Ladd leaned in close to his uncle's face. At a distance where he could feel the breath from his nose, with his eyes opened abnormally wide, he spoke. He just *spoke*, calmly.

"You're the one who's talking like you know, aren't you, Uncle? You don't know a thing about me. Battlefields? Those aren't our *style*. Those are places where warriors gather, *warriors*, warriors! Guys prepared to die in order to kill, guys who fight like they're gonna die because they don't want to die, guys like that, see? Frankly, there's nothing fun about killing those guys. Get me, Uncle?"

Placido was no longer able to object: While he'd rattled on, at some point, Ladd had pulled a rifle out from who knew where and had jammed its muzzle against Placido's jaw.

"Looking for enemies stronger than we are—that ain't how we roll. That doesn't mean we only go after women and kiddies or weak guys, though."

Using the muzzle of the gun to toy with his uncle's jaw, Ladd explained his aesthetics.

"The guys I kill, the guys that are *fun* to kill, are the ones who are completely relaxed. Get me? The type who are somewhere absolutely safe, without the *tiiiiiniest* suspicion they might die in the next second. Guys like that. Like, for example—"

The eyes that watched his uncle changed completely. The cheerfulness that had been in them a moment ago vanished, and he glared at his uncle—contemptuously, pityingly, lovingly—with the sort of eyes that dealt death equally to anyone who met them.

"He…Hey, wait, wait, Ladd. Stop, stop!"

"Yeah, for example—"

The final stop for Ladd's gaze was the tinge of terror that had risen deep inside Placido's eyeballs. When he'd seen that tinge appear, Ladd's face twisted happily, and he began to tighten his trigger finger.

"—guys just like you right now, Uncle."

"For the love of God, *stoooooop*——!"

There was a hollow *click*.

…And that was all.

In the hushed room, only Ladd's quiet laugh echoed briefly.

"Ha-ha, ha-ha-ha, ha-ha! Ha-ha, as if I'd actually kill you. It ain't loaded, Uncle. You've taken real good care of me up till now. Even a murderer like me has *that* much decency. See?"

Ladd's wired mood hadn't changed a bit. Placido's heart had already been completely swallowed up. He fell to his knees on the floor, drawing in deep breaths, over and over.

"Well, we need to hit the road. We probably won't meet again, but take care, Uncle."

As if to declare he had nothing else to say, Ladd spun, turning his back on the man.

"D-don't you ever come back!!"

For Placido, who'd been completely whipped, that parting shot took all his resources. However, Ladd shattered even that hint of pride.

"Nah, I doubt I'd be able to even if I wanted to."

"Eh?"

"See, Uncle, you're, what's-it-called, all washed up. You groused about Luciano's reformers' proposal the other day, remember? And y'know, I bet you're on their hit list now."

Lucky Luciano. He was right up there with Capone as a made man who symbolized the era. He was working to modernize the mafia and was taking steps to get rid of outfits with old ideas. In other words, he was promoting an inventory clearance of guys who talked about things like "duty" and "tradition."

"Wha…?"

"Lucky Luciano's killing hundreds of mafia bosses just because their attitudes are outdated. That's a hell of a lot scarier than a murderer like me. You really don't want to be on that guy's bad side. Right, Uncle?"

At his receding nephew's words, Placido's body was once again dominated by trembling and nausea.

"Th-that's nonsense…"

"Just be real careful not to end up like Salvatore Maranzano, a'right?"

Ladd's warning intentionally invoked the name of a mafioso who'd been killed in New York a few months earlier, while in his own home. It wasn't clear whether it was Ladd's kindness or cruelty talking.

"Well, maybe you feel safe because you've got great guards here, but it sounds like the police and the tax men also have their eye on you after this latest mess. As a 'sacrifice,' see, to take back the town of Chicago from the mafia."

Ridiculous. That's a bluff. It's nothing but nonsense. That was what Placido wanted to think, but at this point, he finally realized something: He hadn't told Ladd a thing about the current mess. And more than that, how did Ladd know he'd quibbled with Luciano's reforms?

Something else occurred to him then. Up until now, the Russo Family had often had to clean up after the kills Ladd had carried out without permission.

However, now that he thought about it, they had all been just within the limits. The number of people Ladd had killed, the places and the circumstances, were all just inside the boundary of what the Family could handle completely.

Then, the moment their ability to deal with the aftermath had evaporated, he did this. It meant, in other words, that Ladd had always intentionally reveled in the pleasures of murder. He hadn't been pushed into action by impulses; he'd been quite cool and calculating.

There had been nothing deliberate about the kidnapping plan from a moment ago. However, at this point, Placido finally managed to understand Ladd's character.

It wasn't that the guy couldn't plan. He just *didn't*.

He was the type of man who always came to action from nothing more than rough ideas, then forced those actions to succeed through on-the-spot calculations made in response to each individual moment.

In fact, he seemed to have put out antennae all through his immediate area and had been actively gathering information.

The result had been today's breakaway. In a word, if he stayed with the organization, he wouldn't be able to relax and enjoy killing. With that determined, he'd summarily abandoned Placido's outfit.

"It's too bad, Uncle. A long time back, even in a sitch like this one, you might've been able to recover, but…"

On his way out, Ladd spoke:

"When I had that rifle on you, you didn't strike back, see. You just screamed. I'd say that disqualifies you as a mafia boss, yeah?"

Fixing him with a look that was completely different from what it had been a moment ago, Placido stopped his retreating nephew.

"W-wait. What happened to the guards?"

"Nn? Oh. Relax. We didn't kill 'em. I said they were good, didn't I? They were ready to die guarding you. Remember what else I said? 'It's boring to kill guys like that.' They're just taking a little nap. They've got a few broken bones, but whatever."

Then he added one final, uncalled-for sentence:

"Lucky you, huh, Uncle? Your sweet lil' grandkid was away at school."

At those words, rage welled up once more, and Placido's face turned bright red again.

"Just get out, *now*! If you're not planning to come back anyway, why did you come here in the first place?!"

"Aaah! Right, I forgot!"

For the first time, anxiety came into Ladd's expression. He directed a brazen question at his uncle, whose fists were shaking.

"Listen, Uncle, that white suit of yours. Could you give me that, to commemorate my marriage to Lua over there? Although I dunno when we're getting married."

Naturally dumbfounded by this, Placido forgot his anger and spoke:

"That's right: Why are you people all in white?"

This dumb question received a dumb answer. The answer was also more than enough to provoke a strong feeling of revulsion in anyone who heard it.

"We're on our way to kill several dozen people in a narrow train, see? If we're in white——the blood will show up better, and it'll look cool."

⟺

"Yeah this, this! The size is perfect. Ain't that great!"

Inside a black double-decker bus that was his personal property, Ladd had dressed himself in formal attire for the coming feast.

As she watched him out of the corner of her eye, Lua asked him a question, sounding puzzled:

"Why didn't you kill that man?"

"Hmm?"

"Normally, you would have killed him, Ladd."

She was talking about Placido, apparently.

"Mm. That's true," he answered easily, humming.

"Why not?"

"You're supposed to let yourself get nice and hungry before a feast, right?"

The sociable murderer responded without a moment's hesitation. Lua lowered her eyes, murmuring quietly:

"You're the worst, Ladd."

"And you like guys who are the worst, don'tcha?"

Without giving an audible answer to that question, Lua nodded silently.

Not bothering to confirm this, Ladd declared the opening of the "feast" to the dozen or so snow-white individuals who were packed into the bus.

"All right, let's go. We'll admire those poor passengers like livestock, we'll despise 'em like maggots, and with love and hatred, we'll crush 'em real, real carefully. Ha-ha, ha-ha-ha!"

The bus sped away.

Toward their last stop and their point of departure: Chicago's Union Station.

PROLOGUE V
BEFORE BOARDING

Ladd's party, uniformly and brilliantly clad in white.

The white group elegantly descended the lobby staircase, which later would be made famous by the baby carriage scene in *The Untouchables*.

From the shadow of a column, a man and woman gazed at their abnormally white costumes.

"Wow, Miria, look at that! It looks like lots of people in white are going to be on the same train we're taking!"

"Pure white for sure!"

"I wonder if they're going to get married on the train."

"Uh-huh, a happy wedding!"

⇔

"We are affiliated with the Chicago Paysage Philharmonic. As the orchestra's instruments are delicate, we request that they be handled with particular care, even in the freight room."

Beside the freight car, a group clad in black tuxedos and dresses was delivering an explanation to a station clerk.

"As a precaution, we will place an orchestra member in the freight car. Thank you for your cooperation."

"Huh? I'm terribly sorry, but that isn't a decision I can make on my own..."

The clerk was at a loss. The man who was negotiating took out a single permit.

"We received permission from the company in advance. If you'd like, you may conduct rigorous physical searches in New York, but..."

"Oh, no, if you've got permission, there won't be any problem, sir."

After exchanging a few more words, the orchestra loaded large crates and parcels one after another. Upon confirming that the contents of the large crates were timpani and horns, the luggage checks also ended safely.

If it hadn't been just before departure, and they'd checked the freight more carefully, or if the clerk had been slightly more competent, they might have noticed.

That the packing material meant to cushion the instruments against impacts included large amounts of ammunition. That all sorts of weapons were hidden beneath false bottoms. That the permit from the company was an outright forgery.

However, even if they'd been suspected, it wouldn't have been a problem. They had many other alternate methods ready.

That was how the Lemures, disguised as an orchestra, managed to carry a vast amount of equipment right onto the train.

"Look, Miria! It's a symphony, an orchestra! Mozart! Paul Dukas!"

"Yes, Beethoven!"

Seeing the black suits loading their instruments in front of a freight car, Isaac's and Miria's spirits soared much higher than was really necessary.

In contrast, one man was looking terribly worried as he watched the proceedings.

"Wh-what'll we do, what'll we do? It sounds like they're putting a guard in the freight room..."

Had their plan fallen through already? Jacuzzi, his face tearful, pleaded with Nice.

"It's fine. It looks as though the cargo we're after is in another compartment."

"B-but…"

"Ruh, relax. I do…something, about guard."

Donny thumped his chest enthusiastically, and Jacuzzi gave a shriek:

"Nuh-nuh-no, no, *no, no*, NO! If you do something about them, they'll *die*, Donny!"

"It's fine, leave to me. Probably."

"'Probably' is not good enough!"

As Jacuzzi panicked more than was really necessary, a light impact ran through his back.

When he gave a small scream and turned around, he saw a boy of about ten who was staggering a bit.

The boy regained his balance almost immediately, looked straight at Jacuzzi's face with its large tattoo, and—

"I-I'm sorry! I wasn't looking where I was going, and I just…"

—apologized, bowing his head slightly.

"Oh, sure, it's fine. It's okay. It's my fault; I shouldn't have been in the middle of the road like this. What about you? Are you okay?"

The young man with the tattoo gave a kind smile, and the kid smiled back at him happily.

"Uh-huh! Thank you, mister!"

With that, he bowed one more time, then ran off toward the entrance to the second-class passenger compartments.

"Aww, how cute! Say, listen, did you see that kid? He was just like Jacuzzi when he was little!"

"Stop, you're making me blush."

"You're still cute now, though, Jacuzzi."

"Eh-heh-heh… Seriously, quit."

As Jacuzzi looked down, embarrassed, Donny got in an uncalled-for verbal jab.

"Aah, Jacuzzi. She say you cute at your age, even though you guy. She making fun of you, right?"

Once again looking as if he was about to burst into tears, Jacuzzi boarded the train, heading for their third-class compartment with his companions.

⇔

At the same time, Ladd's white-clad group boarded a second-class carriage, taking only hand luggage.

"All righty! Second-class compartments are great, yeah? Not at the bottom, not at the top; it's a really half-assed place, and I love it! It's like, gray bats swinging in space, see?"

That said, the second-class carriages on this luxury train were fairly posh in their own right, and on an ordinary train, they would easily have passed as first-class cars.

"I wonder what sort of rich fat cats ride first class in a place like this? Ah, I guess one's that orchestra of black suits, huh… It's pretty nifty how they contrast with our duds. I wonder who else is in there; did anybody see?"

One of Ladd's friends responded:

"I saw a mother and daughter get on a minute ago."

"Nn? You mean a lady and a girl? That don't necessarily mean they're mother and daughter."

"No, I recognized their faces."

"Oh, yeah?"

Possibly out of interest, Ladd stopped and waited for his subordinate to speak.

"I saw them in the papers. I'm pretty sure they were Senator Beriam's wife and daughter."

Senator Beriam. He was a powerful senator who was involved with the anticrime measures that had accompanied the Depression, and who was often mentioned in newspapers and on the radio these days.

Ladd seemed to like that answer enormously: His face twisted into a happy grin.

"Oho. The senator's, hmm? I bet they're really enjoying life. Riding in their first-class compartment... I bet they think they're gonna have a real safe trip."

His eyes were like those of a dog confronted with a feast, and his lips warped further and further.

"Sounds like we've got our first victims all picked out for us, huh?"

Just then, the door at the front of the car rattled open. Ladd's group was standing in the middle of the corridor, and they involuntarily looked that way.

The person standing there was swathed from head to toe in gray cloth.

He wore a gray coat over gray clothes, had a gray cloth wrapped around his head, and a thick muffler covered the lower part of his face, hiding it. His eyes were in the shadow of the cloth, and it wasn't possible to discern their attitude from the front.

Closing the door quietly with hands encased in thin gloves, he walked right past Ladd and the others, who watched him suspiciously.

After the man had exited into the next car, one of Ladd's men spoke, an expression of relief on his face:

"What the hell was *that*, huh?"

"It looked like the kinda magician that shows up in operas and stuff."

Completely ignoring their own clothes, they whispered together about the man, whose costume had been far too eerie.

In the midst of this, only Ladd's heart danced with onrushing expectations and unease for the journey.

"Interesting, man oh man is this *interesting*. An orchestra, a senator's family, and a magician? Great, that's great—it's variation like that that makes fun *fun*. In the end, the source is the same, but there's nothing wrong with having several kinds of sauce, yeah?"

However, Ladd hadn't caught on yet.

To the fact that there were all sorts of other people on this train with him as well.

Or the fact that those sauces included strong poison.

⟺

The Lemures—disguised as an orchestra—had split into groups of ten, with one group each boarding first, second, and third class. Each had been given a wireless radio to hide among their luggage; they would use these to stay in close contact with one another. They were articles created by using unique technology to further modify what was currently the smallest type of wireless.

Their objective was to retake the person who had made those modifications: their great leader, Huey Laforet.

If it was for that, they didn't begrudge their own lives, or the lives of other people.

"Comrade Goose. We've confirmed that Senator Beriam's wife and daughter are on board."

"I see."

As they confirmed reports from their subordinates, Goose and Chané were headed to their own post in a first-class compartment.

Then, just when they'd checked the coupling that linked the freight car with the passenger cars, they realized there was a woman on its other side. She was still young and wore women's trousers and a top reminiscent of a coverall. On seeing her, Goose's first impression was—

That's a functional costume. It's similar to Chané's everyday wear.

—a very pedestrian one.

Just then, abruptly, his eyes met hers.

As if nothing had happened, the woman moved away from the coupling and disappeared into the shadow of the train.

"That woman…"

On seeing her eyes across the coupling, Goose had realized that the woman was not an honest citizen. Shoplifting or pickpocketing, or possibly murder. It had only been for a moment, so he couldn't be sure, but it had seemed as though she'd had the eyes of someone who'd been through a scene of carnage in connection with some crime.

Beside him, Chané seemed to have noticed the same thing: She was staring after the woman with narrowed eyes.

Goose investigated the coupling carefully to make sure it hadn't been tampered with. As a result, he managed to confirm that it had not been.

"Just my imagination, hmm? All for the best, if so…"

At that, Goose also left the scene as though nothing had happened.

Even after that, Chané continued to watch the area around the train. Then, suddenly, a voice addressed her from behind.

"Miss, we'll be departing soon… Did you drop something?"

When she turned, the *Flying Pussyfoot*'s original conductor uniform, whose basic color was white, seemed to jump out at her. A white conductor's uniform, exempted from railway corporation regulations in order to show this train's uniqueness. The young man who wore it was gazing at Chané, looking concerned.

Silently, Chané shook her head. Then, walking quickly, she disappeared into the passenger compartment.

"She was really pretty. Thinking there's someone like her on board makes me suddenly eager to get to work."

Once he'd made sure that Chané had entered the carriage, the young conductor flung his arms up and stretched hugely.

"All right: I guess we're off. Nothing wrong with the train today, either."

Saying something that ran completely counter to the actual situation, the easygoing conductor headed for the last train car...

...with no knowledge of the fate that lay in store for this train just up ahead.

And then the departure bell rang out.

BACC
19
THE GRAND PU

ANO!

31

NK RAILROAD

LOCAL
THE MAN WHO WOULDN'T CRY

One could say that the history of American growth had always coincided with the development of transportation and shipping methods.

The era of westward expansion. Most of the people who crossed the continent had an unquestioning faith in the philosophy of the frontier spirit. The thing that most satisfied the desires of these pioneer-invaders was the development of the railway engine and the completion of the transcontinental railroad.

Even after the frontier era came to an end, railroads continued to constantly evolve. The Great Depression notwithstanding, the 1930s would become the peak of the golden age of railways. This year, the number of people out of work surpassed eight million, and the "Hunger March" mobbed the White House. It was the job of the railways to transport the people who participated in that demonstration, and to carry what little food and products there were. As a result, the glory of this great age of railways would continue until it was replaced by the prosperity of automobiles and airplanes.

All roads led to the rails. These eternal roads, which had been laid everywhere by the frontier spirit, still continued to transport the undying American Dream.

At least, that was what fortunate people believed.

*　　*　　*

The *Flying Pussyfoot*—a train built by a fortunate corporation that had been lucky enough to come through the Depression—could well be called a curiosity.

Its basic build mimicked that of England's Royal Train. All first-class compartment interiors were embellished with marble and similar materials, and the second-class compartments were built in a corresponding fashion.

On a regular train, each carriage would have been divided into first-, second-, and third-class compartments. Ordinarily, the areas over the wheels, where vibrations were the fiercest, were kept for third-class passengers. However, on this train, the cars themselves were first, second, or third class: After the engine came three first-class carriages, then a single dining car, then three second-class carriages, one third-class carriage, three freight cars, and a car with a spare freight room and the conductors' room. This was the internal breakdown of the train. Except for the dining car, all cars had a corridor on the left, according to the direction of travel, and it was possible to check the numbers on the door of each passenger compartment before entering. There was no freight car on this train; instead, there were three cars with spacious freight rooms. As usual, the corridors were on the left.

It was an ostentatious nouveau riche train, one that prioritized design at the expense of functionality. The third-class compartments, which had been built in a perfunctory manner, actually seemed pathetic, and the flattened, sculpture-like ornamentation on the exteriors of each carriage made this even more striking.

The train's greatest distinguishing characteristic was that it was independent from the usual railway corporations' operation. It was run by borrowing the rails from the railway companies and could truly be called a present-day royal train.

Then came December 30, 1931. On this luxurious train, a tragedy unfolded.

⟺

Several hours had passed since the train's departure, and the surroundings were already wrapped in darkness.

"How are you doing, newbie?"

With his back to the landscape outside the window, the middle-aged conductor spoke.

"Oh… Mm. I'm okay."

Giving a slightly delayed response, the young conductor looked up.

Although they'd entered the middle stage of a long journey, it was the first time his more experienced colleague had spoken to him. Thinking this was odd, the young conductor examined the man's face.

Come to think of it, this was the first time he'd taken a good look at his face, period.

The young conductor was a bit appalled by his own lack of interest. The face reflected in his eyes wore a smile that seemed somehow mechanical. It was as though the man was forcing himself to smile; it deeply warped the thin lines that had begun to be etched into his face.

"I see… That's good to hear. Sometimes, if you spend too long watching the receding landscape we see from here, it plants a terrible loneliness and fear in you."

"Oh, yeah, I know what you mean."

"All sorts of terrors lurk in this unease. In the dark or inside tunnels, it's even worse."

"That's right! You're totally right! The other conductors tell scary stories quite a lot, and man, it's gotten so I'm afraid to be alone at night!"

The young man had latched on to the elder's subject, and he began blabbing away about things he hadn't been asked to discuss.

"I tell ya, the other conductors are seriously mean. I keep telling them I'm no good with stories like that, but they say things about bee-men with talons, or how they keep hearing bells from empty passenger compartments…"

For someone who was supposed to be "no good" with such things, his eyes shone very brightly as he spoke. His true colors—his desire to see scary things—showed vividly in his expression.

"And then, let's see… Stories about the Rail Tracer, and stuff."

"Hmm?"

The older conductor had been traveling all around the country for a long time, but apparently he'd never heard the name of that ghost story before.

"Oh, you don't know that one? The story about the Rail Tracer, the 'one who follows the shadow of the rails'?"

To be honest, he wasn't interested, but they were coming up on the "arranged point." It wouldn't hurt to listen.

With a smile as though he were plotting something, and also as though he felt some pity, the older conductor decided to listen to the younger's tale.

"Well, it's a real simple story, you see? It's about this monster that chases trains under the cover of moonless nights."

"A monster?"

"Right. It merges with the darkness and takes lots of different shapes, and little by little, it closes in on the train. It might be a wolf, or mist, or a train exactly like the one you're on, or a big man with no eyes, or tens of thousands of eyeballs… Anyway, it looks like all sorts of things, and it chases after you on the rails."

"What happens if it catches up?"

"That's the thing: At first, nobody notices it's caught up. Gradually, though, everybody realizes that something strange is going on."

"Why?"

"People. They disappear. It starts at the back of the train, little by little, one by one… And finally, *everybody's* gone, and then it's like the train itself never existed."

When he'd heard that much, the old conductor asked a perfectly natural question:

"Then how does the story get passed on?"

It was a question considered absolutely taboo with ghost stories like this one, but the young conductor answered it without turning a hair:

"Well, obviously, it's because some trains have survived."

"How?"

"Wait for it. I'm coming to that. See, there's more to the story."

Looking as if he was having fun, he began to tell the crux of the story:

"If you tell this story on a train, it comes. The Rail Tracer heads straight for that train!"

At that point, the older conductor felt abruptly deflated.

Oh, so it's just a common urban legend. In that case, I'm pretty sure I know what he's going to say next.

That was what the man thought, and in fact, he did hear the words he'd anticipated.

"But there's a way to keep it from coming. Just one!"

"Wait a second. It's time."

Feeling annoyed by his colleague, who was enjoying himself far more than was strictly necessary, the older conductor interrupted him.

It was time for the periodic check-in, so he flipped the switch on the contact transmitter. Then he turned on a lamp that would tell the engineer all was well.

At that, bright light streamed into the conductors' room from both sides.

The tail lamps on either side of the very end of the train made it possible for people by the tracks to tell that the train had passed by.

However, on this train, larger lamps had been specially installed below the tail lamps.

Operating regulations for the *Flying Pussyfoot* stated that the conductors had to periodically contact the engineer. This was so that if the rear car was cut loose and the conductor stopped making contact, for example, the engineer would know that something was wrong.

While it might have been an ostentatious, inefficient system, possibly it was also part of this curious train's special presentation. The conductors followed this system without complaint, lighting the lamps on the end of the train at set times.

…However. For the older conductor, this time held an even more important significance.

After he'd seen the senior conductor turn off the switch, the young conductor cheerfully began his ghost story again.

"Uh, sorry. So, to be saved, you——"

"Oh, wait, hold on. Hearing the answer first would be boring, wouldn't it? I know a similar story; why don't I tell that one first?"

The young conductor happily agreed to the sudden proposal:

"So we'll trade ways to be saved at the end, right? Sure, that sounds like fun."

Looking at the young conductor—whose eyes seemed happy—with a gaze that was half pitying and half scornful, the older man began to speak...

...about his own true identity.

"Well, it's a real common, simple story. It's a story about Lemures... Ghosts who were so terrified of death that they became ghosts while they were still alive."

"Wha? ...Uh-huh..."

"But the ghosts had a great leader. The leader tried to dye the things they feared with their own color, in order to bring them back to life. However, the United States of America was afraid of the dead coming back to life! And, would you believe it, the fools tried to shut the ghosts' leader up inside a grave!"

The content of the conversation didn't really make sense to the less-experienced railman, but anger had gradually begun to fill the face and tone of the speaker. The young conductor felt something race down his spine.

"Uh, um, mister?"

"And so. The remaining ghosts had an idea. They thought they'd take more than a hundred people hostage—including a senator's family—and demand the release of their leader. If the incident were made public, the country would never accept the terrorists' demands. For that reason, the negotiations would be carried out in utter secrecy by a detached force. They wouldn't be given time to make a calm decision. They'd only have until the train reached New York!"

"A senator… You don't mean Senator Beriam, do you? Wait, no, you can't— Do you mean *this* train? Hey, what's going on? Explain yourself!"

Maybe he'd finally realized that something was wrong: The young conductor took a step back, retreating from his senior.

"Explain? But I am explaining, right now. To be honest, I never thought my cover of 'conductor' would prove useful at a time like this. In any case, when this train reaches New York, it will be transformed into a moving fortress for the Lemures! Afterward, using the hostages as a shield, we'll take our leave somewhere along the transcontinental railroad. The police can't possibly watch all the routes at once."

"Wh-who's the leader?"

Asking an awfully coolheaded question, the young conductor took another step backward. However, the train wasn't very big, and at that point, his back bumped into the wall.

"Our great Master Huey will be interviewed by the New York Department of Justice tomorrow. For that very reason, this train was chosen to become a sacrifice for our leader!"

The train was scheduled to arrive at noon the next day. If the negotiations succeeded, they probably planned to put their leader on the train and flee with the hostages.

The young conductor now knew what this man, the one who'd been his senior colleague, really was. As he gazed steadily into the other man's eyes, he asked a question whose answer he already suspected:

"…Why are you telling me this?"

The answer was about what he'd expected.

"Master Huey is merciful. I merely emulate him. Knowing the reason for your death as you die: You're very lucky."

Then, taking a gun from inside his coat, he wrapped up his story:

"Now then, regarding the all-important method of salvation… 'Everyone who heard this story died immediately. There wasn't a single way to be saved'!"

As his story ended, he took aim at the young conductor's nose and fired.

A gunshot.

The sound traveled along the rails, echoing sharply…
Exhaustively…
Across the entirety of the line…

And so the monster awakened.
The monster named…

…the Rail Tracer.

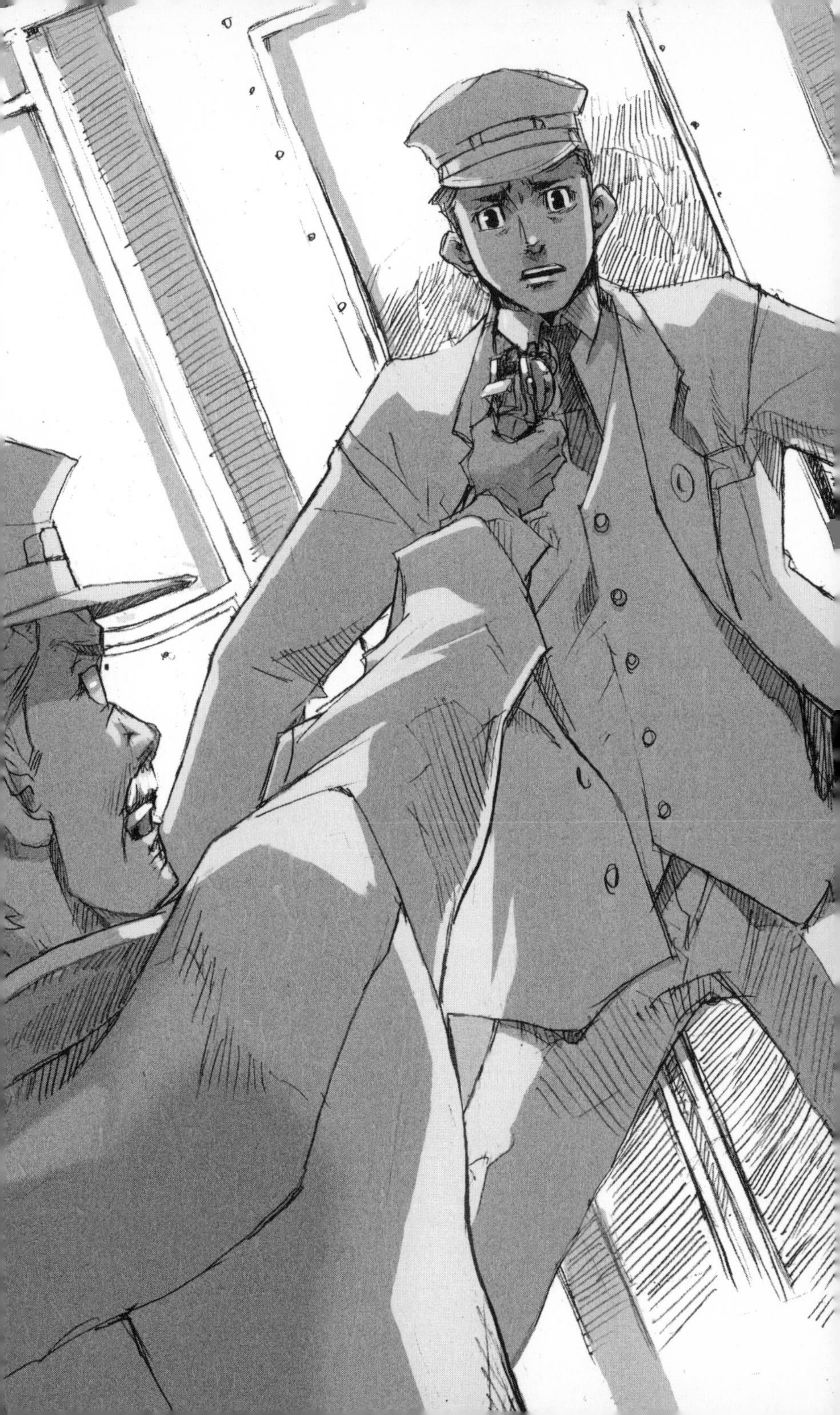

⇐⇒

A short while earlier.

The train had made it to sunset without incident, and people from a variety of passenger compartments were enjoying their dinners in the dining car.

The design motif for the dining car had also been based on the Royal Train, and the calm shades of the woodwork formed an exquisite harmony with the overlay of gold ornamentation.

The dining car was available to anyone, regardless of which compartment they were in, and while passengers from the third-class compartments ate, they too could feel like kings. This was one of the things that made the train popular.

Rows of tables took up half the dining car, while the other half held a kitchen and counter seats. Several cooks bustled around busily in the kitchen, making maximum use of the small space to create rich flavors and fragrances.

All sorts of food—from French dishes and Chinese cuisine to the Creole specialty jambalaya—were lined up on the tables, boldly asserting themselves.

While people were engrossed in the food, there was one group of men who hadn't gotten involved with the meal.

"Look, I'm telling you, this isn't the place for this conversation. You understand, Jacuzzi. We got customers here."

"He's right, Jacuzzi. I know you get it. And actually: Get it."

At a counter seat in the dining car, two men were reproaching Jacuzzi. They were behind the counter; one was dressed as a cook, while the other was dressed as a bartender.

The cook was an Asian man, and the bartender was a young Irish guy. Both were Jacuzzi's friends, and the informants who had turned him on to this freight robbery.

"No, um, I know, I know, I really do know. It's just like you say, Fang and Jon. But listen, it wasn't okay when I came by this evening, either, so I was wondering when we'd be able to talk…"

The Asian man was Fang, and the Irishman's name was Jon. A

duo consisting of a Chinese immigrant and an Irish one. According to the common sense of the day, it was an impossible combination.

Both men were rogues who'd caused trouble in their immigrant communities.

Jacuzzi had indiscriminately adopted people like these as companions, and before he knew it, he'd become the central figure of a gang of delinquents. It wasn't as though he'd wanted to be the boss, but Jon and Fang and his other friends never objected to it. That said, they didn't show him any particular respect, either.

"Well, there's no help for it. There are always customers in here. Plus, there are people who keep ordering Chinese, so I can't get away. If I leave, the kitchen chief's gonna kill me."

As he spoke, Fang heaved a sigh. As if in response, Jon gave a big sigh, too.

"I'm the only bartender here, and as long as there's someone in the counter seats, I can't leave, either. Show some understanding."

"Waaah… Does this train ignore Prohibition entirely?"

"Normally, yeah. We're completely dry today, though. Today's conductor is really strict about laws."

"Then there's no work for a bartender, is there?"

At Jacuzzi's question, Jon shook his head slightly.

"That couple's been ordering nothing but honey green tea for a while now. All they order are nonalcoholic drinks with honey. Just give up."

"Nn. *Those* customers. The ones who've been camped here since right after departure, ordering nothing but Chinese food."

As Fang spoke, he gestured with his jaw toward the end of the counter.

Jacuzzi looked that way. A strange couple was sitting there.

In a word, the man was a Western gunman. He wore an old-fashioned vest and coat, and there were several holsters strapped to his waist and chest. However, not one of them held a gun. He carried a lasso on his back, too, so it was hard to tell whether he was a gunman or a cowboy. On top of that, for some reason, he wore three sheriff's badges.

As if to match the man's costume, the woman was also dressed like someone out of a Western: She looked like a saloon dancing girl from a hundred years ago. Her hair was straight, and she wore a red, Spanish-style dancing costume and a bright-red, broad-brimmed hat.

The two of them suited the atmosphere of their location, but they seemed far removed from the atmosphere of the era. The couple was creating their own unique world at the corner of the counter.

"Or do you want to go run them off for us, Jacuzzi?"

"I-I'm kinda scared. What if they're weird people?!"

"I don't want to hear that from a guy with a tattooed face."

Jon delivered a perfectly natural verbal jab.

"Th-that's so mean…"

As Jacuzzi began showing signs of waterworks, Nice cut into the conversation from behind him.

"Well, don't worry about it, Jacuzzi. Never mind that; why don't you try talking to those two? They look interesting."

"N-Nice, 'they look interesting'? That isn't a real reason."

"They might be movie stars, you know, dressed like that."

At that, Jacuzzi took another good look at the couple in the corner.

"Now that you mention it…"

"You see? It would be kinda cool to be friends with movie stars, wouldn't it?"

Hearing this from her made him feel like trying it, and Jacuzzi timidly approached the couple.

Watching him go, Jon muttered to Nice:

"Nice, don't pick on Jacuzzi too much."

In response, changing her attitude completely from what it had been with her boss, Nice turned back to Jon and Fang with words that were too courteous.

"It isn't like that, Master Jon. I merely wish Jacuzzi to become more sociable."

"Man, you haven't changed at all, Nice," Fang said. "That overly polite speech of yours is still the same, too."

"Then it's as I suspected: Courtesy does not suit my appearance…?"

As she rubbed her eye patch, which was embellished with gold thread, Nice nodded, looking a little embarrassed.

"Uh… No, that's not what I meant."

"Frankly," Jon cut in, "no, it doesn't, but that's also one of your virtues, you know. …To the point where it makes me wonder why you talk so casually to Jacuzzi."

"It's because he says he won't stand for anything but casual speech. He's quite stubborn about such things."

With that, Nice smiled happily, then turned her gaze toward the boy in question, who'd engaged the couple.

The pair behind the bar also glanced at Jacuzzi, then muttered critically:

"Stubborn, huh…?"

When they looked, their leader seemed to be begging the couple for something with tear-filled eyes.

"You meant 'spoiled brat,' right?"

Taking the seat beside the mystery couple, stiff with tension, Jacuzzi spoke:

"Um, uh, erm, g-g-g-good day. Oh, no, I guess it's 'good evening.' Um, I, er, excuse me, I'm sorry."

When he didn't know what to say and it came out incoherent, the man finally seemed to notice him; he stopped the hand he'd been eating with and turned toward the boy.

As he chewed, his mouth working, he stared steadily at Jacuzzi's face, and as soon as he swallowed, he said:

"Miria, what'll I do? A guy I don't know just randomly apologized to me."

At that, from behind him, a woman's perky voice spoke up.

"In terms of winning and losing, I guess you won!"

"I see. A win, huh?! Great! I don't really get it, but that was a good match. Thanks!"

At that, he abruptly took Jacuzzi's hand and shook it firmly.

What'll I do? They really are *weird people.*

Jacuzzi begged Nice and Jon for help with tear-filled eyes. However, Nice only gave him an easygoing wave. Hearing the cook's yell from the kitchen—"Do your jobs, dirtbags!"—Jon and Fang hastily returned to their own tasks.

"Uh, umm..."

"Still, mister, that's really cool! I've never seen anybody with a tattoo on their face before!"

"Yes, talk about culture shock!"

"Could you possibly be a movie star?!"

"That's *amazing*!"

If things were like this, their positions were the complete opposite of what he'd expected. Anxiety began to erode Jacuzzi's thought patterns with breathtaking speed.

"Nuh-nuh-no, I, um, I'm not, I'm, uh, I'm not a movie star or anything, I just make and sell liquor... No, that's not it, I lied, um, erm, it's a lie, it isn't true, I'm just a delinquent, or, um, something, and anyway, I'm just a normal person, I'm sorry, I'm sorry!"

Although there wasn't a single reason for him to apologize, he teared up and bowed repeatedly.

"Hey, Miria. He apologized to me again."

"That's two wins in a row!"

"I see... To think you'd let me win twice. You're a really good guy!"

"Yeep......huh?"

"You're a good person!"

"Come, come, don't cry. When good people cry, it makes *us* cry."

"Yes, it's contagious!"

When Jacuzzi raised his head, there were tears in the eyes of the couple in front of him as well.

As they held a handkerchief out to him, he realized that this had gotten rather strange.

"It's all right, mister. Dry your tears and have some of this Chinese food."

"It's all-you-can-eat!"

From the kitchen, he heard Fang's voice say, "No, it's not!" When Jacuzzi looked bewildered, they just went ahead and shoved food into his mouth.

"Mgrph..."

Carried away by the current of events, in spite of himself, he swallowed.

The taste of the steamed chicken Fang had made spread through his mouth. Come to think of it, this was the first time he'd eaten anything Fang had cooked.

"...It's good."

Before he knew it, he'd stopped crying.

"————And so then I just let him have it. 'Hang it all,' I said!"

"Wow, Isaac, amazing, that's amazing!"

"Ah-ha-ha-ha-ha!"

"Ah! Jacuzzi laughed out loud. I haven't heard that in forever!"

By now, the dining car counter had turned into the site of a miniature banquet.

At some point, Nice had joined the conversation as well, and they were making the atmosphere in the dining car even more cheerful.

Although the night had begun to deepen, the dining car was as crowded as ever. However, there were no members of the black orchestra or the white-suited group to be seen.

"By the way, Mr. Isaac, you haven't ordered anything except meat for a while now."

Speaking with startling frankness, Jacuzzi pointed out that his orders were lopsided.

Nice had never seen Jacuzzi be so fearless around people he'd just met. No doubt he'd taken that much of a shine to the strange couple; the fact that he wasn't afraid showed how much he trusted them.

To think they'd get so far with Jacuzzi in such a short time...

What in the world were these two? Nice felt a little jealous, but more than that, she'd begun to like the couple as well.

"Oh, meat? It's fine, no worries. After all, this is beef."

"Domestic beef!"

"What's that supposed to mean?"

"Well, cows are herbivores, right? That means, if you eat meat from those cows, you're eating both meat and grass!"

"Wow! Isaac, you're really smart!"

"Huh... Really...?"

Ignoring Jacuzzi, who seemed puzzled, Isaac and Miria kept whooping it up in their own little world.

"Right, that's right, if you eat something that ate something, they say you eat that other thing, too. It's not just food, either: If you pick up something that already had something, it all belongs to you! For example, if somebody picks up a bag that has lots of money in it, that person has both the money and the bag!"

"Whee, they're rich!"

"Yes, in the Far East, I believe the law is stated this way! Erm, 'Maybe you did, but—'"

"'—I ate *you!*'"

"Wow. Is that right... 'Maybe you did, but I ate *you*,' huh?"

"That's great, Jacuzzi. You heard something interesting!"

Having learned a rather mistaken tidbit of Eastern knowledge, Jacuzzi happily stuffed his mouth with beef.

A familiar impact ran through his back.

"*Mghk-ghk-gak!*"

Swallowing a piece of beef he hadn't managed to chew thoroughly, he hastily washed it down with some water that had been nearby.

Then, from behind him, a voice that was also familiar flew his way:

"Aah! Mister, again...! I'm really sorry!"

When he turned around, coughing, there was the boy he'd met before boarding. The one thing that was different from earlier was that he had a girl about his age beside him.

"Oh, no, it's okay, it's fine, I'm completely fine. What about you two? Are you all right?"

The boy nodded, smiling just the way he had earlier.

The girl hid behind the boy, gazing timidly at Jacuzzi's tattoo and Nice's rough eye patch.

"Ah-ha-ha. If you're okay, everything's fine. Is that girl your little sister? *Hhrk...*"

His throat still hurt a little, but Jacuzzi forced a smile. Possibly because he'd noticed this, the boy apologized one more time—"I'm sorry"—and then answered Jacuzzi's question.

"Uh-uh, she isn't. She's my friend. I just met her; we're in the same room!"

The girl also nodded at his words, silently. Her eyes were still fixed on Jacuzzi's tattoo. Apparently, to an ordinary kid, Jacuzzi looked a bit scary.

Just then, a woman appeared behind the children.

"Excuse me. I'm afraid my daughter's been rude to you. I do beg your pardon."

She was probably around thirty years old. The clothes the lady wore were expensive without seeming pretentious. Her well-bred speech didn't hold a shred of diffidence or contempt. It only soaked quietly into Jacuzzi and the others' hearts.

Calling her daughter's name, the lady scolded her mildly:

"Mary, you mustn't look at others' faces as if they frighten you."

"Th-that's telling it like it is…"

Because the words had been spoken in a voice like that, Jacuzzi couldn't get mad or cry; all he could do was smile wryly.

"Oh! I beg your pardon; how could I…"

"Oh, no, I, uh, I'm the one who should apologize!"

"Why?"

Failing to hear Jon's reasonable verbal jab, Jacuzzi once again plunged straight into crybaby mode.

"Miria, they're both apologizing. What happens in a case like this?"

"A referee call!"

"I see. So the result of the match depends on us!"

"It's a huge responsibility!"

Isaac and Miria were also saying irresponsible things.

Fed up with watching this, Nice changed the subject, intending to throw them a rope:

"Are you traveling as a family?"

Showing no fear of Nice's eye patch, the lady answered; her expression was mild.

"Yes, my daughter and I are on our way to meet my husband. We're sharing a room with this boy, and we thought we'd go have dinner together, but all the seats seem to be taken."

At that point, a question suddenly struck Nice, and she asked it:

"Is the little boy by himself?"

"Yes, he's—oh, good gracious. I haven't asked his name yet."

Hearing this, the boy gave his name, a bit bashfully.

"My name is Czeslaw Meyer—"

Speaking that hard-to-pronounce name, the boy paused for a moment, then continued:

"—Please call me Czes. I'm on my way to New York to see my family."

Next, the lady and the girl paid their respects as well.

"I'm Natalie Beriam, and this is my daughter... Go on, Mary."

Prompted by her mother, the girl timidly stepped forward.

"I'm Mary Beriam."

She kept glancing at Jacuzzi's and Nice's faces from time to time; they really did seem to bother her. She didn't seem very interested in the Western gunman right beside them.

After that, as the circumstances seemed to call for it, Jacuzzi, Isaac, and the rest also introduced themselves, and the perimeter of the banquet widened to include a bit more of the car.

"Czes, you bumped into Jacuzzi's back a little earlier, too, didn't you?"

Patting Czes's head, Nice smiled cheerfully with her one eye.

"Mister, I'm really sorry."

"No, really, it's fine. You didn't do anything wrong."

As he spoke with Czes, Jacuzzi gained quite a lot of mental leeway... Although it was pitiful that he couldn't manage that sort of leeway with anyone who wasn't a child.

At that point, abruptly, Isaac and Miria spoke loudly:

"That's right. If you'd done something bad, the Rail Tracer would have eaten you already!"

"Chomp! Just like that!"

"—That's how my old man used to threaten me, anyway."

"It frightened you, didn't it!"

"Huh? The R-Rail Tracer? Wh-what's that?"

Maybe because he'd instinctively sensed that it was something scary, Jacuzzi's expression and tone abruptly changed to those of fear.

"What, you don't know about it, Jacuzzi? You see, the Rail Tracer is..."

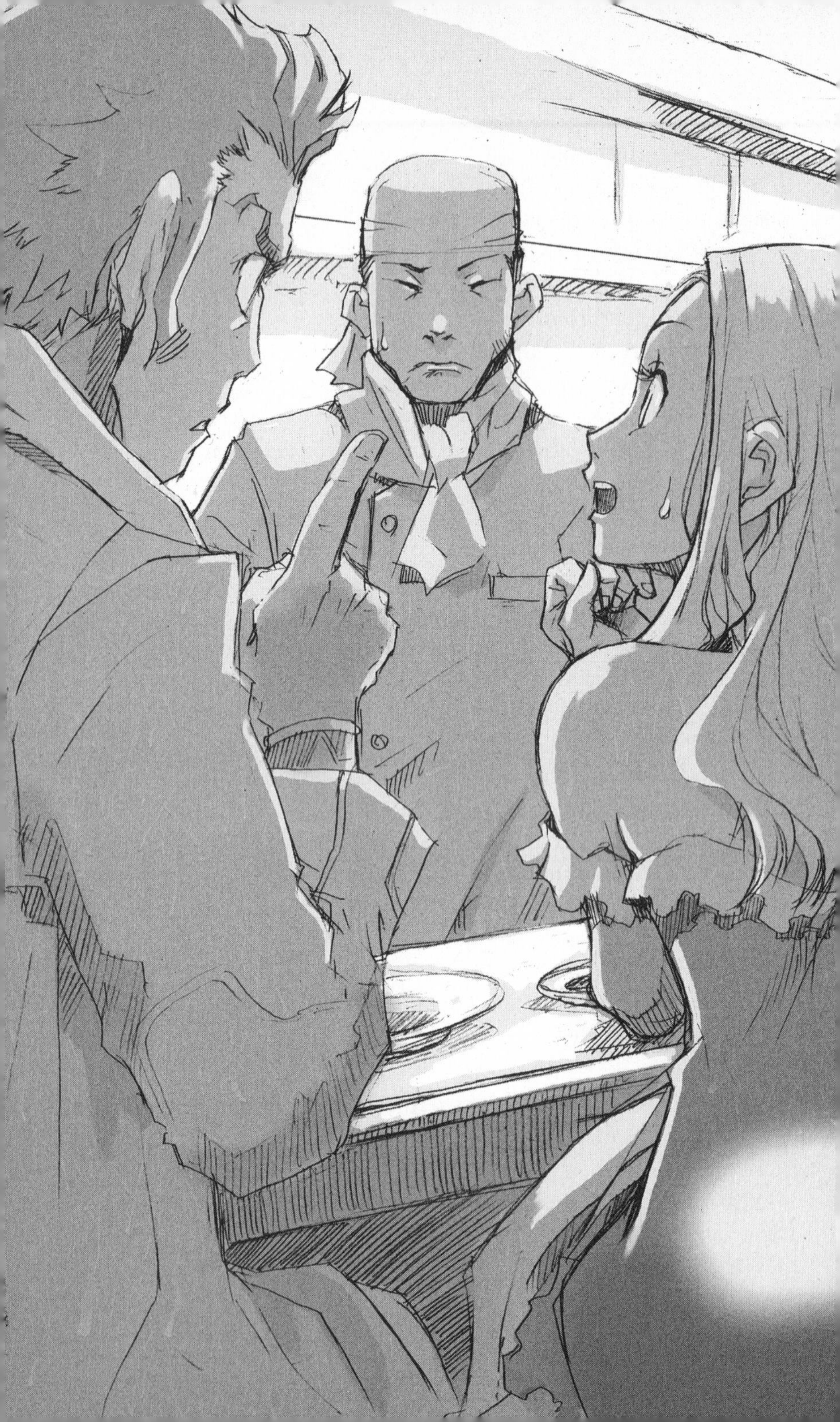

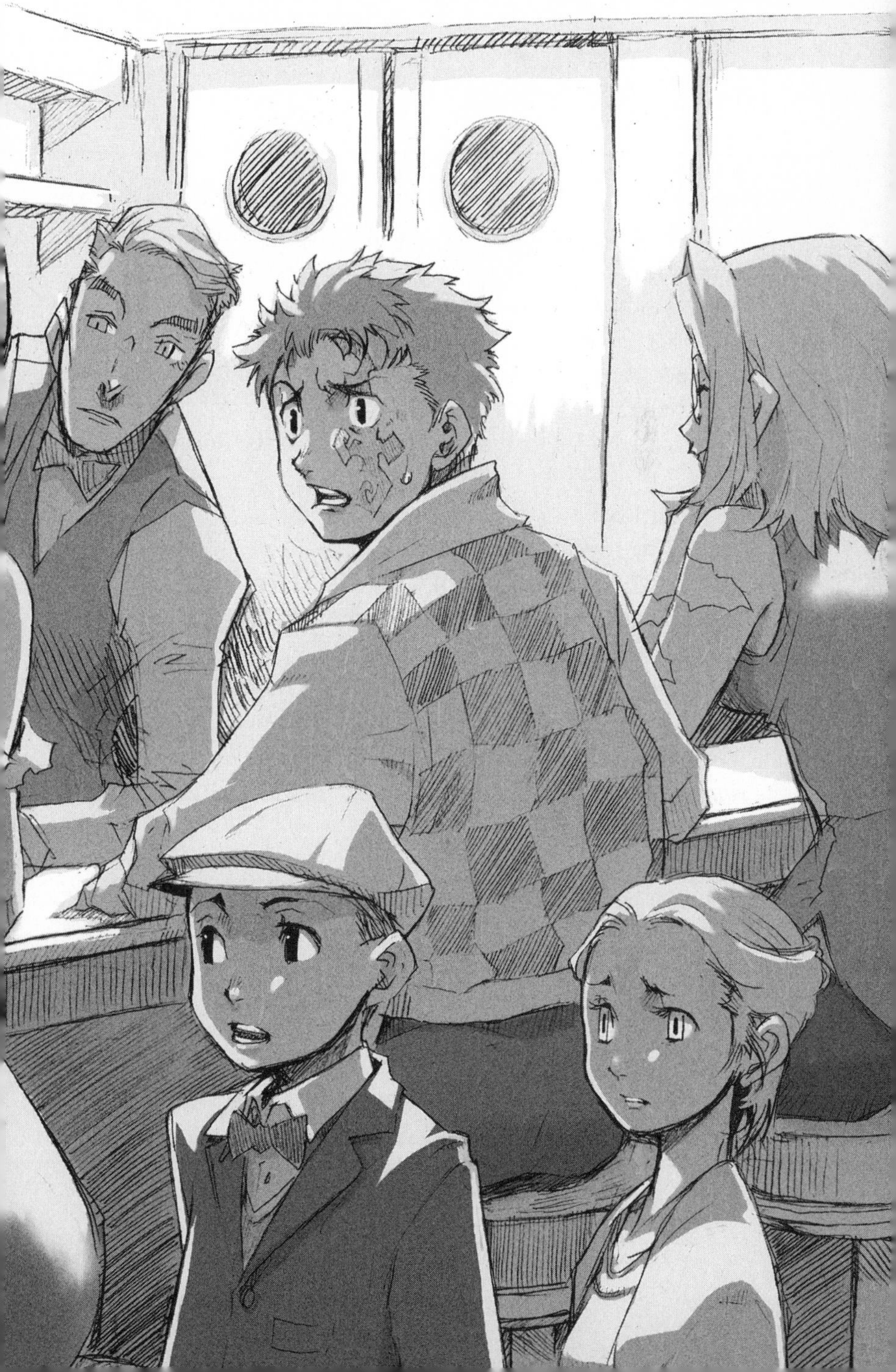

"...And so, if you tell this story on a train...it comes to that train, too. ——The Rail Tracer!"

"Eeeeeeeeeeeeek!"

At Isaac's story, Miria gave a fake-sounding scream.

"~~~~~~!"

Meanwhile, Jacuzzi gave a wordless shriek, while the rest of the group wore expressions that seemed to say, *Yeah, that's a pretty common story.*

"Th-th-th-that's awful! We're gonna disappear! Wh-wh-what do we do?!"

As if advising Jacuzzi—who was actually scared—Isaac slowly began to tell the end of the story.

"Relax, Jacuzzi. There's just one way to keep the Rail Tracer from coming!"

"Yes, only one!"

On hearing this, Jacuzzi's face lit up.

"R-r-really? T-t-tell me what it is! Hurry! Hurry, *hurry*, hurryyy!"

"Sure thing! Listen, in order to be saved, you... Uh, in order to be saved— Hmm. In order to be saved, see..."

Dark clouds began to gather over Jacuzzi's hope.

"In order to be saved... What was it you had to do, Miria?"

"Who knows? I'd never heard that story before, either!"

You mean you chimed in like that when you didn't know the story? Nice and the others quipped silently.

Of course, for Jacuzzi, this was no time for smart remarks.

"N-n-n-noooo! Th-th-th-th-this is terrible! I-i-if you don't hurry up and remember, then—! If you don't, we'll all die, we'll disappear!"

Jacuzzi was trembling in earnest, and his teeth were chattering loudly. In contrast, Jon the bartender muttered in a very calm tone:

"I've heard that story before."

"R-r-r-really? What do we do?! What do we need to do?!"

"Nah, I forget what you're supposed to do, too."

"Whaaaaat?! Don't *do* this to me, Jon!"

"Now, hang on. Calm down, Mr. Customer. I heard it from the

conductor on this train, so just ask him. There are two of them on board; the young one's the one to ask."

No sooner had he heard those words than Jacuzzi clambered down from his chair and took off.

When he'd gone a little distance, Jacuzzi turned around, forced his lips to curve, and yelled to Isaac and the others.

"I-it's okay, Mr. Isaac! I'll hurry and go ask! J-just leave it to me!"

He was probably doing his level best to set everyone at ease, but when said with tear-filled eyes, it had the opposite effect.

That said, besides him, the only ones who believed the Rail Tracer story were Isaac, Miria, and Mary.

Weaving his way between tables, Jacuzzi ran toward the rear of the train. Nice got up from her seat at the counter, intending to go after him.

"Um, please excuse him! He isn't a bad person! He's just a little cowardly…"

As Nice defended her friend and broke into a run, Mrs. Beriam smiled softly.

"Yes, I know. I think Jacuzzi is kinder than anyone else."

Mrs. Beriam had noticed: Jacuzzi truly believed in the Rail Tracer, and he was seriously frightened. Even so, under the circumstances, he'd never once blamed Isaac.

Isaac and Miria had picked up on this, too.

"Say, Miria. Jacuzzi's a really swell guy, isn't he?"

"Yes, really and truly!"

"We'll have to let him win later, too!"

"Yes, we will!"

"Later on, then, I'll apologize to him with everything I've got! Twice or so!"

"Then I'll apologize once, too!"

At that point, smiling, Isaac made a declaration:

"I see! In that case, Jacuzzi wins three times!"

"He's the champion!"

⇔

"Aah, what's wrong, Jacuzzi? Why you panic?"

Right outside the dining car, he'd run into Donny and the others, who were just on their way in. The two friends Nice had chosen and brought along were behind the big, swarthy man.

"Oh, uh, it's terrible! This train might disappear, so I'm going to see the conductor!"

"Aah?"

Saying something incomprehensible, Jacuzzi took off, heading for the back of the train.

A moment later, Nice came running up.

"Ah, excellent timing. Jacuzzi's gone to the conductor's room; I'm on my way to bring him back, and I'll check on the freight room while I'm at it. Donny and Jack, you come with me. Nick, you take care of the dining car!"

Even as they exchanged glances over her words, Donny and the man she'd called Jack ran after Nice.

Meanwhile, the man called Nick had drastically misunderstood.

"What was that, Miz Nice…? What am I supposed to do with the dining car?"

Nice had meant *Keep an eye on people*, but Nick was used to robberies, and unfortunately, he came to an entirely different conclusion.

"Oh. In other words, I bet she wants me to make sure the guys in the dining car stay quiet during the 'job'… Yeah, that's gotta be it. Well, sure. We can't have them spotting us, kicking up a fuss and stopping the train."

While he was thinking, a guy in a white suit went into the dining car. Even as he hesitated, the number of people in the dining car might continue to grow.

On that simple thought, Nick took out his trusty knife.

Then, carefully, he began walking forward.

Toward the target he'd been given: the dining car.

⇔

"Weeeeell now, well now, well now, well now? Our show's about to begin! And their show's about to end!"

In a second-class compartment, Ladd was hugging a pillow and rolling around on the floor.

"Whoops! It's the time we settled on already! *Man*, this is fun, *man*, am I happy! I'm so worked up I bet I won't sleep tonight!"

The man rolled around and around and around and around the small passenger compartment. The others watched him, Lua with a cold expression, his other friends cackling with laughter.

"...If you're looking forward to it so much, you should have gone yourself...," Lua muttered in a scarcely audible voice, to which Ladd was quick to reply:

"Weeeeell, there wasn't any help for it, was there? We drew lots, and I lost! Aah, dammit, that rat Vicky, I'm jealous, jealous, *jealous*!"

Ladd's group's first act had been to gain control over the passengers gathered in the dining car. They'd drawn lots to determine who would go, and as a result, the man named Vicky had been handed a gun.

"Aaah, man oh man. There is no God in this world. I bet Vicky himself killed him a while back!"

As he grumbled, Ladd began to do a headstand in his suit. Lua murmured again, quietly:

"...You could go check on him, you know..."

"That's *it*!"

Springing up from his upside-down position, he smacked Lua's cheeks lightly and frolicked around.

"You're right! I can just go look! I'm an idiot! I don't have to wait around in the room! Since I lost the draw, I thought I'd just have to sit on my hands here! Great, I'll get right over there, then."

After yowling some terribly self-centered things, Ladd leaped right out into the corridor...

...where he crashed into somebody.

"Whoa, watch where you're going, you little bra—"

As he was on the point of bawling him out, Ladd stopped.

"Aaaaah, aah, I-I-I'm sorry! Excuse me! The train's in trouble! S-s-so, um, I have to hurry and get to the conductors' room...um... A-a-a-anyway, I'm sorry!"

The young man dashed off toward the rear of the train.

"That guy... Wasn't that...?"

There was no way he could have mistaken that tattoo on his face. It was the kid from the wanted poster his uncle had handed around a few days earlier.

"Hmm? What's that about? Hey! Lua!"

Sticking his head into the passenger compartment, he recruited his beloved for a small job.

"Could you take somebody and go see what's up in the conductors' room for a sec? If a kid with a tattooed face is in there, grab him for me."

Lua nodded silently, then took one of their companions and started for the rear of the train.

"Mm, is this getting interesting? I hope it gets more interesting. Actually, I need to *make* it interesting."

Lips curving up happily, he headed for the dining car, not taking a single gun. On the way, he passed a woman with an eye patch and glasses and a big man who was over six feet tall. They were running, with tense expressions on their faces, and they swiftly passed Lua and her companion, who were just strolling along.

"What's this? Something pretty interesting is going down on this train, huh? That trouble the tattooed kid was talking about... I wonder what that was... Man, this ain't good. I'm getting way too worked up here. If I don't cut loose soon, I'm gonna explode."

He walked slowly, slowly, humming as he went.

Toward the dining car, where a horrific show was sure to have begun.

⇔

"Comrade Goose, all preparations are complete. The Beriams are in the dining car."

In the first-class compartment where the black suits were gathered, Goose took a report from a subordinate in the middle of the room. At present, only three members each were left in second class, third class, and the freight room; all the rest were assembled here.

"Time, is it? All right. According to plan, split up into teams of three and begin your work. I will be waiting here. Report in every hour without fail. Those who do not will be presumed dead."

His expression was completely closed, and he continued to issue orders mechanically, to the point where one wondered whether the muscles in his mouth were the only ones he was using.

"The appointed time is here. At this point, the 'conductor' should be making his move. Now, no matter what happens in the rear cars, the train will not stop. Spike, use the wireless and relay this to the units in the second- and third-class rooms as well. First, gain control over all passengers and all cars. The final touch will be the locomotive. At the very least, gain total control before the cars are switched."

By law, steam engines were forbidden to travel in the area around Pennsylvania Station in New York. This made it necessary for steam locomotives to have the cars they drew recombined with an electric locomotive. That coordination point was where they would claim Huey, and the time limit for the lives of half the hostages. They'd need to leave the other half alive, to use during their flight.

"All right. We will now commence Master Huey's rescue."

At their leader's order, the black-suited orchestra clicked their heels on the floor. The result was a truly warped, beautiful performance that echoed sharply in the first-class compartment.

"This is a ritual. A ritual to bring Master Huey back to us once more. This train is an altar, its passengers mere sacrifices. Do not forget that."

Goose, expressionless from beginning to end, commenced the Lemures' march.

"Let pandemonium begin. At this point in time, neither justice nor evil exist. All power is here. Once we have saved Master Huey, that power will be transformed into justice. That is the purpose of this fight. Let us swallow all the mundane passengers, the train, and the country, into ourselves."

Then the black suits became black shadows, scattering to every car on the train.

Multiple shadows, wearing the violence known as machine guns. Three of these directed their feet toward one car.

Cheerful talk sounded in that car, and light that was brighter than the rest filtered from it. The black shadows ran, bent on turning that light the color of blood. The dining car, which held Mrs. Beriam, the maneuver's greatest target. Its door was already right in front of the shadows.

⇐⇒

Vicky was in a great mood.

"Fill this dining car with screams." He'd never dreamed that such an important, pinnacle role would come to him.

Vicky, dressed in white, quietly thanked his own good luck.

To congratulate myself, maybe I'll kill somebody first, as an example. Should I take that weird Western-wannabe couple, or the kiddies next to them, or the hot tomato by them...? Whoops, mustn't do that, that mom and kid are the ones Ladd likes, aren't they... But I could probably at least shoot the daughter dead a little, right? I'll just kill her a little, just a tiny little bit; she won't die from being a smidgen killed—

Basking in lunatic delusions, the gent looked around the train car. Several people glanced at his pure white outfit, but compared to Isaac and Miria, its impact probably wasn't that great. They turned their eyes back to their dinners as though nothing had happened.

Speaking of weirdos, he didn't see the magician from a little while back. He was probably in a third-class compartment.

There was just one person who made him uneasy. A woman in coveralls by the window.

That ain't no amateur.

The woman was acutely alert, and when he turned his eyes slightly in her direction, the wariness in her eyes grew noticeably stronger.

She was casually observing not only Vicky, who'd just entered the dining car, but everyone else around her as well. The instant their eyes met, Vicky was run through by the sharp light deep in her eyes.

Who the hell is this broad? She's bein' supercautious about something.

At first, it bothered him, but apparently it wasn't anything to do with his group.

Well, like it or not, she's about to get pulled into this.

Without letting it worry him particularly, as if he'd lost interest, he crossed to the center of the dining car.

All right, then. Shall we get this thing started?

Soundlessly, Vicky slipped the handgun from his jacket.

⇔

"Right, let's go."

Guns at the ready, the men in black flung the door open.

⇔

"Okay! Let's do this!"

Drawing his piece from inside his jacket, Nick flung open the dining car's door.

⇔

Inside the dining car, three yells went up.

Each voice carried well, and the words reached everyone in the car.

The men in black tuxedos, who'd come in through the forward door, yelled:

"Everyone on the ground!"

In their hands, they brandished machine guns.

*   *   *

The man in white, who'd been in the center of the dining car, shouted:

"Everybody reach for the sky!"

In his right hand, he held a shiny, copper-colored handgun.

The man in ragged clothes, who'd come in through the rear door, called:

"Hey, hey, hey! Nobody move!"

In his hand, he held a single fruit knife.

One of the passengers, dripping with cold sweat, muttered:

"Wha…What do you want us to do…?"

Surprisingly, the ones who were quickest to react to the situation were Isaac and Miria.

The pair made the two children beside them duck and cover, and then——

—they dropped to the floor, stuck both their hands up, and froze, motionless.

⇔

As Ladd sauntered down the corridor, he heard gunfire from the direction of the dining car.

"Whoa, whoa, whoa, he's going at it, he's shooting, he's really into this…"

Heart leaping, he headed for the dining car, skipping as he went.

However, he stopped in his tracks after a second.

Following the single fire, there had come what sounded like several dozen shots in a row.

"Hmm? Machine guns?"

For a moment, his expression went tense. But, in the next instant, he'd recovered his smile and returned to frolicking. His skips were slightly lighter than they had been before.

"Well, that's its own kind of interesting, ain't it?"

When he reached the carriage before the dining car, a young guy who looked like a thug came running toward him from the other end of the corridor.

He was glancing back at the dining car again and again, and he dashed past Ladd without even looking at him.

"What the hell?! Nobody said a thing about this, Miz Nice!"

Screaming something along those lines, the thug ran off.

"Hot damn, hotdamnhotdamnhot*damn*, what's up, what's shakin' in the dining car?! Is he killing? Getting killed? Either way, it's seriously 'whoa' and 'hold the phone' and *damn* this is exciting, hey, hey, hey, hey, hey…"

Ladd was unable to hold still, and before he knew it, he'd broken into a run.

As he got closer to the dining car, he started to hear crying and screams from inside. What lay behind this door, heaven or hell?

When he threw open the sliding door of the entrance, he was pierced by looks from a majority of the people inside. As they gazed at Ladd, some of their eyes were pleading, others seemed to cling to hope, while still others simply despaired.

In the center of the dining car, Vicky lay facedown. His back, which should have been white, was dyed bright red with his own blood.

On the opposite side of the car were three men with machine guns. He could tell from their clothes that they were part of the orchestra.

One of the men seemed to have taken a bullet from Vicky: He was crouched down, holding his bleeding shoulder. The remaining two were brandishing their grim trench sweepers, threatening the sobbing passengers to make sure nobody made a break for it.

However, the glares of the gang of three were focused solely on the man in white who'd suddenly appeared.

Apparently, as far as Ladd was concerned, the situation had turned out to be hell.

And yet, he kept smiling.

"Eh, no help for that."

He strode right into the middle of the car.

"I'll just remodel a bit, make it into heaven."

Muttering softly, he raised both hands high.

"Hang on a sec, hold it! I dunno what's going on, but as you can see, I'm not packing anything! I'm not your enemy, so just calm down!"

Naturally, the black suits didn't relax their guard. From his clothes, he had to be a friend of the guy who was dead in the center of the car. That was exactly what gave Ladd a chance at success.

One of the black suits approached, keeping his gun muzzle trained on him.

"You… No; who are *you people*?"

"Hey now, we're suspicious characters, but we're not your enemies."

Just then, another of the men approached Ladd as well. They probably meant for one to keep the gun on him while the other restrained him.

The only one left at the end of the car was the wounded one. Even as he held his shoulder, he kept the gun in his free hand trained on the passengers, with a glare.

The instant the two approaching black suits fell into a single-file line, Ladd raised his voice in protest again.

"Look, I told you, I'm not your enemy!"

By the time the words were out of his mouth, he'd kicked the black suit's gun up so that the muzzle pointed at the ceiling.

"Wha…?"

The front kick had caught the man completely by surprise, and he hadn't even had time to pull the trigger. Ladd had also raised his hands, and so he gripped the center of the gun barrel lightly, then pushed it over hard—forward, from Ladd's perspective—so that it pointed back over his adversary's shoulder.

It was pointing behind the panicking black suit, toward the other one.

Of course the man in Ladd's grip had struggled, but in the blink of an eye, the gun barrel had been pushed to point behind him. The thin part of the barrel bit deeply into his shoulder.

Leaving one hand on the gun barrel, Ladd grabbed the butt of the weapon. Using the black suit's shoulder as the fulcrum, he yanked the gun sharply toward him.

"What?!"

The force made the black suit's finger slip off the trigger. Ladd's finger, from the hand that had been holding the gun barrel, slid into its place.

A roar.

The upside-down gun spat out a huge amount of lead.

That lead pierced the body of the rear black suit: his jaw, his lungs, his heart, but mostly his head. The man, his upper body transformed into a fountain of blood, twisted sideways and crumpled to the ground. At the same time, the volume of the screams that echoed in the car swelled.

"Why you—!"

From the back, the previously wounded man trained his gun on them, but his remaining comrade blocked the shot. Not only that, but Ladd had grabbed the man's collar with his left hand and hauled him up—his feet now rose slightly off the floor. With a strength that was impossible to imagine from his slender frame, Ladd was suffusing the man's face with blood.

The black suit fought, kicking and struggling, but he didn't know any effective techniques for combat this close. He tried to gouge Ladd's eyes with his free hand, but Ladd anticipated the move and bit a chunk out of his hand.

As he spat out blood and flesh, Ladd called to the wounded black suit at the back of the car.

"Well, what'll you do? Run for it? Shoot me through your friend? Kill yourself? Yack for a bit? Have some tea? Grab some food? How's business? No way it's good, huh? Well, what're you gonna do? Reorganize? Run for office? Wage war? Kill each other? Are you scared? Sad? Or are you mad?"

He rattled off a string of pointless questions, then cackled to himself. Abruptly cutting off that laugh, he poked a gun out of the shadow of the man he was using as a shield.

"Answer at least one of 'em, why! Don't! You!"

In lieu of an answer, the wounded black suit turned his back on them both.

The man dashed out of the dining car. Ladd didn't follow him. Instead, he dropped his shield onto the floor.

"Well, this got pretty interesting. It's getting pretty damn interesting..."

The lone remaining black suit coughed hard several times, then glared at Ladd and called out triumphantly:

"You fool! To think you'd let my comrade escape! I don't know who you people are, but don't think you can make enemies of us and survive!"

"Y'know, the mafia fellas I killed said stuff like that before they bit it, too. Not that it matters."

Without seeming particularly interested, Ladd tossed the machine gun onto the floor. The passengers who were near where it fell gave small shrieks.

"Idiot!"

Seeing this, the black suit suddenly stood up. Grabbing the knife he'd had hidden in his boot, he swung it in a powerful horizontal slash.

According to the black suit's prediction, the blade should have slashed the white suit's throat, but——

"Wh...What?"

Ladd's head wasn't there anymore.

The moment he thought he glimpsed hair at the bottom of his field of vision, it was already too late: A heavy impact ran through his guts.

"Booby prize."

The pain came to him dully, and an urge to vomit welled up inside him.

Smirking, Ladd had rammed an uppercut into the man's side. In contrast to his grinning face, the black suit was moaning and dripping with greasy sweat.

"Y-you damn... Boxi..."

As he fell forward, a loosely clenched fist flew up at him from below.

"*Nghaa!*"

"Nn? No worries. It's fine. I'm tons weaker than Pete Herman."

As the man fell backward, Ladd grabbed the hem of his clothes and hauled him back up.

"I don't have the strength or techniques of Jack Johnson or Jack Dempsey, either."

Left hook. Followed by a weird, unnatural noise: *gatch*.

"I wonder... Is the name Jack lucky for boxers or something? Huh?"

Several blows were paid out, one-sidedly.

"I said 'Herman' and 'Dempsey' all casual-like, but do you know boxers' names? Of course you know; all Americans know."

Punch.

"If you say you don't know or something, I'll never forgive you."

Punch.

"I'll never forgive you."

Yet another punch.

"I'll never"—*punch*—"ever"—*punch*—"forgive you."—*punch*— "Well"—*punch*—"it's not like"—*punch*—"I'll forgive"—*punch*— "you"—*punch*—"even if"—*punch*—"you know, though."

Taking an uppercut at the end of a complete joker's rush, the man lurched backward again. At that rate, he should have been down long before now, but Ladd had intentionally kept hitting his opponent in ways that kept him from falling.

Now his head crashed back into the wall.

The door was right beside him. In the midst of the repeated strikes, the black suit had been driven all the way to the end of the car.

"Oh, you finally dropped the knife, huh? Man, I was so terribly, terribly scared that I hit you too much by accident."

The knife had been dropped way back at the very first attack, but Ladd spoke shamelessly, with a patently fake attitude.

"*Aah...*"

"Whoa. You're still conscious? I guess I really don't have any punch strength. That's a hell of a shock, yeah? What're you gonna do about it?"

Ladd grabbed the black suit's collar with both hands and shoved his back right up against the wall.

"Well, I was sure you wouldn't shoot me dead on the spot. You wanted to know what us white suits were up to, right? Hmm? That's why you came up close to me, right? To catch me."

Then he pulled the black suit to him and hugged him hard.

"*Thank you*, seriously, thank you! Thank you for doing just what I thought you would."

Rubbing his cheek against the black suit's head, he yelled out words of gratitude; his eyes looked set to tear up any second.

"You're real good guys! What did I tell you? I'm not your enemy! As long as there's love—enemy or friend, it don't matter! Aah, I'm on your side, and I love you, all of you, from the bottom of my heart! ———But die."

He slammed the black suit up against the wall again.

Even though there was blood dribbling from his victim's mouth and nose, and the whites of his eyes were showing, he was still conscious.

"You...fool... Making ene...mies of us—*bwuh!*"

A clenched fist hit him right under the nose. He felt something break, under the skin; probably a front tooth.

"What's this 'us' business you keep rattling on about? It's kinda snobby and annoying and irritating, and I'll slaughter you."

"As if feebleminded...fools like you...could block...Master Huey's... path..."

A fist flew at the black suit's right eye. And at his left eye. The whites of his eyes had already been showing, and those eyes would probably never be able to register light again. That said, in order to know for sure, he'd have to live through this.

Ladd's expression abruptly grew quiet, and he whispered in the black suit's ear.

"I dunno who that Huey fella is, or who you really are, and frankly, I don't give a rip."

In combination with that statement, he slammed a fist into the stomach of the black suit, whose consciousness was nearly gone.

"But there are several things I know for sure. One is, everyone in the black-suit orchestra on this train is an enemy, and they've got about a gazillion crazy guns."

Ladd's fists struck home rhythmically. As his tone grew stronger, the force behind his fists grew as well. The fists also shifted their target from stomach to chest, and from chest to face.

"And most of all! I bet you're thinking this, right now! 'We've got all these awesome weapons, and there's no one on this train who can defy us. We're the toughest. In other words, we're safe!'"

As the white suit's voice reverberated in the car, the curtain quietly came down on the black suit's consciousness, and on his life.

Whether he'd noticed this or not, Ladd's fists didn't stop.

"I bet that'll be fun! That's gonna be real fun! Killing guys like that! Dragging out their guts! Squishing 'em and grinding 'em down until they look like sausage meat!"

The squishing noise was coming from Ladd's fists. His punches had gotten stronger and stronger, and by this point, he'd crushed all the bones in the man's face.

As he was showered by sprays of blood, Ladd's face truly shone. It was the face of a man who'd accomplished something. To a normal person, it would have looked like nothing more than the crazed smile of a murderer, and in fact that was exactly what it was.

When Ladd turned, looking invigorated, everyone in the car averted their eyes at once. He had figured they would all just run, but when Ladd glanced at the exit on the opposite side of the car, he understood.

A group of white suits was camped there. They had guns aimed and ready and were eyeing the passengers.

"Hey, Ladd, what the hell's going on here?"

"We heard somethin' that sounded like machine guns, so we came to check up. Fill us in, Ladd."

They were easygoing voices that didn't match the situation. Waving a hand at them, Ladd sauntered down the middle of the car. As he passed by the counter, he spotted a lady who was lying down, covering the children with her body. He spoke to her.

"Missus Beriam?"

Fixing Ladd with a strong gaze, the lady nodded slowly.

Warping his mouth and eyes in a dangerous smile, Ladd delivered a leisurely announcement:

"Lucky you: Your turn's been pushed back. We'll finish off the whole orchestra first, and then you're next. Well, I'll be looking forward to it."

Without forgetting to pick up the guns that the black suits and Vicky had dropped, he rejoined his friends.

"Let's go, fellas."

"Whaddaya mean, 'Let's go'? What are we gonna do about these guys?" one of his friends asked, pointing at the passengers in the dining car.

"Leave 'em. Forget that. You're not gonna believe how awesome this is. Just c'mon back to the room."

"Yeah, sure, but Ladd, your hands. They okay?"

Ladd's hands were dripping with blood. The passengers had assumed it was his victim's blood, but the flesh on Ladd's fists had split in places. After he'd paid out that many blows without taping his hands, this was a perfectly natural result. On the contrary, it was practically a miracle that he hadn't taken more damage.

"Yeah, it's fine. I dislocated a few joints, but nothing's broken. And hey, I'm still good to go. From the feel of it, I could beat another five guys to death."

"Just give up and tape 'em already."

With an attitude as though nothing had happened, without bothering to wipe off the dripping gore, Ladd's group quietly disappeared from the dining car.

Then silence filled the car. Even the crying voices had stopped dead. In this tense space, only two idiotic voices echoed quietly.

"Say, Miria, how long do we have to stay like this? I've been hearing gunshots and scary people's voices from up there for a while now, and it's, uh, kinda nervous-making."

"Yes, it's a horror show!"

"Besides, you know, this is a pretty tough position to hold."

"Yes, frankly, it hurts!"

⟺

At first, the passengers who'd been left behind stayed silent. After a short while, the ones who'd begun to understand the situation gradually began to clamor. None of the passengers had tried to leave the dining car yet. There might have been white suits or black suits lying in wait outside either exit.

Before long, complaints ballooned, and the cooks and bartender, who were train personnel, began to take the brunt of them.

What happened? What sort of joke is this? Where are the conductors? Let me off! Stop this train!

Fang and Jon, feeling disinclined to put up with them, retreated into the kitchen. Immigrants were roundly discriminated against in this era, and they probably understood that if they tried to handle things, it would backfire.

Even so, there was someone who turned an unjust attack on them.

"What's the matter with this train, anyway?! Keeping a yellow monkey and a stinking Irish hick in its kitchen!"

Possibly because he'd used up all his complaints about the uproar of a few moments ago, one man began singling out Jon and Fang for grief. He was a fat, flabby old guy with a little mustache. He was far too undignified to be called "portly" or "pleasantly plump"; he was an utterly unsightly man.

Jon and Fang could hear his yells all the way back in the kitchen, but they ignored them as if they were used to it.

The man bore down even harder on a different young cook, who wasn't sure how to deal with him.

"I paid a lot of money to ride this train! What's with that face?! If you have a problem with me, gimme back my money!"

As his fist struck the counter, something was laid down on top of that fist. It was a stack of bills bundled together in groups of one hundred.

"Wha…?"

"Is that good enough for you?! You, uh......you nasty guy!"

"You're the worst!"

When the man with the little mustache looked to the side, a cowboy and dancing girl were standing there, glaring daggers at him.

"Wh-who *are* you people?"

"If it's money you want, I'll pay you back for your tickets! That means you're not a customer anymore! Isn't that right, Miria?"

"Yes, he's stealing a ride!"

Isaac and Miria raised their voices in protest against the man with the little mustache. A bit surprised by this, Jon and Fang peeked out of the kitchen.

"You fools! Do you have any idea who I am...?"

Even as he protested, the man with the duster on his lip reached out for the bundle of bills.

"*Silence!* You've been going on about nonsense like 'monkeys' and 'hicks' in a restaurant where people were enjoying their meals! I bet you were planning to find fault with them and extort money!"

"Ooh, what a lowlife!"

"You're unbelievable, you money-grubbing ghoul!"

"Make like a ghoul and get back in your grave!"

Saying things that were just as unfair as the mustachioed man's protest had been, they threw another stack of bills in his face.

"G'wan, get lost! If you don't, then my hundred...my hundred-*million* pistols will spit fire!"

"We'll give you lead poisoning!"

Just then, from deep in the kitchen, from a place that could never be seen from the customers' positions, a voice spoke. It was a voice like a bear's, low and ponderous.

"Jon! Fang! You heard them! That guy's not a passenger or a customer of this kitchen anymore! Hurry and toss 'im out!"

On hearing this voice, which was like the roar of some ferocious beast, the mustachioed man's pompous attitude imploded.

"Yessir, Head Cook."

"Pain in the butt..."

Even as Jon grumbled, he and Fang picked up the struggling

mustachioed man from both sides. Then, with beautiful efficiency, they went out through the car's rear door.

At that, the ferocious beast's voice abruptly became gentlemanly and delivered a certain announcement to the dining car:

"Now then, I'm afraid we've put all of you through something terribly trying! Upon our arrival, everyone present at this time will, of course, have their train fare refunded to them in full by our headquarters. In addition, you will be paid commensurate reparations, although we do not feel that this could ever be apology enough—"

The voice went on to say the most important thing:

"Now, when we are unable to communicate with the conductors' room, we request that you think and act independently, with the goal of reaching New York alive. That is all!"

The bit he'd said at the very end there had been horrendously irresponsible, but everyone was too scared to complain. In this way, once again, quiet times returned to the dining car.

"Would you unhand me?! Filthy immigrants! You'll soil my clothes! You'll give me your diseases!"

As he spouted nasty comments, the man with the little mustache was turned out into the corridor. As they were about to leave, Jon lowered his stance and glared at the man. Although there was no telling when it had gotten there, his right hand gripped an ice pick.

The irate passenger had bluffed all over the place, but that one glare shut him up. Jon had once been affiliated with the Chicago underworld. Going up against the likes of such a passenger didn't make him the least bit nervous.

"Listen up, you whiskered pig. Half of this transcontinental railroad was built by us Irish, and they treated us like slaves while we did it. And actually, they *made* us build it. Do you understand that?"

"The other half was us Chinese."

"In other words, half of everything on these rails belongs to the Irish."

"Add in the Chinese workers' share, and it's everything."

Jon began saying something even more unfair than what the

mustachioed man and Isaac had said. Neither of them had personally built the railroad, and in any case, they'd become Jacuzzi's friends after their compatriots had chased them out.

"So, you whiskered pig, everything here is ours, including your life. Don't you forget it."

Smacking the mustachioed man's cheek lightly, Jon and Fang started to go back into the dining car.

At that, possibly because he'd suddenly grown uneasy, the man's attitude changed abruptly, and he clung to Jon slavishly.

"W-w-w-wait! Those white suits… They're out here! Please! Let me in!"

"Don't worry. It didn't look like they had any stinking hicks or yellow monkeys in their group. Make friends with them. If you come in here, we'll kill you."

With that, the door shut without mercy.

When they entered, the passengers seemed to have regained some of their composure. A glance around showed that the three corpses had disappeared from the dining car. Possibly the other cooks had carried them out. At this point, everyone was quickly wiping the bloodstains off the floor and the walls.

As they went behind the counter, their eyes met Isaac's and Miria's.

"Thanks."

Jon offered it in an undertone, and they didn't seem to hear him.

"Hey, welcome back! I've gotta say, your chef sounds like a real tough guy!"

"Yes, the strongest legend!"

Isaac and Miria heaped excessive praise on the individual in the back of the kitchen.

This chef considered cuisine his top priority in life, and so, while he was cooking, he never left his post, no matter what. …To the point that there was an anecdote about how, even when a gas explosion had occurred right next him, he hadn't abandoned his pan. Naturally, during the firefight a short while earlier, the chef had continued to stir the stew pot, all by himself.

"Still, that was one nasty customer! There's really no excuse for making false accusations like that!"

"Yes, he was just too mean!"

"I mean, this place doesn't stink at all, and there are no monkeys anywhere! Ye gods, how dumb does he think we are?!"

"The guy who makes fools of people is the real fool!"

As Jon heard out their proclamations, a doubt flickered inside him.

Wait... Were these guys actually protecting us, or...did they just not understand what the slang meant?

Breaking out in a cold sweat, Jon hastily canceled that thought.

⇔

"Who are those men in the white suits?"

Goose frowned over the obstacle to the operation that had suddenly presented itself.

He'd heard that there was a group of men in white suits in the second-class carriages, but he'd never imagined that his subordinates, who'd had machine guns, would be defeated. He didn't know what sort of group they were, but it was evident that they were far from ordinary.

"In any case, temporarily call back everyone whose hands are free."

At that order, several members withdrew, while one switched on the wireless set and attempted to contact the rear cars.

"Good Lord. First Nader and now the group in white. Should I consider this some sort of trial?"

"I can't imagine we'll reach it that easily, can you, Goose?"

At Spike's question, Goose glanced at the corner of the room—where Chané was, silent, with her arms folded—and answered quietly.

"You're right. It isn't possible to reach Master Huey's heights by any normal path."

As he turned his back on Chané, Goose's lips twisted into a smirk.

⇔

"So, hey. Ladd. What the hell is that orchestra?"

Ladd answered his friend's question with a rapturous expression:

"A feast. I dunno anything else, and there's absolutely no need to. Right?" he said, absently, bewildering his companions.

"Anyway, just kill them all."

At those words, delighted cries escaped his friends. Now that Vicky was dead, there were ten group members left. They were packed like sardines in the second-class passenger compartment, even though it wasn't a small space.

Although they had far fewer people than the orchestra, that wasn't what they were feeling.

"It's outta sight! We get to kill two or three apiece! Not only that, but these are relaxed guys who think they're squarely on top!"

The delighted cries became cheers, and the second-class compartment was engulfed by their mood.

"Still, what a farce… Except for the ones in the dining car, the only people in the second-class compartments are us and those black suits."

Three corpses lay in the room next to theirs. While Ladd was in the dining car, his friends had finished them off.

It was the three-man group from the orchestra—the Lemures—that had been sent to occupy the second-class cars.

Each had been killed in a different way. The only thing they had in common was that none had been allowed to die in the first attack.

"All right, it ain't safe for us to be all huddled up like this, so let's scatter. I'll tell Lua and the other guy."

Taking nothing but his rifle, Ladd threw open the door to the corridor.

"We'll meet up again whenever! Just come back here whenever you think, 'Yeah, I did good!'"

Nobody objected, and the group of white suits fanned out into the train. In order to destroy the black shadows, and to devour the train themselves.

⟺

Neither Goose and the black suits nor Ladd and the white suits had noticed it yet.

The fact that the train carried an even stranger shadow.

The one to notice that fiendish monster's existence was the most cowardly guy on the train.

"What......is this......?"

All the color had drained from Jacuzzi's face. He stood transfixed, unable even to tremble.

He'd run into the conductors' room, out of breath. And what he'd seen there was——

"It's a lie, it has to be a lie, you can't really be dead, please, please, wake up and say it's a lie! Mr. Conductor! *Please!*"

The end of the train was dyed red.

What he saw there were the bloody bodies of the conductors.

There were two corpses.

One conductor had been shot dead.

The other's body had been disfigured before he died.

His head was twisted at an impossible angle, and his face and right arm were completely gone.

It was as though they'd been ground off, or maybe chewed off by something. The cut surfaces were incredibly dirty, and it was likely that no blade had been used. If one had been used, it had probably been some sort of rough-toothed saw.

The incandescent lamps cast a warm light over the horrible scene. As he gazed at the pool of blood that covered the floor, Jacuzzi muttered quietly. There were no tears in that voice. What did it hold: determination or resignation?

"It came, I was too late, it already caught up..."

As it reflected the light, the color of the blood was nauseatingly pure, almost like wine.

Then Jacuzzi murmured the monster's name:

"The Rail Tracer..."

⟺

In the dining car, Mrs. Beriam was telling her daughter something.

"Listen to me, Mary. Go with Czes and hide, quietly. It's all right; if you stay hidden until noon tomorrow, I'm sure Papa will come to save you."

Their surroundings were surprisingly calm. The passengers were all seated, and their faces held varied mixtures of despair and hope. Sobs could be heard from a few places, but aside from those, things were very quiet.

Although, as you'd expect, no one was ordering food anymore.

"All right, Czes. Please take care of Mary."

"Uh-huh!"

The boy nodded decisively, then took the girl's hand and left the dining car. After the door was open, she saw him walk away, looking around carefully as he went.

"Are you sure you don't need to hide, too, ma'am?"

In response to the question Jon had asked her across the counter, Mrs. Beriam smiled gently.

"Yes, it's all right. I don't know why, but both the people in black and the people in white seem to be looking for me. If I hide, too, it will cause trouble for the people in this car."

"I see. Well, it might be safer in here, anyway, and even they probably wouldn't kill just the kids."

…Although he couldn't be positive about that white-suited boxer.

Jon kept those words shut up inside himself. Mrs. Beriam had probably already realized that. It was likely she'd sent them away for that very reason, so that the enemy wouldn't know where they were.

Just then, Isaac and Miria abruptly spoke up.

"Okay, we'll be back!"

"We're off!"

At that, they both clambered down from the tall chairs.

"'Off'? Off to where?"

Isaac and Miria answered Fang's question without a shred of hesitation.

"Where? To find Jacuzzi."

"To find Nice, too!"

"It's dangerous, you know."

He did try to stop them, but naturally, Isaac didn't reconsider.

"That's why we're going to find them!"

"Yes, it's a rescue!"

"I have no idea what's going on here, but if I see black suits or white suits or a weird guy with a knife, I'll just threaten 'em with my pistols and run!"

"*Amazing!*"

Patting his empty holsters, Isaac gave a proud whistle.

"Oh. Huh. I see."

Jon wasn't trying to stop them anymore. In any case, he was acquainted with the "weird guy with a knife," and it made him feel too awkward to continue the conversation.

Why did Nick pull a stunt like that, anyway?

While he was wondering about it, Isaac and Miria exited through the car's rear door.

As if to replace them, the front door opened. In unison, the passengers screamed and ducked down.

A group of black suits with machine guns had come through the door.

"Good evening. Madame Beriam, I presume?"

The leader spotted Mrs. Beriam and spoke to her. The other black suits were glaring around at the passengers, machine guns in hand.

"My name is Goose. I believe you'll understand; there's a certain matter in which we require your husband's cooperation. Would you come with me?"

Mrs. Beriam stood, directing an intense glare at the man who'd introduced himself as Goose.

"Please promise me you won't harm anyone else."

"Ha-ha-ha. You must know that you are in no position to set terms. Well, I will tell you that the fate of the passengers depends on the answer we receive from your husband and the government."

He began to escort her away at gunpoint, but someone essential was missing from her side.

"And where is your child?" Goose asked the lady, grimacing a little.

Mrs. Beriam looked down, biting her lip hard. She curled both hands into fists, squeezing them tightly.

"What is it?"

When Mrs. Beriam raised her head, her eyes were wet with tears, and blood was flowing from her lip and hands.

"My daughter... Those people in white—— They took her away...!"

I see. So that's her angle.

Jon, who'd taken cover behind the counter, was impressed by Mrs. Beriam's idea and her acting skills. He really couldn't visualize either from the mild person he'd seen a moment before.

"The white suits, hmm? Who are they?"

Open hatred was apparent in the phrase *white suits*, but Goose promptly made a cool-headed decision.

"I don't know. They seem to have been looking for me as well, but first they took...my daughter... Oh, oh, Mary...!"

"I understand your feelings, but..."

Without seeming particularly moved by her vivid acting, Goose gave an unconcerned sign to his subordinates.

"For now, come back to our room."

Together with his subordinates, who held their guns at the ready, Mrs. Beriam left the dining car.

"All right. I want teams of two to watch this group, in shifts."

After he'd issued orders to his subordinates and was about to exit, Goose noticed the sound of wind flowing through the dining car. When he looked toward the source of the sound, he saw that one of the windows beside the tables was open. It was a small thing, but Goose's instincts were insistently telling him something. He turned his gun on the man closest to that window.

"You. Who opened that window?"

"Yeeee!"

Finding himself abruptly at gunpoint, the terrified man shrieked and began to speak like Jacuzzi.

"N-nuh, nuh-nuh, no, no, you've got it wrong! Th-th-that window— A woman in coveralls—!"

"A woman in coveralls?"

"Y-ye, ye, *yes!* When the shooting started, she just pushed the window open a-a-and climbed out! It's true, I swear! I'm not lying, so please don't shoot meeeeee!"

Without listening to any more of the man's story, Goose put his head out the window. When he looked up, he saw that part of the ornamentation on the outer wall was within arm's reach. Above that, several sets of the same ornamentation formed rows of bumps and dents, and it looked as if it would be possible to climb up to the roof.

A woman in coveralls.

Goose had an idea about that. It was the woman he'd seen by the freight car, before boarding. Who on earth could she be?

Adding the item "woman in coveralls" to his mental watch list, Goose left the dining car without a word.

⇔

Meanwhile   Somewhere in New York City   An illegal casino

"Firo, hey. Wouldja make it a little easier to score on the roulette wheels here?"

"Berga, you come to someone else's turf and ask for *what*?"

In the midst of a dazzling clamor, two men were talking. One was a big, stern-faced guy; the other was a young man. The big man, the one called Berga, was one of the bosses of the Gandor Family, a tiny New York mafia outfit. Since his organization was run by a triumvirate of brothers, no one was technically "the top."

Firo, the young guy, was the youngest executive of the Martillo Family, which was part of the organization known as the Camorra. He was also Isaac and Miria's friend.

In addition, Firo had been put in charge of running this underground casino, and as a rule, it would have been unthinkable for Berga—the boss of another organization—to be there.

Firo and the three Gandor brothers had grown up in the same tenement and were practically family. That said, when it came to the interests of their syndicates, they never colluded.

"Anyway, Berga, this is no time for you to be here, is it? I heard the situation with the Runoratas is a ticking bomb."

Firo gave the name of a mafia outfit that had recently begun throwing its weight around in New York.

"Well, that's *why*. If I hang around on our turf, they might take a shot at me, and I know for a fact the Martillos wouldn't sign on with the Runoratas."

"Just stay home. Don't drag us into it."

As he responded to what Berga was saying, Firo abruptly raised his right hand and made some sort of sign.

At that, people gathered around a man who'd just won big at a poker table in the corner of the room. One of them grabbed the man's arm and held it up.

Several cards slipped out of his sleeve.

An expression of despair came into the man's face, and he was dragged off to an inner room.

"I'll be heading home for the day in a minute or so. I have to go to Penn Station tomorrow to meet somebody. Frankly, I want to get to bed early. You go home, too, before the Runorata fellas see your face."

On hearing that, Berga looked puzzled.

"What, you too?"

"Me 'too'?"

"We're supposed to pick up you-know-who tomorrow, too."

"Who's 'you-know-who'?"

"*You* know, c'mon! I know you know. That's who you're going to get tomorrow, ain't it?!"

In contrast to Berga, who was unfairly yelling, Firo responded coolly.

"Calm down, Berga. I'm going to pick up Isaac and Miria. You met them at my promotion party last year, remember?"

"Huhn? Uh… Ah, aah! Oh, for cryin' out loud. You mean those idiots?!"

"You're one to talk. …Quit with the scowl. And? Who are you going to pick up? Say the name, all right? Gimme the name."

At that, smirking, Berga answered Firo's question.

"Claire."

When he heard that name, Firo's eyes went wide.

"Claire? You mean *the* Claire?"

"What other Claire would be Claire besides Claire?!"

"I see… Well, that's something to look forward to. So Claire's coming… Then the Runoratas have as good as lost."

Firo nodded to himself, predicting the defeat of the Runoratas solely by the existence of this Claire person.

"Nah, you don't know that yet."

"No, I know. That natural-born contract killer is coming back. There's practically no one in this business who doesn't know the Vino name by now. If you manage to lose anyway, you're complete idiots."

He muttered this in an undertone. When you talked about a currently active killer using their real name, it wasn't the sort of conversation you wanted people to overhear.

"Yeah, well, Claire does awesome work. The genius turns up everywhere and can kill in absolutely any situation!"

"Don't yell it, moron. Well, true, those physical skills and the ability to assess situations are something else. It seems impossible for those skinny arms to be as strong as they are, though."

To them, the name Claire seemed to indicate someone who had reached the heights of a certain type of strength, someone who could be said to be the physical embodiment of that strength.

At that point, as if something had just struck him, Firo turned to Berga and asked a question:

"Say, is the train Claire's riding in on the *Flying Pussyfoot*?"

"Yeah! That's the one! What, are those idiots on the same train?"

On hearing that answer, Firo suddenly went quiet. After a short silence, he looked up and informed Berga of a certain fact:

"Actually, Maiza's going to meet it tomorrow, too."

A little hesitantly, Firo brought his superior's name into the conversation.

"Huh? To pick up the idiots? Maiza, in person?"

"No, not them. He has another acquaintance on that train…"

After hesitating a little, he muttered under his breath:

"Maiza's old friend—one of the alchemists who became immortal two hundred years ago."

⇔

Ladd had headed for the conductors' room to look for Lua. In order to reach it, he had to go through the third-class carriage and the freight rooms. It was likely that the black suits had taken control of the third-class compartments already.

How should he kill them? As he was entertaining himself with speculation, someone squirmed on the connecting platform between the cars.

Ladd leveled his rifle and spoke to the back of the man on the platform.

"Whoops! Don't move, you giddy bastard. Did we scare you? You're being pretty sneaky—"

At that point, he realized something: The shadow wasn't a black suit. It was the gray "magician," the one he'd seen when they boarded the train.

The magician turned to face him and spoke. He didn't seem especially afraid of the rifle.

"You're not a friend of the group in black suits, then?"

It was a man's voice.

"Not so much."

Ladd responded to the magician's words without lowering the weapon. Would he prove to be an enemy or an ally?…

"I climbed up to the roof to feel the night wind, and before I knew it, my room had been occupied."

From his voice, the man was probably somewhere between forty and fifty. He wasn't young, but nothing about him seemed particularly old, either.

The connecting platforms on this train didn't have walls or roofs; all they had were railings to keep people from falling off. There was an iron ladder beside the entrance to each platform, and if they wanted to, it was possible for absolutely anybody to climb up to the roof of the train.

The magician looked up slightly, gazing at the night sky as if reluctant to part from it.

On seeing his eyes, Ladd lowered his rifle.

"Say, Mr. Magician. All the compartments in the second-class carriages are empty now; use whichever you want."

At that, under the cloth that covered his face, the magician smiled quietly.

"Thank you, man in white. Ha-ha-ha, 'magician,' that's good. Well, I suppose it's a similar profession."

With those words, he passed by Ladd, black bag in hand.

"Hmm? What's in the bag?"

"Would you like to see? I doubt there's anything that would catch your interest."

Turning, he opened the mouth of the bag and showed it to him.

Inside were all sorts of large and small medicine vials, implements he'd never seen before, and books in languages Ladd couldn't read.

"Yeah, you're right: not interested. Move along. ...Oh, right. If you get stopped by anyone who's wearing the color I'm wearing, tell 'em you've got Ladd's permission. They should let you through then."

With a slight nod, the magician closed the top of the bag and went into one of the second-class compartments.

As he watched him go, Ladd clicked his tongue softly.

"Aah, dammit to hell. What's with those eyes? He's got eyes that look like he could die at any time and be fine with it. Or maybe eyes like a guy who's already dead. That's the type I'm worst with."

After griping for a while, he remembered Lua and decided to hurry to the conductors' room.

"Although, if he were a dame, he'd be my favorite type."

Remembering his girlfriend, who had the eyes of a dead fish, Ladd stood on the connecting platform and looked up.

"The roof, huh? Nice…"

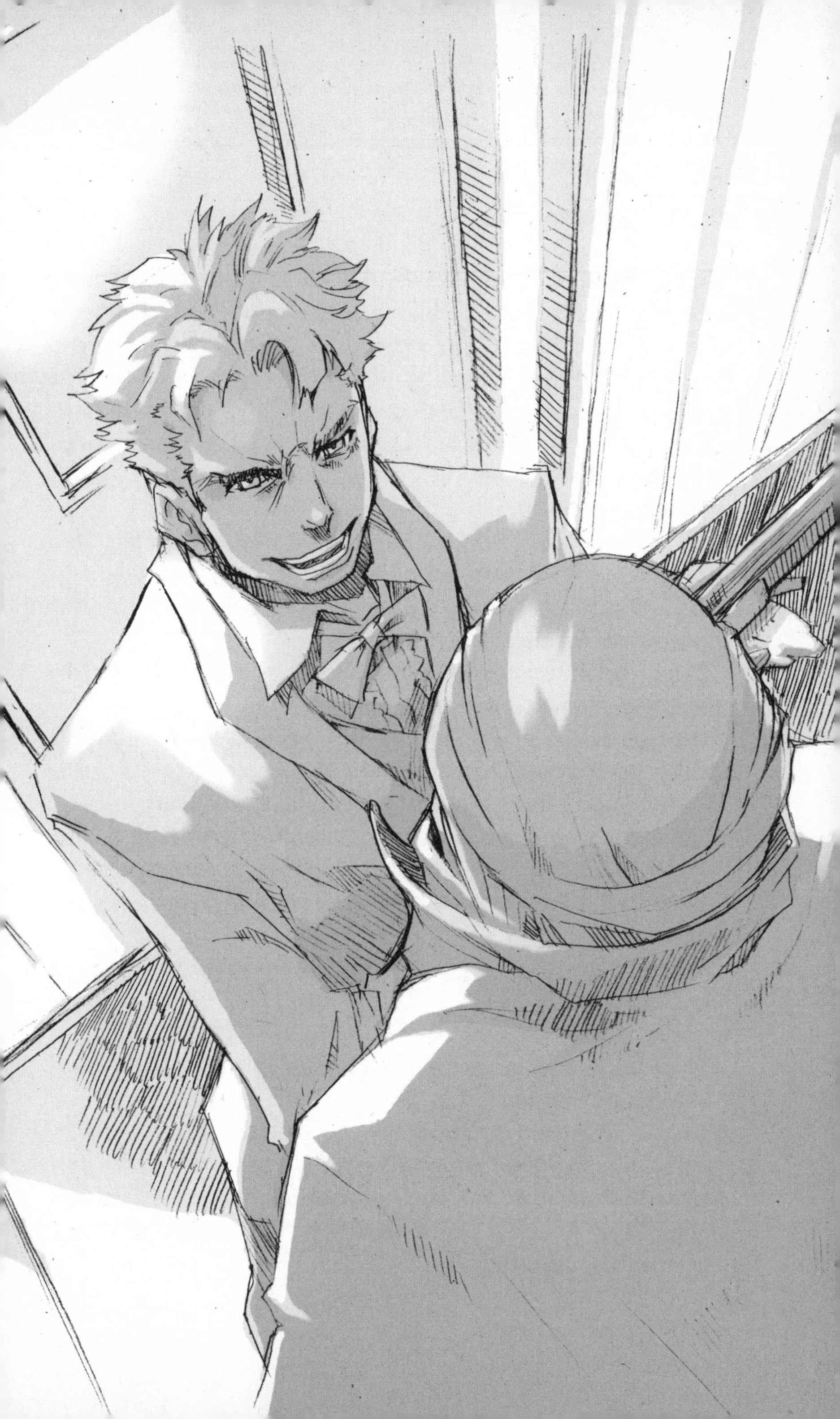

⟺

First-class compartment

When Goose and his men returned to the first-class compartment with Mrs. Beriam in tow, Spike was in front of the transmitter, a sour look on his face. Goose wanted to ask him, immediately and in detail, about what was going on, but it wouldn't have been wise to let Mrs. Beriam sense that there was trouble. He ordered his men to take the lady to another first-class room, and then, finally, grilled Spike about the situation.

"What is it? Trouble?"

"No, not with the transmitter. It's just that there's no contact from the group in the freight room."

There should have been three men in the freight room guarding the remainder of their stowed equipment.

Using the transmitter's handset, Goose sent the code for the freight room.

However, no matter how long they waited, the transmitter's speaker stayed silent.

Scratching his head, Spike mentioned a likely situation:

"I bet I know what this is. Think those white suits took them out?"

"Spike. Right now, we need to confirm the facts, not speculate."

Goose put together a new team of three and sent them to check on the freight room.

When he happened to glance at the corner of the room, Chané was gone.

"Spike, where's Chané?"

"Oh, it looks like she went out to hunt some albinos. She took several weapons with her."

Chané the Fanatic. Although she was a member of the Lemures, she obeyed orders from no one except Huey, their leader. Even during this operation, she was only cooperating—silently—in order to liberate Huey. She might even have thought she was merely using Goose and the others.

After he was certain that he couldn't sense her presence in the area, Goose turned to Spike and told him his true intentions.

"Let's have her make herself as useful as possible. She won't live past noon tomorrow in any case."

⟺

A couple was walking down the corridor of a second-class carriage. Although the lights were on, the glow seemed fragile in the face of the absolute darkness that enveloped the train.

"Ooh, it's gloomy! It's scary."

"Yes, and it's cold! And creepy!"

Miria agreed with Isaac's timid remark in a voice that was quiet, but very firm. In response, Isaac switched gears completely, putting up a bold front.

"Whaaat?! I'm not cold or creeped out! Just relax and follow me!"

"Wow, Isaac, you're so dependable!"

No one responded to their voices. Only silence weighed heavily on the corridor.

"It sure is quiet. You'd think there was nobody here. I wonder where the guys in white suits from the second-class compartments went to."

"Yes, and this is the only road there is!"

"The Rail Tracer might have caught up to us already."

"Yeeeeeeeek!"

"We've got to hurry... Even if we've got guns, even if we're tough, nothing will work against the Rail Tracer!"

"Yes, it's an invincible monster! Frankenstein! Count Dracula!"

"Miria, Frankenstein was the scientist's name, not the monster's name."

"Was it? Then what was the monster's name?"

"Um, let's see— Mary Shelley, wasn't it? Formally, I think it was Mary Wollstonecraft Godwin Shelley."

"Wow, Isaac, you know *everything*! ...But that sounds sort of like a lady's name!"

"Ah, but there are all sorts of guys who have names that sound like girls' names. Besides, it's a monster! That means anything goes!"

Possibly he'd gotten carried away: He proclaimed this in a loud voice.

The answer came in the form of machine gun fire, echoing in the distance.

"What was that? Was it from the third-class carriage?"

"No, farther than that! It sounded like it came from the freight room."

⟺

Suddenly, the transmitter in Goose's room began to make noise.

"..........≠≠≠......≠≠≠≠...........≠≠lp me! ......≠ght room speak≠ ...... Fr≠ght room speaking! Somebody, anybody! Come in!"

The static was horrendous, and Spike hastily twirled the knob, adjusting it. Ordinarily, they made contact via telegraph, so the fact that there was an audio transmission at all meant that this was a true emergency.

"Spike here. What's going on?"

"Help me! Help me! Send reinforcements right away! The other two are both dead! No, I mean, I just can't see them anymore, so I can't say for sure, but they disappeared! They're gone! It made them disappear!"

"What? Who are you fighting?! The white suits?!"

"White suits? N-n-no, it's nothing like that! It isn't human! N-no, I mean, I couldn't see it clearly, but... Anyway, it's a monster! I can't win... I can't...win..."

"Hey, what happened? Hey!"

The voice from the transmitter was getting farther away. Apparently, he'd turned his back on the transmitter and was facing off against something.

"Stop...... Stay back...... Stop, stop, *stooooooooop!*"

From beyond the transmitter, the roar of a machine gun echoed. As it passed through the equipment, the sound was transformed into a weird burst of static that split the air in the first-class carriage.

In spite of himself, Spike clapped his hands over his ears, but the next instant, the gunfire stopped.

In its place, there was the sound of something being thrown to the floor, and he began to hear a tiny, moaning voice. Soon, the moaning stopped as well.

The other side of the transmitter and this side. The double silence weighed eerily on the hearts of the black suits.

However, from time to time, they could hear a sound. A sound as if something was walking through a puddle.

Spike and the others could vividly imagine the truth of the situation. It wasn't a puddle of water. It was blood, from the body of the man they'd just been talking to.

Something was walking through it. The something that had just killed their comrade. The thing sent an overwhelming sense of its presence through the transmitter, planting a definite fear in the terrorists' hearts.

"Call back the unit that just left for the freight room."

Goose's grave voice sent a shiver through the still air.

Someone besides the white suits was trying to get in their way. With a sour expression, Goose struck the wall with his fist.

However, privately, Goose had a hunch he knew the identity of the something. They still didn't have enough information, so he was far from certain, but…

The woman in the coveralls who disappeared from the dining car——

⇔

A stall in a second-class carriage bathroom. In the janitor's closet beside it, Mary Beriam was holding her breath.

"I'll go on ahead and see how things look, so you hide here, Mary. Whatever happens, don't move. It'll be fine. I'll be right back."

With those words, Czes had gone away, and he hadn't come back. Mary felt as though her heart would burst with anxiety.

After a short while, she began to hear voices from the corridor. Cheerful voices that seemed terribly out of place in this situation.

That's Mr. Isaac and Miss Miria. On identifying the owners of the voices, Mary hesitated, wondering whether she should leave the closet.

Just then, she heard distant machine gun fire. Mary flinched, covering her ears and crouching down. The terror paralyzed her, and even if she'd wanted to call for help, her voice wouldn't come.

While this was going on, Isaac and Miria's voices had vanished.

⇔

"You've got to be kidding… What is this?"

"*Muah*, Jacuzzi. What this?"

The sea of blood in the conductors' room. As he stood there, stunned, Jacuzzi heard familiar voices behind him.

On hearing those voices, life returned to his eyes.

"Guys… Oh, you're okay. That's great… I-I'm really glad, really, guh–, *hic*, glad…"

"Donny and I are, somehow."

"Ah…oh. Now that you mention it, where are Nick and Jack?"

In response to that question, Nice looked down uncomfortably.

"They both got caught. Remember that orchestra group in black? Apparently, they were train robbers, too."

"Uh—huh?"

"*Aah*, Jack caught. White people caught, too. Nick caught, too."

"Um…what?"

When he asked them for details, he learned that, first, Jack had said, "I'll go on ahead and tie up the guards in the freight room," and had gone from the corridor into said freight room.

Of the three freight cars, the orchestra was using the foremost one, which meant that the treasure Jacuzzi and the others were after was in either the second or third car.

Nice and Donny had waited for Jack in the second car, but no matter how long they waited, he hadn't come back.

Then, when they'd gone to see what was up, Jack had come out of the freight room with his hands tied behind his back. Not only that, but a man in black carrying a machine gun had appeared behind him.

"Jack and the other man came toward us, so first we hid in the shadows of the room, but then Jack got tossed into the second freight room."

"Oh, but, and then, two more guys with machine guns came out into the hall. Then a white man and woman came. They got caught. Last, Nick came running. Got caught. That all. The end."

"D-d-don't end it! What happened then?! Are Jack and Nick okay?!"

"Calm down." Nice sighed. "Right now, one of the three men is guarding the hostages. Since they're guarding them, it means they're not dead, so I think they're probably both okay."

Apparently, at first they'd thought Jacuzzi might have been caught as well. They'd kept an eye on things for a short while after that, but when they realized that the black suits showed no sign of moving, they'd decided to check the conductors' room first.

"—And so, when we got to the conductors' room, we found this horrible scene. What happened? I know you didn't do it, Jacuzzi, so relax."

"Wah, thank you, b-b-but-but it's terrible: It's Rail Tracer, the Rail Tracer came! We have to get out of here fast or we'll be erased, too, so let's save Nick and Jack somehow and then run—"

Just then, from far away, they heard the sound of a machine gun.

"They're firing...?"

Behind Nice's glasses, her single eye warped slightly.

"Wh-wh-what was that? What was that gunfire? What did they shoot? Did somebody die? C'mon, tell me!"

The roar had seemed to split the air. What did it mean? Various guesses were born inside Jacuzzi's head, then rapidly boiled down to a conclusion.

"Waah, wah, *hic*... Niiice, Donnyyy..."

They had to run. They had to escape from this train as soon as possible. His brain had a solid grasp of this fact. However, at the same time, his heart had begun to settle on a different conclusion.

Fang's and Jon's faces rose in Jacuzzi's mind. They were followed by the faces of Isaac and Miria, Czes and the Beriams, and the faces of people he'd merely passed by in the dining car. Then the corpses of the conductors that lay in front of him rose in his mind, overlapping with the scene before his eyes.

Before he knew it, he'd swallowed the answer "run away," and other words had surfaced.

"Let's run the group in black and the Rail Tracer off this train... *Hic*. Huh? Wh-what did I just say? No, no, we really need to get away, but, but——"

They were a gang of hopeless delinquents; they'd made and sold liquor, and even if the other guys had been mafia, they'd been people, and they'd killed them. Then and there, they'd become inexcusable villains. And he was the cause of everything.

However, all along, Jacuzzi had only done what he thought was right. He'd thought the law that banned liquor was wrong, and he'd hated the way the mafia used it to rake in money and kill. In consequence, he'd tried to sell cheap, good-tasting liquor on his own. That was all. And yet.

Before he realized it, ne'er-do-wells had collected around him, and he'd become their boss.

Their friends had been killed, and they'd fought the Russo Family tooth and nail. And yesterday, although killing them hadn't been Jacuzzi's original intention, as a result, they'd avenged their friends.

Now Jacuzzi was on this train. He was here to steal a certain something from its cargo. It was something Nice had wanted, and if they just threw away the contents, it would be safe to sell it. Most important, they couldn't let "that thing" arrive in New York.

If "it" reached New York, it was likely that lots of people would die. He'd hated the idea of knowing that and doing nothing about it. It made him a terrible hypocrite. Even Jacuzzi knew that. Still, it felt as though, if he didn't do it, his existence would lose all value, and it scared him.

And now, he was on the brink of pulling his friends into yet another hypocritical act.

I want to save the passengers. For the leader of an organization—someone who needed to make his comrades' lives top priority—not to mention the leader of a gang of robbers, this was a naïve, foolish thought, the sort of idea he must never have.

However, Nice and Donny would probably smile and agree to it. He knew this. He knew it and was planning to use their personalities. It was so hypocritical it made even him feel nauseated, but even so, he didn't care.

I broke the law and killed people. I'm a bad guy. All I've done, this whole time, is try to stick to my path. At this point, what does a little hypocrisy matter?

He was finished with his excuse. There was no chance anyone else would accept one that convenient; Jacuzzi knew this better than anyone. Still, he made the excuse to himself. The logic couldn't have been more selfish, but he didn't care.

After all, in the end, he was nothing but a bad guy.

After a short silence, he made a declaration. How much courage had he focused into this one moment in order to put his resolution—the sort of resolution that so-called allies of justice could probably have said without even thinking—into words? As usual, Jacuzzi's eyes were brimming over with tears. Even so, the fear had completely disappeared from his gaze.

"Let's get rid of them, by ourselves. The black suits—and the Rail Tracer."

The doubt had vanished from Jacuzzi's face. The light had disappeared from his sharp gaze, and in combination with it, the tattoo on his face looked even better.

After confirming that Nice and Donny had smiled and nodded in agreement, Jacuzzi left the blood-dyed room behind him.

His tattooed face wore a devil's expression, while the tears he cried were hotter than anyone's.

⟺

Mary was unable to stir from the janitor's closet.

It had been quite a while now, but Czes showed no sign of coming back.

Could he have been captured?

In the darkness, her unease grew and grew, and tears rolled down the girl's cheeks.

After another short while, she heard footsteps approaching in the corridor. Could it be Czes, or maybe Isaac and Miria, or maybe——?

In an attempt to hear the footsteps better, she tried to put her ear closer to the wall. Just then, part of her body touched a mop, and it fell.

Tunk. The sound was small, but it carried well.

Mary thought her heart might explode. That was how clear and loud her heartbeat had become.

Please don't let them have heard that...

The girl's wish was in vain: The footsteps stopped.

After a short silence, she heard the door to the bathroom open. They probably weren't sure exactly where the noise had come from. At that point, the possibility that the footsteps belonged to Czes disappeared.

Her terror swelled; her tears spilled over; she wanted to scream and run right this minute.

Swallowing down all these thoughts, the girl concentrated on holding her breath. Picturing her mother's face, she desperately waited for time to pass.

However, time yielded a cruel result.

The footsteps she'd begun to hear from in front of the bathroom slowly approached, then stopped in front of the door to the janitor's closet.

There was no way to lock the door from the inside. One light tug on the knob, and the bulwark that protected her would be lost.

Still, the door hadn't opened yet. It was still okay, still okay, and besides, it might be Mr. Isaac, or Mr. Jacuzzi, or Mama—of course it might be Mama! It must be; Mama, Mama had come, Mama, Mama, Mama…

In the girl's mind, the person in front of the door right now was her mother. Hope simmered within despair, and at this point, her mother's figure was the only one in her world.

Slowly, the door began to open.

Mama!

She wanted to scream the word and leap out, but she couldn't.

The hand that had appeared through the crack in the door belonged to a man. What she saw after that big hand was a sleeve as white as snow.

The world with her mother that she'd created began to crumble. The sound of its collapse turned into the girl's scream.

However, her mouth was covered by the hand of the man in the white suit.

"Foooound you."

With a nasty smile, the man opened the door all the way. His eyes drooped at the outside corners.

"You mustn't scream, hee-hee. Sorry 'bout this, Ladd, but it's okay if I take the girl, ain't it?"

Mary struggled with all her might, but the man in the white suit was built tougher than an ordinary adult. She knew it wasn't any good, but even so, she kept fighting.

"Quit fighting, hya-hya! I'm gonna throw you out the window before Ladd finds us."

He tried to drag her out of the closet.

"Unlike Ladd, all *I* like is torturing weaklings to death. Hee-hee-hee……hee?"

Abruptly, the man's laugh cut out. He stopped moving for a few moments, and then the strength that had been focused on Mary suddenly weakened. When, with a desperate effort, she shoved him away, the man simply fell over backward.

His body had fallen faceup, and centered on that body, a red puddle began to spread across the corridor.

Not understanding what had happened, Mary slowly raised her eyes from the man's corpse.

There was a woman standing there.

"Eeek—"

On seeing her, Mary gave a small scream.

The woman wore a black dress, and in her hand she held a knife that dripped with blood.

However, that wasn't what had frightened Mary. She'd been gripped with a fathomless terror at the sight of the woman's eyes.

Mary had seen the eyes of the woman in the black dress—Chané—right from the front. The color of those fantastically dark, deep, pure eyes.

When she saw those eyes, Mary found herself completely unable to believe that this person was human.

Ironically, a name that was completely off target leaped from Mary's lips. At this point, she must truly have thought Chané was "that."

"The......The Rail Tracer..."

⟺

"Okay, first we'll get rid of the guard. I'll be the decoy, so when he comes through the door, grab him."

"*Mrrg*, got it. Leave to me."

In the corridor outside the room where Jack and Nick were being held, Jacuzzi knocked on the door.

If everything was the way Nice and Donny had seen, there should be one guard inside. He took two steps back from the door and stood at the ready, leaning against the corridor window.

However, no matter how long he waited, there was no response from inside. Did the group use some sort of code among themselves? He approached the door and knocked again. As before, there was no reply.

Making up his mind, Jacuzzi set his hand on the door's handle. There was a tiny creak, and the door opened with surprising ease.

A gloomy freight room. There were two shadows, deep inside it.

One was crouching and seemed to be in pain; the other, who was bound with ropes, was glaring at the open door, but—

"Nn? Jacuzzi! Is that you, Jacuzzi?!"

"Nick? Oh, good, you're oka—"

His delight was immediately cut short. Jack was hunkered down beside him, and his face was red with blood.

"Jack!"

"Don't worry. He's not gonna die."

Nick looked down, resentfully.

"No, I'm worried! What on earth happened?!"

"That's what I want to know. Forget the black suits—what the hell is that punch-drunk lunatic in white?"

Then Nick began to tell them about what had happened after they'd been caught by the black suits.

When the black orchestra members had tied Nick up and taken him to the freight room, several other people were already there.

"Jack!"

"Hey, Nick. They got you, too, huh?"

Of the three bound individuals, one was his friend Jack. The other two were a young man and woman in white.

They'd tried to talk to the white-clothed pair, but they wouldn't say a word. With no help for that, Nick tried to talk to Jack, but the guard with the machine gun glared at them, so they gave up.

After a little while, the guard opened the door and went outside. He'd probably gone to call a replacement. A little more time passed, but the guard didn't come back. Just as Nick and Jack were struggling, trying to figure out a way to cut the ropes, someone abruptly flung the door open.

When they hastily looked that way, a man in white stood there. No, *white* wasn't quite accurate. Red stains spread across his clothes here and there, creating a warped, mottled pattern.

"Thank you, fuck you, here comes the enemy!"

He was hyper to the point where it was patently idiotic. Striking a weird pose, the man entered the room and spun around once.

"What's this, what's this, what's this? Not one single guard! Man, that blows! Still, I'm glad you're okay, Luuuaaa—"

"What, you're not worried about me?"

The trussed-up man in white spoke for the first time. Meanwhile, the woman murmured "Thank you" in a voice as faint as a mosquito's whine.

They had no clue who this guy was, but they were saved. Nick and Jack looked at each other and smiled, but the man only untied the snowy pair, then started out of the room.

"H-hey, c'mon, untie us, too."

At that, the man glanced at them, looking mystified.

"Huh? Why? What's in it for me? Are you? Gonna do? Something for me? If you were dolls, I'd expect a kiss, but you're fellas, meaning 'no way in hell.' Actually, why don't you just die right there? If you leave the planet, a doll might be born to replace you. Great, g'wan and die. It's your destiny to die! If you fight destiny, you die, see?"

Spinning around and around in place, he kept pointing fingers at them sharply. At that taunting attitude, Jack's face turned bright red, and he raised his voice angrily:

"What the hell, bastard?! Just hurry and untie these ropes, perv!"

Without rising to the bait, the wired guy cackled and left the room with his companions.

"Get back here! I'm still talking to you, loser!"

"Give it up, Jack. Let's just think about getting these ropes cut."

And then it happened.

The instant Nick called Jack's name, someone stuck their head in through the freight room door. It was the hyper guy who'd just left.

"What's this? Did you say 'Jack'?"

Tripping over to Jack with short, quick steps, he nimbly untied the ropes.

"What're you playing at?"

Nick was the one who'd asked the question, but the guy was already blind to everything except Jack's face.

"So your name's Jack, huh? Now, see, *that's* interesting! It's time we figured out whether all guys named Jack are good at boxing. Diiiing!"

Right as he rang the gong with his mouth, the man buried his fist in Jack's face.

"After that, it was awful. He just kept whaling on Jack... Then we started to hear gunfire from the cars up front, and at that point, he finally stopped thrashing him."

On hearing gunshots, the face of the man wearing the red-and-white-mottled suit had warped cheerfully, and he'd walked off in the direction of the sound with his compatriots.

"If he'd kept that up, he might've beaten him to death."

At Nick's mutter, Jacuzzi examined the fallen Jack's face again. He could hear him wheezing, but his face was so swollen he couldn't even tell what color his eyes were.

Jacuzzi narrowed his eyes, quietly clenching his fists. On seeing this, Nick moved a little ways away from him and whispered to Nice and Donny.

"Hey... Did Jacuzzi switch on?"

Nice nodded and answered Jack, also in a whisper.

"Yes. It hasn't happened since the time the Russo Family killed eight of us."

"He was crying *and* awesome that time."

"Mm-hmm. He robbed eighteen Russo establishments on his own. In one day. And he cried the entire time."

The Russo Family had learned Jacuzzi's face through that incident, and they'd passed around wanted posters. In the end, Jacuzzi hadn't regained his fear until after the funeral for their dead companions was all over.

They hadn't been able to put them in proper graves. They'd just buried them in an empty space in a corner of a public cemetery, without permission. Still, even that had been better than burying them under the floor of a room in the slums. A few days later, they'd forced a priest they knew to say prayers for them and had conducted a simple funeral. After all of that was over, Jacuzzi had finally retaken his "fear," and he'd kept apologizing and apologizing to their dead companions for something.

"What's up? It doesn't look like he's snapped as bad as he did then, but what happened?"

"Erm, well… I'll explain later."

Before she could explain the scene in the conductors' room, Jacuzzi had begun to walk, heading out the door. He was carrying Jack over his shoulder. He didn't seem to care one bit that his clothes would get bloody.

"Ahm, I carry Jack."

Donny followed his lead, and the delinquents left the freight room.

As they did, Jacuzzi noticed something. Compared to the length of the car, the room was quite small. In addition, the color of the rear wall was very slightly different from the color of the floor and ceiling.

Jacuzzi was sure of it: Their prey was behind that wall.

"What's wrong, Jacuzzi?"

"It's nothing, Nice. Let's go."

He didn't tell the others about that fact. They still had time, and even if he'd told them now, they'd have had to leave it until later.

However, depending on the situation, they might be able to come and retrieve it. He understood that, too.

The train's top-secret cargo, the thing they were after.

A large quantity of a new explosive with several times the force of conventional types, and bombs that had been manufactured from it…

$\Longleftrightarrow$

"Wouldja look at this? Whaddaya think, whaddaya think? Ain't it interesting? It is, ain't it? Hot damn, what is it, what *is* this? Hell, I wish I'd just come through below the normal way instead of walking on the lousy roof."

The very first room in the chain of three freight cars. In the corridor in front of its door, Ladd was doing a happy little dance.

"...What is this...?"

Lua was gazing in through the open door. Her dark eyes were clouded even further.

Just then, from down the corridor, someone yelled:

"There they are! That's them!"

They'd tried to stop Nick from yelling, but it was too late. Nice and Jacuzzi looked around hastily. However, except for the fact that the white suits had turned to look at them, they didn't sense any particular abnormalities.

"What? Where are the black suits?"

Warily, Jacuzzi's group approached the white suits.

They were going to grill the white suits about Jack, and depending on the situation, they planned to attack them.

However, Ladd's words stopped that idea in its tracks. Victory went to the swift: As soon as he saw Jacuzzi's face, Ladd called to him.

"Hey, there! Was Jack a friend of yours? Is that loser who threw in the towel at my machine 'guns' still alive, *Jacuzzi*?"

"*Ngh?!*"

Agitation alighted Jacuzzi's face. Why did this guy know his name?

"Whoops? I guess I forgot to introduce myself. I'm Ladd Russo. That explains why I know your name, don't it? If it doesn't, you're a complete moron, but that would be its own kinda interesting!"

"Russo...!"

Tension ran through Jacuzzi's group. They didn't know how this guy was related to the boss, Placido, but there was no doubt that he was one of their sworn enemies, the Russo Family.

"Oh. Huh. So you did know. That's boring. Well, never mind. What do you people think you're doing on this train? Or actually, who do you think you are? We're about to fully occupy this train, or rather, kill half the passengers, or rather, depending on how things go, massacre all of 'em, and anyway, if you don't want us to kill you, you'd better jump off and die. Don't even think about getting between us and our fun!"

As he said these unreasonable things, he gestured as if he were chasing a dog away: "Shoo, shoo."

Splish.

Jacuzzi had been about to say something, but that sound echoed in his ears with awful clarity.

"Huh…?"

He'd heard the sound when Ladd had turned toward them to make that gesture. The sound of water splashing.

The ripples spreading at Ladd's feet told all there was to tell of the sound's identity.

A red puddle spread from the entrance to the freight room. It was the same thing he'd just seen in the conductors' room.

"Curious about what's in this room? C'mon and take a look. …If you've got the guts for it."

Snickering, Ladd taunted Jacuzzi. However, the boy and the others weren't about to carelessly approach the white suits.

"You're pretty cautious… Folks say caution and cowardice are two different things, but they also say caution is cowardice. Which is it?"

Ladd cackled his jibe. In contrast, Jacuzzi quietly glared back. His eyes were calm.

"We don't have time to deal with you people now. Afterward, though, we'll make you pay. Count on it."

"Oho, you're sounding pretty tough there, lil' crybaby. You don't look like you did a minute ago. Did the conductor say something mean to you in his quarters?"

"Both of the conductors are dead. Just to make sure: You didn't do it, did you?"

At Jacuzzi's words, the expressions on the faces of Ladd's group visibly changed.

"They're *dead*? Both of 'em?"

"Yeah."

"Both of them. You're sure? There wasn't anybody else there?"

"Hmn?"

Why was he so fixated on that? Frowning, Jacuzzi noted Ladd's response.

"…Let's go. To the conductors' room."

Saying this to his two companions, Ladd strode toward their group.

Tension ran through Jacuzzi and the others. Nick held his knife at the ready, and Nice took a small explosive and a lighter from her waist. However, Ladd didn't even seem to see them: He walked right on past them, with his hands in his pockets.

"You got lucky. For now, I don't have time to deal with you, either."

His mood was a lot more subdued than it had been. Ladd's tone even betrayed agitation about something.

When he'd passed them completely, Nick asked Jacuzzi a question:

"Hey, you're sure it's okay to leave him?"

"Yeah, for now. There are other people we have to take down first."

Assuming he couldn't have been serious about massacring all the passengers, Jacuzzi decided to prioritize defeating the black-clad orchestra and the Rail Tracer.

Besides, he was concerned about the contents of the freight room that was leaking blood up ahead.

Jacuzzi moved forward. Just when he was almost in front of the door, Ladd yelled at his back:

"Oh, just so's you know, we weren't part of what went down in there!"

When he looked back, Ladd and the others had already opened the door to the connecting platform and were on their way through.

Wordlessly, Jacuzzi turned back, stepping onto the carpet of blood. Then he turned his eyes to the interior of the freight room, and——

At first Nick thought a barrel of bootleg wine had tipped over in transit.

Meanwhile, Jacuzzi and the others had already witnessed these conditions in the conductors' room. As a result, they understood the situation in this room immediately.

Red. What an absolutely brilliant red. A truly warm red spread across the floor, reflecting the light of the incandescent lamps. However, the instant they saw the object in the middle, that warmth was transformed into a chilling nausea.

The thing that lay in the center of the room wore a black tuxedo.

They knew right away that it was a "thing," not a person. They didn't even have to make guesses regarding the profuse amount of blood. There was a much easier way to tell.

The lower half of the black-clad corpse didn't exist.

The cross section certainly wasn't a clean one. The closest term for it was *torn off.* That was what it seemed like. After a short silence, Nick made a sudden dash for the corridor window.

They heard the sound of the window being opened, followed by violent retching. Jacuzzi and Donny just gazed at the corpse, while Nice's lone eye observed the area in meticulous detail. Lots of luggage from the orchestra was lined up on either side of the room, and several of the boxes had already had their seals broken. One of the boxes held some kind of machine, but they couldn't tell what it was supposed to be used for.

Then Nice looked up, and her gaze fixed there.

"Say, Jacuzzi…?"

When Nice tapped his shoulder and he turned, she was staring up at the ceiling.

As if her eyes had drawn his, Jacuzzi looked up, too, and gulped.

The only things there were simple bloodstains. Compared to the horrible scene on the floor, they were nothing.

The problem was, what would have had to be done in order to get such a huge number of bloodstains onto the ceiling?

There was a massive spray of blood on the ceiling. However, it didn't seem as if it could possibly have spurted up from the corpse below.

Jacuzzi was crying, but he wasn't afraid of the Rail Tracer anymore. Still, he had to be even warier than before about what sort of monster they were dealing with.

That wasn't the only abnormal thing about the room.

There was a door on the opposite side of the corridor, a big cargo opening used for loading freight from the outside while the train was stopped. It was a sliding door, and it stood half open. The scenery they could see through it was steeped in darkness, and it looked as though a big pit yawned in the wall.

The train seemed to be traveling through a wood at the moment, and the faint moonlight cast an eerie illumination over the passing trees. They seemed almost like the arms of someone beckoning from the hole.

Even stranger were the footprints on the floor.

The blood hadn't covered the entire floor; there were places where its original color was still visible. However, those places were dotted with red, shoe-shaped footprints.

When he saw them, Jacuzzi thought that Ladd's group must have come in and walked around. However, that idea was disproved almost immediately.

The footprints clearly indicated their destination.

After walking here and there around the room, the owner of the footprints had walked away from the scene with no hesitation whatsoever.

…Through the door in the wall that opened onto darkness.

Having emptied his stomach of all its contents, Nick finally regained his composure.

Then, just as he was turning back to Jacuzzi's group, out of the corner of his eye, he caught sight of something odd. He felt as if there was something beyond the door at the very front of the corridor, the one that led to the connecting platform. Something bright red.

"Hey, guys. C'mere a second."

Nick's voice was tense. On seeing his expression, Jacuzzi and the others realized that something was up.

Cautiously, they came into the corridor. Nick spoke; he'd broken out in a cold sweat.

"There's something on the forward platform."

Just then, an eerie feeling settled over the group. They could feel an intense gaze from the connecting platform Nick had just mentioned.

"Jacuzzi, let's all turn that way on three. One, two......three!"

Except for Jack, who was slung over Donny's shoulder, everyone's eyes turned to the forward connecting platform.

And they saw it. Unfortunately, they saw it.

A red shape, sliding away to the side of the platform.

The thing had gone sideways, and this put it in their blind spot. It had moved quickly, so they hadn't been able to make out its form, but something red had most definitely been there.

Cautiously, Jacuzzi and the others made their way over to the platform, but already there was nothing to see.

The next carriage held a row of third-class passenger compartments. They couldn't see a red shadow in there, either.

"It might have climbed up onto the roof."

Jacuzzi's group looked at each other and nodded, then climbed up after it.

"Donny, you can't do it carrying Jack, so you go through the corridor. Keep a real careful eye out for black suits."

"Roger. I handle it."

Donny nodded firmly, then made his way down the corridor; Jack was still slung over his shoulder.

"Okay, Donny. Wait for us at the next connector."

Jacuzzi told him this from up on the roof, then began making his way through the ferocious wind pressure with Nice and Nick.

⇔

What on earth had that gunfire a minute ago been about?

Isaac and Miria were carefully making their way along the train's long hallway.

The third-class carriage, the only one in this long train: The moment they opened the door to enter that car, a huge shadow blocked their way.

It was a big, brown-skinned man more than six feet tall, carrying a bloody man over his shoulder.

Donny was moving through the corridor of the third-class carriage. At this point, nothing was happening, but he really couldn't let his guard down.

Just as he reached the door that led to the car in front, it suddenly opened.

Through the door appeared a man who looked like a gunman and a woman who looked like a dancer.

The woman's clothes were a brilliant red, as if they'd been dyed with blood.

The couple and the man looked at each other. An awkward silence ensued.

"……Excuse us."

Slowly, Isaac closed the door.

"Wh-wh-wh…What was that man?! C-c-c-could that have been the Rail Tracer?!"

"Eeeeeeeeek! We're gonna get erased!"

"Uwaaah, those red clothes, that woman, was she maybe, the Rail Tracer?"

Leaning against both sides of the door, the two groups broke out into simultaneous cold sweats.

Each heard the other's voices, and silence fell again. Only the wind and the noise of the train rattled the door of the car.

Before long, having made up his mind, Isaac timidly spoke to him: "Erm… Hello?"

"Please answer us!"

"Aah."

After Miria chimed in, they heard a low voice. From the way it sounded, it had to be the voice of the big man.

"Um, are you the Rail Tracer? …Uh, sir?"

"You're a monster! ……No, I mean, are you a monster, mister?"

"*Mrk*, woman over there not Rail Tracer?"

Silence again.

"Hey, Miria. Are you the Rail Tracer?"

"No, I don't think so! Probably not!"

"All right, I believe you! …For which reason, mister, that doesn't appear to be the case."

"Yaaay, Isaac believed me!"

"Aah, I see. That good."

They heard a relieved sigh from beyond the door.

"By the way, you aren't the Rail Tracer, then?"

"You're not?"

"Aah, no."

"Then who's the person on your shoulder?"

"Are you going to eat him?"

"Guah, this guy my friend. He hurt, we save, I carrying."

At that, Isaac and Miria rattled the door open, and their tones changed just as drastically.

"Oh, is *that* all! So you aren't a monster! And here I went and acted all respectful! Sorry about that, guy!"

"Yes, so you weren't a monster!"

"On the contrary, you're a good guy who looks out for his friends!"

"Aah, what you two?"

Donny finally seemed to have let his guard down as well: He questioned the two, a little shyly.

"Me and Miria? Ho-hoh, we pretend to be nothing more than a gunman and Miria, but we're actually—you guessed it—Isaac and Miria!"

"Isaac, you're so cool!"

"Muh, mu-muah?"

Confusion was born inside Donny's head.

"Uh, what you two doing?"

"We're looking for a friend of ours."

"'Cos, you see, we have to find that friend before he gets eaten by the Rail Tracer!"

On hearing this, Donny was convinced that these two weren't enemies. At the same time, he realized that the story of the Rail Tracer was more widespread on this train than he'd thought.

Donny didn't know that the two in front of him were the culprits behind the the Rail Tracer commotion. In addition, he didn't have the slightest inkling that the "friend" the couple was looking for was his own boss.

"*Aah*, I see, you two, good guys."

At that, conversely, Isaac's face clouded.

"Good guys, hmm? That's a huge misunderstanding. Still, someday, I'd like to be called that."

"So we'll do more good things! It doesn't matter if nobody acknowledges us until we're dead! We'll do good things forever and ever, until we're satisfied! We'll do bad things, too, but we'll do even more good things!"

"Mwuh?"

At the sight of Miria's smile, which seemed to contrast with Isaac, Donny felt embarrassed for no reason. He didn't understand what Isaac and Miria were saying, but in his heart, Donny was convinced that they really were "good guys."

"Aah, I see. Well, hope you find friend."

"Yeah, thanks! I hope the fella on your shoulder feels better soon!"

"Yes, 'pain, pain, go away!'"

With that, Isaac and Miria started for the rear cars.

"Muah, white-suit guys, dangerous guys. If you go near, bad."

When he bellowed at their receding backs, urging caution, they yelled back, "Thanks!" "Yes, thank you!" and waved.

Donny waved back, watching the pair go, then went out onto the connecting platform and waited quietly for Jacuzzi and the others to arrive.

⇔

At the same time, separated by a single door from the corridor where Donny, Isaac, and Miria were——

"Hey, did you just hear voices out there?"

A guy in a white suit—one of Ladd's men—spoke.

One of the third-class passenger compartments. Inside, the slaughter game had already reached its end.

There were five figures in the room. Three of them were on the floor, one was crouched in front of them, and the last one was standing beside the door.

As the crouching figure looked down at the three perfectly still shapes, it was emitting crazed, derisive laughter.

The moving figures were white suits.

The figures that were no longer moving were black suits.

"Hey, are you listening to me?"

"Hee-hya, hee-hya-hya-hya-hya-hya-haaaa-ha-hya-ha-heeee-hya—hya—hya—!"

"C'mon, gimme a break. You and Ladd are fine as long as you get to kill, but for me, it's money. I want to make sure we get that money, so get it together, will ya…?"

"Hya-hya-hee-ah-hah! Ha-ha-ha! Ha-ha!"

Having finished off three black suits, these two were taking a breather in Room Three. Either that, or they might have been enjoying the lingering sensations of the kill.

Giving up on calling to his partner, who kept right on laughing, with no help for it, he put his ear close to the door by himself.

"Hya-ha-ha-hee-hya-hya! Hee-oh-ah-haaah!"

He thought he heard a man's voice, followed by a woman's cheerful voice…

"Hee-hee! Hee! hee! Hee-hya! Ha-ooh-heh-ooh-ah-hee-hee! Hya!"

"Hey, shut up a minute!"

Without turning around, he barked at his companion, who was laughing like a lunatic.

"Hee-hya-hya! Ha-ooh-ha! Ha————yee."

Abruptly, the laughter stopped.

He finally calmed down, huh?

Without paying any particular attention to that, the white suit focused his hearing on the voices beyond the door.

The man and woman's voices were receding. Apparently they were headed for the rear cars.

"Hey, let's go."

He had a hand on the doorknob, but his companion didn't respond.

"Hey——?!"

He turned around and was struck dumb.

His friend wasn't there.

Although it certainly wasn't small, the design of the third-class compartment was startlingly bleak, and there were no places where people could hide.

"Hey! Where are you? Where'd you go?"

He looked for his partner, but there was no answer, and he saw nothing.

…Only…the wide-open window really concerned him. He was pretty sure that window hadn't been open a moment ago.

The window was pointlessly big. A lone person would probably fit through it easily.

"C'mon, now… Don't tell me he fell out."

Nervously, the white-suited man started toward the window.

He had to lift his leg high in order to step over the black suits' corpses, and in that moment…

…"it" appeared in the window.

Splitting the darkness, a deep red shadow touched down in the room.

A very brief time passed, and——

——all the figures had vanished—or more precisely, had been *erased* from the room.

Men in white and men in black. Everyone equally.

⇔

"Sorry we're late, Donny. Walking on the roof is pretty hard. At first, we were practically crawling."

Jacuzzi and the others climbed down from above the connecting platform.

"Aah, Jacuzzi, you okay?"

Jacuzzi answered the brown-skinned giant's question clearly:

"Yeah, there was nobody up on the roof. No Rail Tracer, either. All we had was moonlight, so we weren't quite sure, but we didn't see a red shadow anywhere."

⇔

"Aaah!"

"Eeek! What's the matter, Isaac?!"

Isaac gave a little scream, and Miria clung to him, anxiously.

"We overlooked something important!"

"Wh-what?"

Looking solemn, Isaac spoke gravely:

"We forgot to buy the souvenir for Ennis…"

Silence. For the space of a breath, Miria looked down. Then she raised her head and spoke:

"Wh-wh-wh-what'll we do? We *can't* meet Ennis empty-handed! I'd *hate* it! We *mustn't*!"

Miria's eyes were damp, and Isaac immediately consoled her:

"Don't cry, Miria. I've got a good idea."

"What is it?"

"Let's buy a souvenir in New York. They say everyone's happy to get souvenirs from New York, no matter where they live."

On hearing this, Miria's face lit up.

"You're right! Isaac, you're so smart! That's wonderful!"

"It is, hmm? Ha-ha-ha-ha-ha…"

As he laughed, they reached the entrance to the second of the three freight cars.

When they'd discovered the pool of blood and the corpse in the first freight room, as you'd expect, they'd panicked, but the moment they'd seen that it wasn't Jacuzzi, they'd regained their composure.

Isaac had crossed himself, then clapped his hands together, beginning to pray.

Miria had mimicked him, and they'd prayed for the dead in the style of contrasting religions.

They weren't terribly disturbed when confronted with that horrible corpse. It was as if they were used to seeing them. Even so, they prayed earnestly for the repose of the dead. When they'd finished, Isaac and Miria left the room as though nothing had happened.

After that, they'd enthusiastically engaged in the sort of out-of-place conversation they'd been having a moment ago, and before they knew it, they'd reached the connecting platform.

The entrance to the second freight car's corridor. When Isaac slowly opened the connector door, he didn't see anyone inside.

Relaxing, he began to go in, and in that instant—

—the sharp report of a gunshot echoed through the car.

"!"

Immediately, Isaac and Miria ducked, then hastily shut the door to the platform.

"Wh-wh-wh-what was that?"

"S-s-s-scary!"

When they peeked in through the window in the door, they saw people in the center of the corridor, leaving the freight room. There were three of them; they all wore white, and one of them sported a mottled red pattern on his clothes. The mottled man held a smoking rifle in his hands.

As Isaac watched their movements tensely, the three began walking toward them.

"Not good, Miria. Let's hide."

"Yes, like the Secret Service!"

The two of them hastily went back to the first freight car, flattened themselves beside the door, and held their breath.

…Held their breath and blabbed away.

"Listen, Miria… Those people must be the 'dangerous guys' the big fella mentioned a minute ago."

"Eeeeek!"

"Don't worry, Miria. They don't stand a chance against my trillion guns."

"Really?"

"Yes. Miria, have I ever stood by and watched you die?"

"No! Not even once! 'Cos, I mean, I'm still alive!"

"You see? And so, well, leave it to me!"

"Okay!"

This time, the two did silence their voices. They focused their attention on the situation beyond the door.

Before long, they heard the sound of a door opening outside. It was probably the door to the second freight car. The distance from there to the door beside Isaac and Miria wasn't even two yards. Voices—and footsteps—were coming closer.

"Why'd you kill him, Ladd? That would've been a pretty good deal."

"Mm, yeah. But did you see the guy's eyes? He had this look on his face that said, 'I'm not gonna get killed.' He was sure we wouldn't kill him! He was making a monkey of the great Ladd Russo, see? It was sort of, y'know, frankly, he made me sick, so I shot him up."

"Yeah, but, c'mon..."

"I don't like it, though. Even right when I blew his head off, he looked cool as a cucumber... What the hell was that about?"

The voices stopped in front of the door. The door showed no sign of opening.

Then the voices gradually receded, moving upward.

What in the—?

When, after a short while, Isaac peeked through the window in the door, there was absolutely no one in sight.

"There's nobody there..."

"It's a locked-room disappearance!"

They opened the door, but there really was nobody there. Only the cutting winter air, which seemed to seep into their bodies.

The cold cooled his head, and Isaac remembered that one of the voices he'd just heard had mentioned a name that bothered him.

"*...Making a monkey of the great Ladd Russo...*"

"*...The great Ladd Russo...*"

"*...Ladd Russo...*"

"Russo...?"

He knew that name.

Isaac and Miria were robbers. Just that morning, they'd stolen a large amount of money from mafia couriers...

"Miria, that money we got today. Which mafia did it belong to again?"

"The Russo Family!"

His bad feeling had been right on the mark.

Then the screws in Isaac's head guided him to an entirely wrong conclusion.

"I see... That group of white suits must be after us!"

"Eeeeeek! Pursuers!"

Miria shivered so dramatically that it seemed as if she really had to be faking it. Isaac hugged her shoulders tightly, nodding firmly.

"It's all right. We'll make a clean getaway. Both from those white suits and from the Rail Tracer!"

"That's another good reason to find Jacuzzi and the conductor as quickly as possible!"

"Well, it won't be long now. There're almost no people past this point..."

Abruptly, Isaac had a thought.

It was true: There were almost no people past this point.

In that case, the one who had fallen victim to Ladd's rifle was——

"Waaaaaugh! Jacuzzi! Stay with me! It's just a flesh wound!"

"Your wound is going to be just fine!"

Yelling unconfirmed information, the pair dashed to the entrance to the freight room in the center of the corridor.

——However.

"Huh? There's nobody here."

"Yes, it's deserted!"

There wasn't a single person in the room. No one living, no one injured, not even a corpse.

"That's strange. From the way they were talking, it sounded as though somebody had been shot dead in here."

"Yes, like someone had brought up some sort of deal, and they'd turned them down and killed them!"

Radiating question marks, the two investigated the room, but they didn't find a single tiny bloodstain.

Under the circumstances, their unease grew.

There was definitely something that was neither a black suit nor a white suit lurking on this train.

As that fancy grew closer to certainty, they moved faster in their search for Jacuzzi.

⟺

Meanwhile, Jacuzzi was in the completely opposite direction from Isaac and Miria. He'd made his way through the second-class carriages and had reached the area just before the dining car.

They stopped at the front of the carriage for a moment, and Nice went out onto the connecting platform to reconnoiter.

Partway there, she found the corpse of a white suit, but she didn't pause for very long.

It had been slashed across the back with a sharp blade, so she'd determined it was probably the work of the black suits.

True, both the black suits and Ladd's group were dangerous, but the most terrifying thing was the Rail Tracer—the "something" that lurked on the train.

"What do things look like in the dining car?"

"Not good. There are two guards, and they both have machine guns at the ready. I don't mean they're holding them; they're ready to fire."

After going to peek in through the window, Nice delivered her report. Jacuzzi considered.

"Does it look as though all the people who were in the dining car earlier are still there?"

"Well..."

Nice hesitated for a moment; then she made up her mind and spoke.

"I'm not sure about the people who were sitting at the tables, but everyone who was at the counter is gone."

"Huh? Wh-what do you mean?"

From what Nice had seen, Isaac, Miria, Czes, and the Beriams—who had all been at the counter—were gone. They might have been in her blind spot, but it was a fact that none of them was at the counter anymore.

"They might have been taken off somewhere..."

Jacuzzi's expression had clouded. Nick asked him a simple question:

"Are those guys friends of yours? Well, that's fine, but... I mean, hey, they might just have made them sit down at a table, y'know?"

Nice objected to that idea. Since she was talking to Nick, even under these circumstances, she meticulously parsed out casual speech and polite speech to the appropriate listener; Nick received the latter.

"Although the Beriams are one thing, that wouldn't be possible with Mr. Isaac and Miss Miria. True, my eyesight is poor, but—"

Adjusting her glasses, she spoke firmly.

"—I could never mistake Mr. Isaac's flamboyant gunman outfit or Miss Miria's bright-red dress for anything else."

What the heck? Nick made a face, and Donny nodded emphatically.

"*Aah*, they're really people that weird?"

Just then, Jacuzzi and the others heard a small moan.

For a moment, they tensed, but apparently the moan had come from Donny's shoulder.

"Jack!"

Maybe the blood on his face had begun to dry; there was a small crackling noise as Jack slowly began to speak.

"...Donny, you bonehead... We just...ran into...those guys, remember?"

Apparently, his mind and sight had recovered slightly by that point; he remembered the exchange between Donny and Isaac.

"What do you mean? Donny? You met them a little bit ago?"

"*Aah.*"

As he desperately focused the memories that slept in his head, a clear vision of a little while ago rose in Donny's mind.

"*Mrrgh*, right, yeah, good guys, couple. Met when Jacuzzi and rest were on roof. Man, gunman. Woman, red clothes. Thought me Rail Tracer."

"Ah! That's Isaac and Miria! It's them for sure! A-and? Where did they go?"

"*Ngh*, looking for friend. Save from Rail Tracer. Said they going to conductors' room."

On hearing this, Jacuzzi felt the blood drain from his face.

To save me? Through this deathtrap of a train?

What a thing to happen. What was that business about how he was going to save everyone, how he was going to beat both the black suits and the monster? He'd talked tough, and yet, in the end, he was putting friends he'd just met in terrible danger.

Not only that—not only that! If they'd gone to the conductors' room while his group had been up on the roof, it meant they must have run into Ladd and his friends.

"*Aah*, no worry, Jacuzzi. I told watch out for white suits. They okay, probably."

"I told you, 'probably' isn't good enough! This is awful... I've got to go back, now!"

Deciding to dash through those dangerous cars yet again, Jacuzzi issued orders to Nice and the others.

"Nice and Nick, you go over the roof and see what things are like on the other side of the dining car. Whatever you do, don't get reckless and do something crazy! Donny, you come with me—no; first take Jack and—"

"*Rrgh, ngh*... Don't worry about me... Just toss me into one of the passenger compartments... That'll be easier on me, too."

It hurt, but under the circumstances, they had no choice but to accept Jack's request.

"—All right. Then, Nice, I'm going. I'll come back, I promise, so don't you guys push yourselves, either!"

Jacuzzi and Nice exchanged a brief kiss, and then he turned back toward the rear cars with Donny.

As he watched them go, Nick casually ribbed the girl beside him: "Hubba-hubba, Miz Nice."

"......That was the first time."

"Huh?"

Watching Nick—who had a seriously weird expression on his face—out of the corner of her eye, Nice went out onto the connecting platform and began to climb up to the roof.

Chasing after her, Nick pressed the issue in a whisper.

"The *first* time? But you and Jacuzzi have been going steady for ten years, right? And you haven't kissed *once*? Man, Jacuzzi, being a coward's one thing, but there are limits. And you, too, Miz Nice..."

He called Nice "Miz Nice," but didn't show any particular respect for his boss, Jacuzzi. Ignoring the grumbling Nick, Nice stood up on the roof.

The wind pressure was nearly suffocating. At some point, the train had left the woods, and a barren wasteland spread under the moonlight. The landscape reflected the moon's light faintly, exerting a subtle allure all its own.

There were no obstacles up ahead, at any rate, but it would be bad if they staggered on curves and ended up stamping loudly.

Just to be on the safe side, Nice and Nick decided to crawl over the roof of the dining car.

⇔

A first-class room at the very front. Into this room, where Mrs. Beriam was being held captive, her daughter was thrown, with her hands tied behind her back.

"Mary!"

The lady gave a cry that was almost a scream. Goose smiled at her, patronizingly.

"Ha-ha. Does that set your mind at ease? We've rescued your daughter from those detestable white suits."

Mrs. Beriam glared at him with steady eyes. Not seeming particularly concerned, Goose pragmatically informed her of their future plans.

"All right. Tomorrow morning, this train will cross a bridge. If a signal rocket goes up from that bridge, for the time being, you two will be saved. *Only* for the time being, however."

"……?"

"There are negotiations, you see. We can't negotiate from the train, so I have subordinates negotiating with your husband."

Clasping his hands behind him, he eyed the mother and daughter appraisingly.

"If your husband proves uncooperative, in order to demonstrate that our actions are no mere threat, understand that we will be leaving your daughter's corpse on the rails."

"No…!"

"Do refrain from telling us to kill you instead. There's no particular reason, but it's a nuisance, so let me state in advance that the answer is no. In addition, note that your daughter will also be killed if we notice attempted police interference on the tracks. Thank you for your cooperation. Just so you are aware, she will be shot, so prepare yourself."

Having said all he had to say, Goose left the room. Mrs. Beriam didn't hurl abuse at his back. His attitude had been enough to show her that it would be pointless, and she knew that if she did something ill-advised, the lives of the other passengers would be in danger.

Seeing her, Chané, who was in the corner of the room, quietly looked away.

With eyes that seemed to be grieving over something, or possibly contemptuous, she gazed steadily into space.

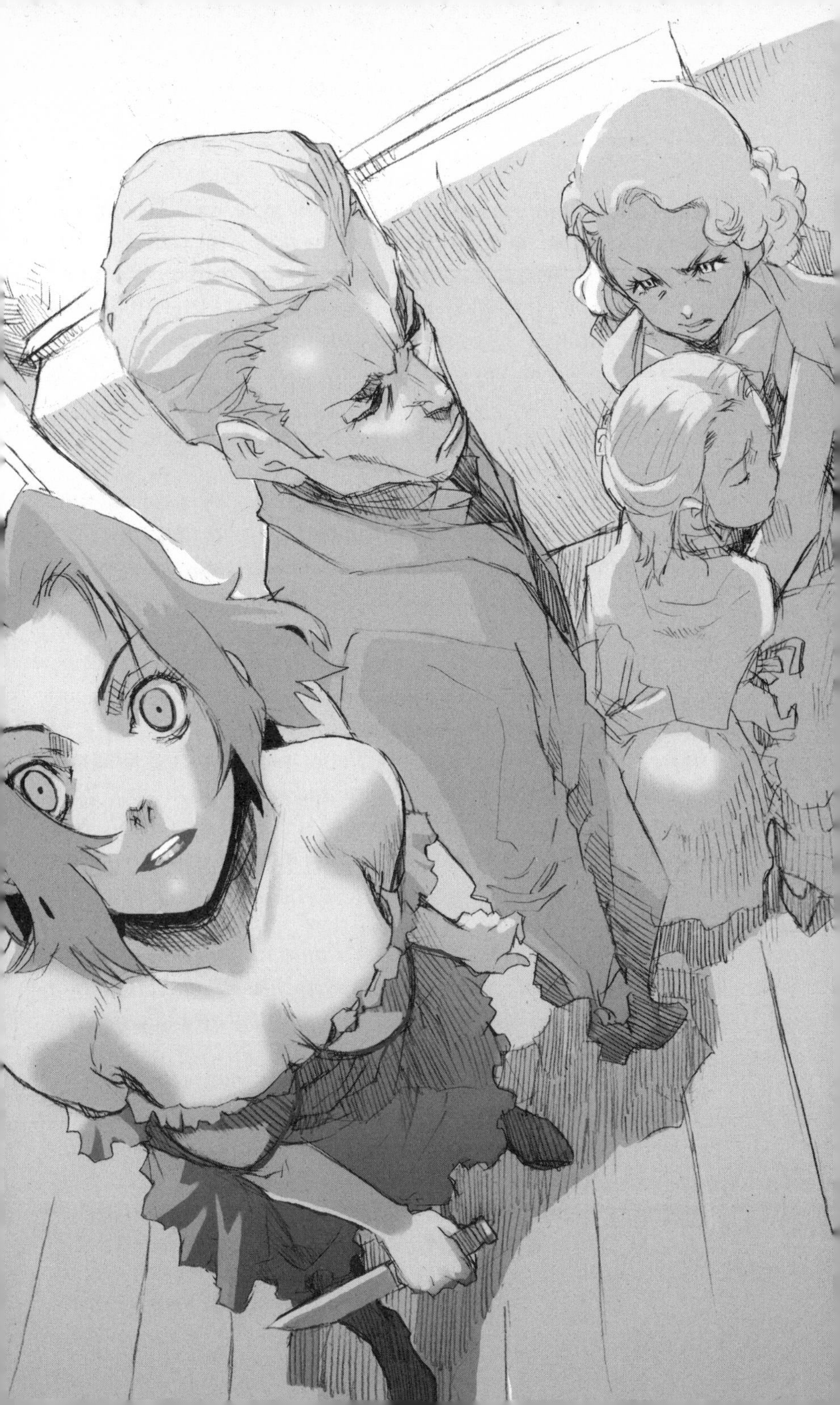

⟺

Jacuzzi and Donny got Jack settled in a nearby second-class passenger compartment, then ran off toward the rear of the train.

Left behind, Jack turned his throbbing face to the ceiling and breathed deeply. He'd said he'd be fine, but his face felt as if it could burst at any minute. His swollen eyelids were pressing down on his tender eyeballs, and they hurt, too.

Aah, I might actually die like this.

It wasn't his life flashing before his eyes, but his brain had begun to project memories from his past onto the ceiling.

One old memory from his childhood was the image of the time he'd buried his parents, who'd died of malnutrition, under the floor of their room. Among the poor, who couldn't even afford graves, this was something everyone did as a matter of course. There were probably thousands and thousands of their mortal remains under the floors of the tumbledown tenements that served as immigrant dens.

After that, he'd teamed up with Nick, one of the neighborhood brats, and they'd gotten up to all sorts of trouble.

It's weird for me to be saying this, but we were such lousy jerks that just looking at us would make you want to beat us to death… If the me from now met the me from back then, I wonder what I'd do with him. Would I beat him to death, or would I quietly hug that brat close and sob like an idiot?

What was it, about half a year ago now? When we met Jacuzzi in Chicago, at first I thought he was just a lame, sniveling punk. He was blabbing about making liquor and attracting people, and I thought if it all went well, I could be the boss and make my own mafia outfit. Man, was I an idiot.

At this point, Jack hadn't noticed it, but on the top bunk of the bunk bed in the corner of the room, a gray shadow had sat up.

Still, when it came right down to it, that guy was the smartest of all of us, and he never abandoned us lousy morons. What a good-natured idiot.

All he does is whimper, and yet in the end, he always worries about us more than himself. He's the type who's never gonna be happy as long as he lives, and that's a fact. And now we can't leave that idiot alone, so we'll probably never be happy, either.

Aah, am I seriously gonna die here? Those jerks Jon and Fang bringing in information nobody asked 'em for... And it's not even gold bars or stacks of bills, either; wanting something dangerous like that is just... No, I guess it's Miz Nice the serial bomber who wants it. Jacuzzi's going out of his way to steal those new explosives because he's worried about the citizens of New York City, guys he's never even met. Man, all of us, even me... We're all hopeless idiots, dammit.

Then the memories that had been projected onto the ceiling abruptly vanished.

Jack's swollen eyelids had cut his field of vision down by half. All his eyes had shown him was the ceiling, and then a big gray mass had leaped into view.

The mass seemed to be shaped like a human. He was dressed oddly, like a magician, and except for a small patch of skin color that was visible on his face, he was completely swathed in gray cloth.

Strangely, Jack felt no fear. Moving his aching jaw, he asked the magician a question:

"...Oh. Are you Death? That Grim Reaper fella? Hold it, I'm still fine, I can still go, I'm not through yet... I'm just gonna rest a little, and then I've gotta go save Jacuzzi and the others. One half of that team's a crybaby and the other half's an idiot, so if I'm not there, it's not gonna go well. So listen, Death, I'm gonna go save him, so Jacuzzi's not gonna die. Don't you dare take him by mistake... How d'ya like...them apples...?"

Saying this, Jack smiled quietly.

The man with a face like a corpse, a pale face decorated with bright-red blood, had definitely smiled.

On seeing that smile, the man he'd called Death also smiled softly.

"I see, young man. You want to live, do you?"

So saying, the gray man opened the bag he'd set down beside him.

"It's good to think you'd like to live while you're still young. To be honest, I envy you."

Someone was watching them quietly.

"It" was pressed to the outside of the window, and in the moonlight, its shape was…

Red. An ominous figure, dyed a deep, dark red.

It was like a bottle in the shape of a human, filled with crimson wine.

⟺

Nice and Nick had made it across the dining car roof and had carefully crossed to the next car via the connecting platform.

It wasn't a distance they couldn't have jumped, but they were worried they'd end up making a ruckus up top, so they'd descended to go to the next car.

The smoke from the locomotive's smokestack was beginning to obscure the moonlight, and the color of the darkness was deepening.

When their hands touched the roof, they turned black with soot. Even so, they crawled on through the darkness.

How much time had passed? For a little while now, they'd been able to see a slight split in the blackness.

It was the coupling. Light was probably seeping out through the window below.

At that point, Nice stiffened midmotion.

Wrong. Something was wrong.

The feeling that something was off swept over her, ranting and raving inside her mind. Something was wrong; something was dangerous.

Trying to discover the true form of that feeling, she adjusted her glasses, straining her left eye.

"M-Miz Nice…"

Nick's eyes were sharp, and apparently, he'd spotted the feeling's true shape first.

A cross wind blew, temporarily clearing away the smoke above the car.

Then they realized the identity of the trouble.

Beyond the light that filtered through. At the tail end of the car, just in front of them.

She was standing there.

Her hand held a naked knife, and her eyes seemed to have absorbed all the darkness around her.

A murderous doll in a black dress.

As she stood in the midst of the soot and smoke, Chané's figure merged exquisitely with the surrounding darkness, to the point where it seemed to exude a kind of beauty.

"…That isn't good."

A trickle of cold sweat rolled down Nice's cheek, but the blustering wind whisked the drops away.

She could probably take one of the bombs out of her shirt. However, it was very likely that she'd be stabbed by that knife before she could light it. As the woman stood quietly in the darkness, her figure showed them, with terrible clarity, that she was not an amateur at combat.

Nice had seen the woman with the orchestra, but if she hadn't, it wouldn't have been at all odd for her to mistake her for the Rail Tracer.

That was how vivid Chané's presence was as she stood on top of the train.

The pressure she exerted on them was so great that they clung to the hope that she might bump into something and fall off.

However, unfortunately, the rails were running through wasteland, and there were no tree branches or tunnel entrances to be found.

Could they forge some sort of opportunity? When, thinking this, Nice looked at their adversary, she realized that the woman's gaze wasn't directed at her.

Behind her… At Nick, maybe?

No, that wasn't it. She was looking even farther back.

Cautiously, careful not to raise her body any higher, Nice looked behind her.

Then her single eye widened in shock.

Reflecting the moonlight as it did, that white suit displayed an astonishingly strong presence against the darkness.

A clunky rifle was gripped at the end of white sleeves.

The next instant, the white suit—Ladd Russo—began to yell in a voice that pierced through the din of the train.

"Heeeeeeey, aintcha cold out here in that dress——?"

Without paying the least attention to Nice and Nick, he continued to taunt the distant black dress.

"You guys are dressed like an orchestra because you're going to perform for me, right? You're going to give a pale, sad, sweet performance for me, all for me, right? Thank you, thank you, thank you so much!"

One would have thought Chané could have attacked while he was talking, but although Ladd's rifle was moving around and around, he always kept its sight lined up with her chest.

"I was just thinking how boring it was now that the first movement was over, and then you climbed all the way up to the roof for me! How should I express my joy? You came just to perform an ensemble of moving, hilarious screams for me! Is this love? Is it really love?! Unfortunately, I've already got a fiancée, but I must respond to that love! When I 'love,' well, it means I kill."

Abruptly falling still, he began to channel force into the trigger.

"I love you—! So die."

With a completely warped whisper of love, he slowly squeezed the trigger.

A gunshot.

Then a ringing metallic sound.

"Whuuuh?"

Wreathed in rifle smoke, Ladd gave a truly dumb cry.

That instant had been burned into Nice's eye. Just before the shot,

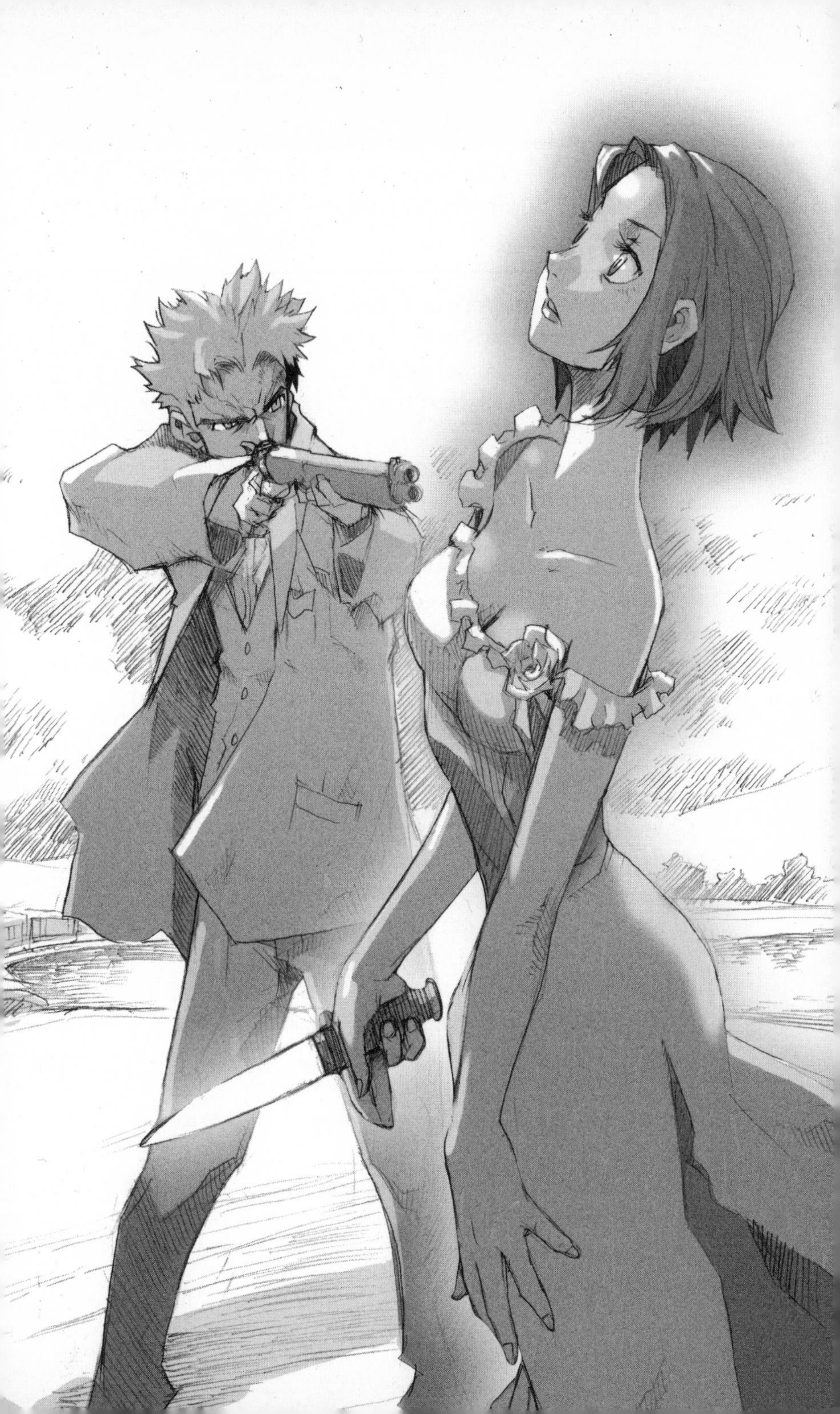

the woman had turned aside, intending to avoid the bullet by spinning. Then, by sheer coincidence, the bullet had connected directly with the blade of the knife she held. Everything up until then had been mere coincidence, but what had astonished Nice was what came next.

The woman didn't drop the knife. She didn't even stagger.

When a bullet hits a knife, the impact is considerable. The strength of the impact depended on exactly how it had struck, but as Chané leveled her knife again, she wore an expression as if absolutely nothing had happened.

"Hey, whoa, are you kidding me? Hey, *are you kidding me*?! You deflected my bullet, you bitch! You sent back the damn bullet!"

Apparently, on seeing Chané unscathed, Ladd had gotten the idea that she'd intentionally repelled the bullet. As if he was a kid who'd been taken to the movies for the very first time, his eyes sparkled, and he started to frolic.

"What the hell are you, hey?! That's nuts! That's completely insane! Even Tarzan doesn't do stuff like that! I thought you were a dame, but are you maybe Popeye, jumped up on spinach?"

Praising Chané while comparing her to cartoon heroes, Ladd kept stomping his feet.

Chané showed absolutely no emotion about this. Her body twisted slightly.

At the same time, Ladd raised his foot high.

The next instant, the knife flew from Chané's hand, and a silver flash headed straight for Ladd's throat.

"Hiyaaah!"

With a spirited cry, Ladd stomped his raised leg down.

As if it had been sucked into the path of the arc drawn by that leg, the silver flash abruptly disappeared.

At that point, for the first time, a change appeared in Chané's expression.

Her eyebrows came together slightly, and her lips seemed to tense a little.

With moonlight all they had to see by, it was hard to imagine that he'd noticed her expression change, but Ladd happily picked up the knife that was under his foot.

"Haa-ha-ha-ha-hyaa-ha-ha-ha-eee-hya-hya-hya! Payback time, payback, payback, you *loser*! How does it feel to have your precious knife ground under my foot? Is it humiliating? Frustrating? Do you want to die? Even if you don't want to die, I'm gonna kill you anyway, hee-hya-ha-ha-ha-ha!"

"He did that on purpose... What a monster."

Nick felt sweat break out on his back. He also fought with a knife, but to be perfectly honest, he hadn't been able to follow that throw with his eyes. The knife had been traveling at incredible speed, and this lunatic Ladd had stomped it down by force with a heel drop.

Unlike Chané, who had deflected the bullet by accident, Ladd's result had been completely intentional.

The hyper guy was waving the knife around, seemingly entertained, but Chané regained her composure and reached behind her back.

"Ha-ha-ha... Huh?"

Ladd's laugh stopped dead. Chané's hands had emerged from behind her back, and each held a knife that was bigger than the earlier one.

"Are you *kidding* me?! Hey, c'mon, you've gotta be kidding me, whoa!"

Ladd turned on his heel and, holding his rifle under his arm, ran away at full speed.

He ran across the jostling roof in a truly rhythmic manner, leaping easily across the couplings with no hesitation whatsoever. As he made for the rear of the train, he looked as if he was truly having fun.

Chané also launched herself into a run, pursuing him across the roof.

Her knives weren't meant for throwing, so she didn't send them after Ladd's fleeing back. With a weighty knife dangling from each hand, she ran over the panels, keeping her stance astonishingly low.

As she sprinted through the darkness, she looked just like a torpedo closing in on its prey.

Passing right by Nice and Nick, who were lying down, Chané ran straight after Ladd. Before long, the train's smoke and the dark of night got in the way, and both figures completely disappeared from view.

Even so, Nice and Nick didn't move. In the instant the woman in the black dress had passed them, they'd been struck by the illusion that death itself had become a solid mass and was rushing at them. As Nice gripped one of the bombs from her inner pocket, she felt her sweaty palm rendering the powder unusable.

That woman and Ladd... Were either of them actually human?

If those were humans, then what sort of thing was the Rail Tracer, the being people called a monster?

As Nice clenched her fists, she was picturing a tattooed, crying face the whole time.

Then, when she raised her head, making up her mind to go forward—

—she saw a man's sly face and the muzzle of an abnormally long-barreled sniper rifle.

"You look like you crawled a good long ways, but..."

Only the upper body of the man in black—Spike—was leaning out onto the roof from the coupling. Grinning, he spoke to Nice:

"Think you could put your hands up and come down here for me? Good job on making the long trip over. ♪"

⇔

"What do you suppose this means, Miria?"

"It's a mystery!"

"Do you think the monster got them?"

"Yes, it's horror!"

Confronted with the two conductors' corpses sinking in a pool of blood, Isaac took in the condition of the room quite calmly.

Miria was responding the way she always did, but she stood back-to-back with Isaac, and she wasn't looking at the bodies.

"Where do you suppose Jacuzzi went?"

"What'll we do? He might've been eaten already…"

Unusually, Miria's voice was subdued. As if determined not to let her cry, Isaac spoke loudly in the most cheerful voice possible:

"Don't think things like that! It's fine! Don't worry! If his body isn't here, it means, you know, he was swallowed whole! That means he's still alive in the monster's belly!"

"But, but, we don't know where the guy that ate Jacuzzi is."

"Don't worry! The Rail Tracer's going to erase the whole train! If we're on this train, we'll see him again someday!"

"Yeah… I hope Jacuzzi stays okay until then."

"I'm telling you, it'll be fine. Jacuzzi's a good guy, see? There's no way a guy who's better than us is gonna die before we do."

"You're right… Jacuzzi!"

Suddenly, Miria shouted his name. Shaking his head, Isaac responded, all cool-like:

"Calling him isn't going to make him show up, Miria."

"No, no! It's Jacuzzi! Jacuzzi's here!"

When Isaac turned, the big man from a little while back and a young, tattooed guy were standing outside the conductors' room.

"O-oh, good… You're both okay…"

Jacuzzi hadn't smiled since he'd seen the corpses in this room, but ironically, in the same place, he regained an expression of relief.

He must have really hurried to get there: He was badly out of breath, and tears were streaming down his face.

"Jacuzzi! That's fantastic! You're okay!"

"You got out of its stomach!"

Even as Miria's words confused him, Jacuzzi drew a deep, relieved breath.

"Oh, that's right: Jacuzzi, I'm sorry."

"I'm sorry!"

"Really, I'm sorry."

The two of them abruptly began apologizing. Jacuzzi didn't understand what they meant by it, and it perplexed him even further.

"Huh? Um, uh, no, that's my line—I'm really sorry I worried you."

Seeing Jacuzzi bow his head, Isaac and Miria exchanged glances.

"Hey, Miria, what's the score now?"

"Three to three! It's a tie!"

"Okay then, let's apologize one more time."

"But, but, Jacuzzi's a good guy, so he might apologize again, you know?"

"That's true. In that case, let's apologize a lot."

No sooner had they said this than Isaac and Miria turned to Jacuzzi and began reeling off apologies without sincerity, meaning, or need.

"Sorry, sorry, sorry, sorry, sorry, sorry, sorry..."

"I'm sorry, I'm sorry, I'm really sorry!"

"Huh? Uh, I, um, I-I-I'm sorry, I don't really get it, but I'm really sorry, I'm sorry. I-I-I-I'll apologize, so please, please stop apologizing, I'm sorry, I'm sorry..."

...And so Jacuzzi's confusion peaked. He kept bowing and bowing, with no idea what to do.

"Arrg. What you people doing?"

Until Donny delivered his verbal jab, the circular cannon didn't stop. It continued to echo, on and on, in the blood-soaked conductors' room.

"A-anyway, let's get out of this place and go to the freight room. I'll fill you in on the details there."

Prompted by Jacuzzi, the party left the conductors' room.

In this space, which should now have been occupied only by the dead, an odd sound echoed.

It was a light rattling sound. At the same time, the door at the side of the conductors' room—the one that led directly outside—rattled and opened, bit by bit.

When the noise stopped, and the door's maw had opened completely...

..."it" appeared from the darkness.

A bright, bright, bloodred shadow.

⟺

"A bright-red monster? Do you intend to stall for time with ridiculous fairy tales?"

In the first-class passenger compartment, Goose spoke, sounding disgusted.

"I'm not lying! There really is a monster on this train!"

Nick yelled angrily, snapping at Goose. He was lying on the floor with his hands and feet bound, so there wasn't really anything else he could do.

"Hmm. Then let me ask a different question."

Turning to Nice, who was also trussed up, Goose asked about their connection to the white suits.

"You say you have no ties to the group in white. In that case, why did you board this train?"

"To visit our friends in New York, sir. There was no other reason."

"Circumstances being what they are, let's dispense with the fabrications, shall we? If that truly was the reason, then why did this fellow attack the dining car?"

"He...attacked the dining car?"

Nice didn't know what this was about, but she could tell that Nick's face was growing paler by the second.

"Hey. You're sure this was the man?"

"Yes, sir. I only saw him from a distance, but from his clothes and his voice, I'd say there's no mistake."

A man in the corner of the room responded to Goose's question. He was the survivor of the group that had first attacked the dining car, the one whose shoulder had been wounded.

"...So he says."

A look at Nick's face told Nice that this was the truth. At the same time, she understood why he'd done a thing like that.

Realizing that the vague order she'd given had been the cause of this troublesome situation, Nice began working out a way to con their way out.

"He's a marijuana addict. I expect he did something so foolish because he'd seen a hallucination of some sort."

"I see. In that case, was the 'red monster' he mentioned also a hallucination? If so, shall we dispose of this socially unfit individual here?"

His lips were smiling, but the light in his eyes said he trusted no one.

She could line up all the lies she wanted, but it would probably be no use against this opponent. Even though she'd only spoken with him once, she understood this quite well. Determining that more tricks would only make their situation worse, Nice decided to tell the truth.

"Huhn... Here I was wondering what it could be, and it's a humble freight robbery? How dull. Well, I don't know how many companions you have, but if you oppose us, we'll kill you without mercy. You'd best be prepared."

With eyes that seemed to have completely lost interest, Goose left the room for a moment.

Nice hadn't told the entire truth here. For one thing, she hadn't let on that Jacuzzi existed. For another, she hadn't mentioned the content of the cargo they were after. Possibly Goose thought they were simply aiming for the cargo of this high-class train in general, because he hadn't pressed her further.

In fact, Jacuzzi's group was after just one type of cargo. Not only that, it was an article stowed in a hidden space in the freight room.

If Goose learned what its contents were, he would probably try to obtain it. She didn't know what their objectives were, but if they got their hands on that, their power would increase dramatically.

Above all else, she wanted to avoid that, no matter what.

For the moment, Nice breathed a sigh of relief. Then she murmured to Nick, who lay beside her:

"My apologies. If I'd only explained the situation to you properly..."

"Nah, Miz Nice, don't worry about it."

Forcing a smile, Nick scraped together some bravado, trying to encourage his esteemed friend.

"Either way, nobody's dumb enough to think we're on the up-and-up after seeing how you look."

"That is absolutely no consolation whatsoever…"

Recalling her own appearance, Nice was dismally convinced. As she sank into mild self-loathing, she began thinking of ways to get out of this situation.

Just then, the door opened again.

Goose, who wore a complicated expression, asked Nice and Nick a certain question:

"A moment ago, you said, 'On the way back from the conductors' room, we saw a corpse in the freight room.'"

This was a fact, and the two nodded earnestly.

"Was there anything abnormal in the conductors' room?"

A doubt had occurred to Goose. He had a comrade in the conductors' room, the informer. According to their plan, the man was supposed to have killed the other conductor. Why hadn't he disposed of this woman when she visited the conductors' room?

At that point, Nice remembered. *Oh.* Come to think of it, she hadn't told him about what she'd seen in the conductors' room.

"Yes, there was something that convinced us of the existence of the Rail Tracer."

"Just tell me the facts. Briefly."

"There were two corpses in a sea of blood. One conductor had been shot dead, and the other had been mauled to death. That is all we saw."

On hearing Nice's answer, yet another doubt crossed Goose's mind.

Just a moment ago, the time when the conductor should have sent the sign that all was well to the engine room had come and gone. …And yet the train hadn't stopped. Why? As far as he knew, they hadn't occupied the engine room yet.

Goose put his head out the window, looking in the direction the train was traveling.

The locomotive, from which light was faintly visible, was attached to the front of the train, and the smoke that streamed from its smokestack showed no sign of weakening.

"What's the meaning of this?"

Goose quickly left the room, put together a unit of five of his men, and ordered them to go check on the conductors' room.

If what the woman said was true, who had killed his comrade in the conductors' room?

Then the tragedy in the freight room, which he'd heard over the wireless, crossed his mind.

Nick's description of the freight room echoed in his ears:

"In the freight room! One of your pals was lying in there with his bottom half chewed off! It's a monster, a red monster—the Rail Tracer did it!"

Even as Goose mentally repeated *Impossible* over and over, a fear of the Rail Tracer was gradually beginning to eat away at him.

Like this train, that terror was slowly but surely eroding his heart.

$$\Longleftrightarrow$$

"I see! I've got it! Right now, the inside of this train is *The Records of the Three Kingdoms*!"

"The greatest three-way relationship in Asia!"

In the last freight room, Jacuzzi and the others had summarized the situation on the train, and once he'd gotten a rough grasp of events, Isaac had abruptly yelled.

"'The Records of the'…what?"

Jacuzzi hadn't heard the term before, and he looked bewildered.

"Oh, *The Records of the Three Kingdoms* is a famous part of Chinese history! It's a story about how amazing samurai split the country into thirds and glared at each other! Um, 'Cao Cao' and 'Liu Bei' and 'Yuan Shao,' I think they were!"

"They get compared to a snake, a slug, and a frog a lot!"

As they related nonsensical Far Eastern trivia, Isaac and Miria gradually grew more and more excited.

"Right now, on this 'tray'—the train—the black suits and white suits and the Rail Tracer are all glaring at each other, right? And so, Jacuzzi! You just have to break down that balance and flip the whole thing over, tray and all!"

"Then you take over the whoooole train! You'll be the king! The lord! His Majesty the emperor! The tyrant!"

"Uh—huh?"

At this abrupt development, Jacuzzi's eyes went wide. True, he'd intended to deal with the black suits and the Rail Tracer, but he'd never thought of calling it "taking over the train."

"B-but…could I do something like that?"

"Don't worry! Even in *The Records of the Three Kingdoms*, there's an amazing guy at the end who united Asia that way!"

"Yes, the champion!"

"So, Jacuzzi! You become 'Yoshitsune'!"

"Yes, Minamoto!"

"Y-Yoshitsune?"

"Yeah, Yoshitsune! He's a fantastic guy who crossed from Japan to China, defeated the three kingdoms, and founded a country called Genghis Khan!"

"That's *amazing*!"

Isaac's Asian history was a very mixed bag of historical fact, fiction, and different time periods, but its energy began to ignite an intense light in Jacuzzi's heart.

"Do you think…I could…be somebody that amazing?"

The guy with the tattooed face murmured quietly. Looking him straight in the eye, Isaac nodded firmly.

"Sure you can! You've beat us dozens of times, Jacuzzi, and you're the defending champ!"

"Isaac's really amazing! Since you beat him, you're *amazingly* amazing, Jacuzzi!"

The pair pressed him even harder, on momentum, but Jacuzzi still shook his head.

Why is it that, when I'm talking to these guys, I can blab away about things I shouldn't ever say to anybody?

Jacuzzi nodded slightly, then confessed who he really was to the pair.

"I do plan to save the passengers and get rid of the black suits, but… I'm not such a great person. I broke the rules and made liquor, and just yesterday——I killed five people."

At those words, Donny, who'd stayed silent until now, spoke up in protest:

"*Mrrg*, no, *we* killed, not Jacuzzi. Besides, they killed friends."

"It's the same thing. If I hadn't done something uncalled for, nobody would have had to die, not our friends nor the guys from the mafia."

On hearing that, Isaac grabbed Jacuzzi's shirtfront and hauled him over. He put his face up close to Jacuzzi's, whose eyes had gone round, and shouted.

At first, Jacuzzi assumed he was going to get hit for saying pitiful stuff, and he shrank back, but Isaac's face wore a smile that was bursting with confidence.

"Hey, don't worry about stuff like that! So what?! Cao Cao and Yoshitsune killed lots of people, tens of thousands, hundreds of millions, trillions and trillions of 'em! Even so, if the people around them say they're good guys, then that's what they are! In other words, see, good guys or bad guys, it all depends on the feel of the situation, the mood! That settles everything!"

"Yes, it's the mood!"

As if a crazy theory like that exists?! Jacuzzi's head thought this, but his heart had already been caught by the pair's mood.

"So you see, Jacuzzi! We're saying you're a good guy! Don't miss that wave! Even if people object, ignore 'em! You just have to pull 'em right into this current with you!"

"Hold your head high, and when you get to the end, believe in yourself! But listen, listen, if you want to create a wave like that, you need at least one of the people around you to think you're a good guy! Then, see, Jacuzzi, that'll mean you did a good thing! We know! So we'll make that wave for you!"

On seeing these two, who were smiling carefree smiles, Jacuzzi felt his own fingers, his hands, his arms, his whole body, tremble. A current of emotion surged up inside him. Was it fear, or…?

"Thank you."

Words of gratitude slipped from Jacuzzi's lips.

There might have been something else he should have said, but he couldn't get any other words to come out.

Ordinarily, Jacuzzi might have said the word *sorry*, but he felt as if saying it now would be an insult, both to these two and to himself.

"But if I'm going to be someone that amazing, who in the world are you two?"

Slightly bewildered, Isaac and Miria responded to Jacuzzi's question.

"We don't really get it either, but the old guy who told us about *The Records of the Three Kingdoms* told us…"

"Listen, listen, it was, 'Become the southeast wind, you two'!"

"The southeast wind…? But that's not a person."

"Well, you're right. They say it's a wind that carries happiness and despair and all sorts of things, all together!"

"So we'll do our best and bring happiness to this train!"

At Miria's words, Isaac nodded emphatically.

"I see. That's a great idea, Miria. All right, then, let's huff and puff and blow the Rail Tracer and the Russo gang away!"

"Faster than this train! Far, far away!"

Laughing happily, the two started to leave the room.

"W-wait! Where are you going?"

Hastily, Jacuzzi moved to stop them. When Isaac and Miria spoke, their faces were brimming over with confidence.

"Where? To find the Rail Tracer."

"Yes, we'll ask him to leave this train and go home! If he won't, we'll get rid of him! If we can't, we'll run away and hide somewhere! If dawn breaks while he's looking for us, I bet it'll be too bright for the monster, and he'll go back home!"

"Aah, monster, probably strong. You get killed. I'd stop, if I you."

As you'd expect, even Donny looked worried. However, Isaac and Miria answered confidently:

"It'll be fine. I'll fill the Rail Tracer full of lead with my hundred guns!"

"Isaac, you're so cool!"

Isaac slapped the holsters he wore all over his body. However, none of them held a single gun.

"A hundred guns? But you're completely unarmed…"

As Jacuzzi pointed this out, eyes round, Isaac nodded once: *Mm.*

"That's very true. I hadn't noticed that," he said, letting himself be persuaded easily.

However, his feet were still pointed toward the exit, and he didn't turn back. Gazing up into empty space, with a significant look on his face, Isaac murmured:

"It's all right. As a great gunman once said, long ago—"

Looking into Jacuzzi's eyes, he nodded firmly, intently, and said:

"—'There's a gun in everyone's heart.'"

"How hard-boiled!"

"No gunman ever said that!"

"Really? All right, then I'll become the first great gunman!"

"That's amazing, Isaac! Just like Billy the Kid!"

Watching the appalled Jacuzzi out of the corners of their eyes, Isaac and Miria quietly opened the freight room door.

"Seriously, don't worry! If things get ugly, we'll run! While we've got the Rail Tracer's attention, you save the Beriams from the black suits, Jacuzzi!"

"We'll be fine! Running and hiding are our best talents!"

Looking at their confident smiles, he began to feel as if there really wasn't anything to worry about. He also understood that, apparently, it was no use trying to stop these two.

And so Jacuzzi decided to see them off with a smile.

"Please don't die, okay? Promise me."

"Yeah, we won't die, we promise! If we break that promise, we'll sign in blood or cut our throats or anything you want!"

"You guys, too, Jacuzzi! You mustn't die, okay?!"

With that, the pair walked off toward the conductors' room to look for the Rail Tracer.

As he watched them go, Jacuzzi swore in his heart that his group would successfully do what they had to do.

"What selfish, willful people, huh, Donny? I don't know who those two are, but they're much bigger villains than I am."

Looking up, he spoke quietly to Donny, who stood beside him.

"Aah?"

"Yeah, this train is full of villains and hopeless thugs, us included."

He stopped and turned back toward Isaac and Miria, just once.

"Those two are several times more villainous than I am, but I bet they're several times better people than I am, too."

"Mmm, Jacuzzi, you lonely?"

Without answering that question, Jacuzzi began walking again.

"Let's go force our own selfish demands through. We might as well become the biggest villains on this train, right, Donny?"

Jacuzzi nodded firmly, agreeing with his own words. When Donny looked at his face, he realized the expression it wore was one he'd never seen before.

"Aah, Jacuzzi, you having fun."

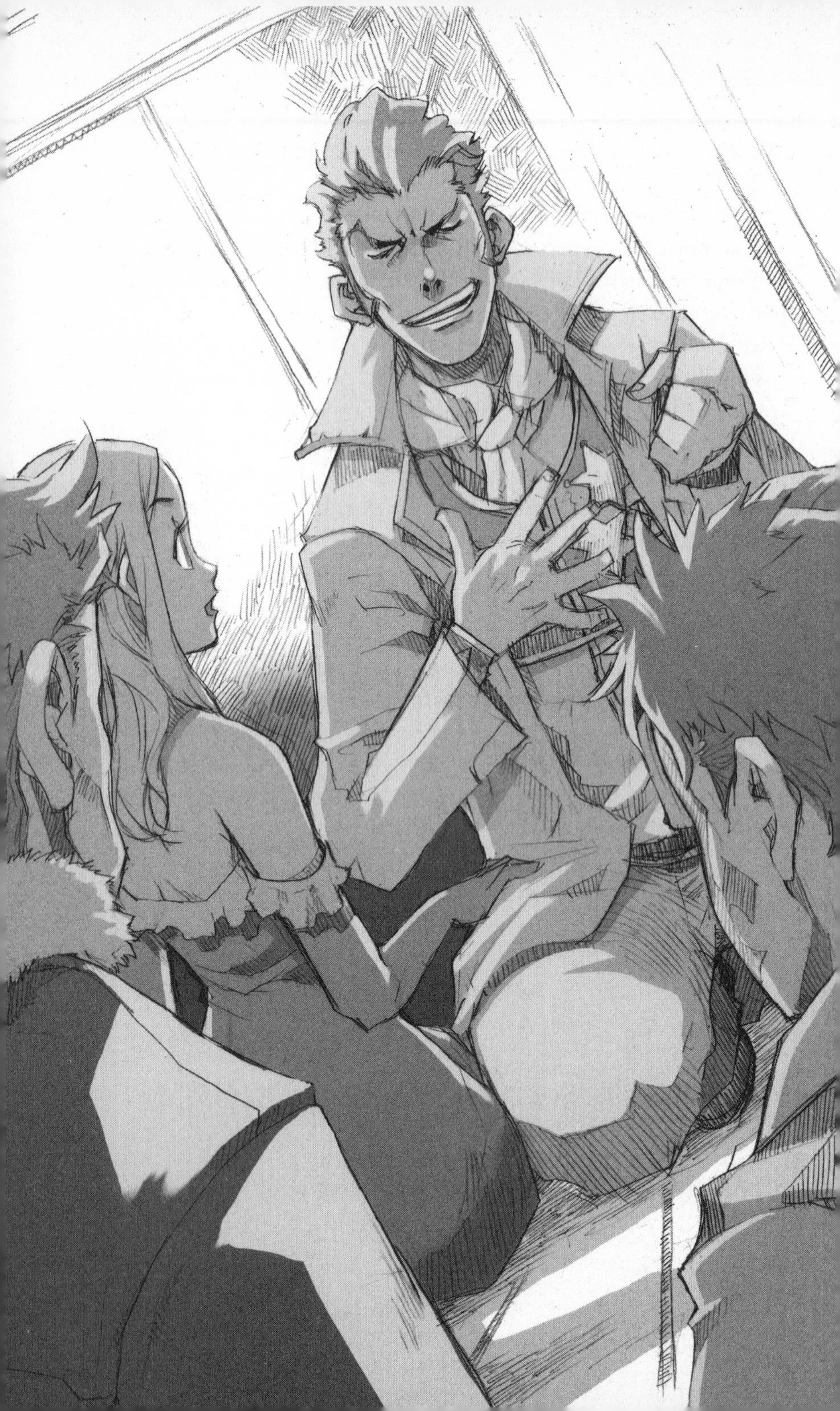

⟺

All cried out, Mary huddled against her mother, shivering slightly.

How much time had passed since she'd been caught? The scary woman had left the room a little while ago, but one guard with a gun was still there.

Come to think of it, what had happened to Czes? Was he all right? He might have gone back to that janitor's closet after she'd been caught; maybe he was worrying about her. Maybe he'd already been caught and killed.

Trembling at her own imaginings, the girl buried her face in her mother's body.

The tears that should have been dried and gone welled up again.

⟺

Having passed through the dining car and second-class carriages, five black suits ran through the lone third-class carriage.

All were armed with machine guns, and they were making straight for the conductors' room.

"Be careful. I hear Chané and one of the white suits headed for the rear cars."

At nearly the same moment as their leader spoke, the violent sound of shattering window glass rang out.

"What was that?"

"It came from one of the passenger compartments!"

The sound indeed seemed to have come from one of the nearby rooms.

"Where's the unit in charge of third class?"

"They say they've lost contact with them, just like the freight room and the second-class compartments."

The black suits gulped, then decided that two would stay in the car, and the remaining three would continue through to the conductors' room check.

After they'd seen the group of three run off, the other two approached the door quietly.

A short time passed in silence, and then, as one man gave a wordless sign, the two of them kicked down the door to the room. ... However.

"There's nobody here."

There was no one there. Only the sound of the wind streaming through the broken window glass reverberated through the compartment.

One man cautiously approached the window and used the butt of his gun to carefully knock out the shards of glass that were still in the window frame.

Once all the glass shards were removed, he stuck his head out, gun at the ready, and looked around.

When the man looked down, his gaze went fixed for a moment. Then he hastily scanned the area.

"What is it?"

"...C'mere a second. Look at this."

Prompted by his companion, the man who'd been called over also stuck his head out the window and looked down.

"*Ugkh...*"

The object they could see dimly by moonlight and roomlight was a weirdly twisted human body.

It was tangled around the metal fittings under the car, and they couldn't see all of it without leaning out.

However, even so, the black suits were sure it was a corpse.

The right arm and both legs had been ripped from the body. ... Or rather, they looked as if they might have been chewed off. The right arm was gone from the shoulder down, and the cut surface was extraordinarily dirty.

It was likely that something they couldn't see from here—either clothing or the left arm—was fastened to the metal fittings.

They should have been fairly used to seeing corpses, but the black suits weren't grimacing because it was a corpse.

It was because the corpse belonged to a young child.

On a battlefield, it would have been one thing, but to think they'd have to see something like this in the United States, and on a train, at that...

Chané and Goose probably wouldn't have been disturbed, and Ladd might actually have smiled. If Jacuzzi had seen it, he probably would have cried and screamed hard enough to send himself insane.

The boy's body had a name.

A name that was just a little hard to pronounce. Czeslaw Meyer.

⟺

"I wonder if Czes is okay."

Mary, who'd finally stopped crying, murmured to herself. Her mother heard her, and she answered her daughter's question instead of empty space.

"It's all right. I'm sure Czes, and Isaac and Miria, and Jacuzzi and all of his friends are just fine. You don't need to worry. I'll take all your bad dreams for you, so relax and go to sleep."

As she spoke, Mrs. Beriam gently stroked her daughter's head.

Tunk   Tunk   Tak-tunk

"!"

Abruptly, there was a sound at the window of the Beriams' room.

A sound as though something hard was striking the glass.

The single guard opened the window, holding his gun in one hand.

".........?"

He looked around, but there was nothing.

He leaned out a little ways, twisting his upper body to see what was above him, and in that instant...

...a black shadow covered the center of the wide, starry sky.

"*Ngh!*"

Two sturdy boot soles touched down on the black suit's face.

The owner of the boots got an underhanded grip on the window frame, then pushed the man's face down with all their might.

"W-w-wait! Ah, ah-ah-ah, waaaaaaaugh——!"

The man's body was pulled through the window, and he fell out of the train. He rolled on the gravel by the rails at incredible speed, and before long, he was swallowed up by the darkness and vanished.

The Beriams, startled by this turn of events, saw the true form of the individual who'd come in through the window.

It was a young woman in coveralls.

Come to think of it, Mrs. Beriam thought, she'd seen this young woman sitting by the window in the dining car. As she was reeling in her memories, the woman spoke to the two of them:

"You okay?"

She asked the question in a brusque tone. She was probably in her early twenties. Her coveralls had been old to begin with, and now they were discolored pitch-black by soot or something. The woman was so dirty she couldn't even be compared to her previous self from the dining car. Yet, she continued speaking to the Beriams:

"You're not hurt? In that case, we're running."

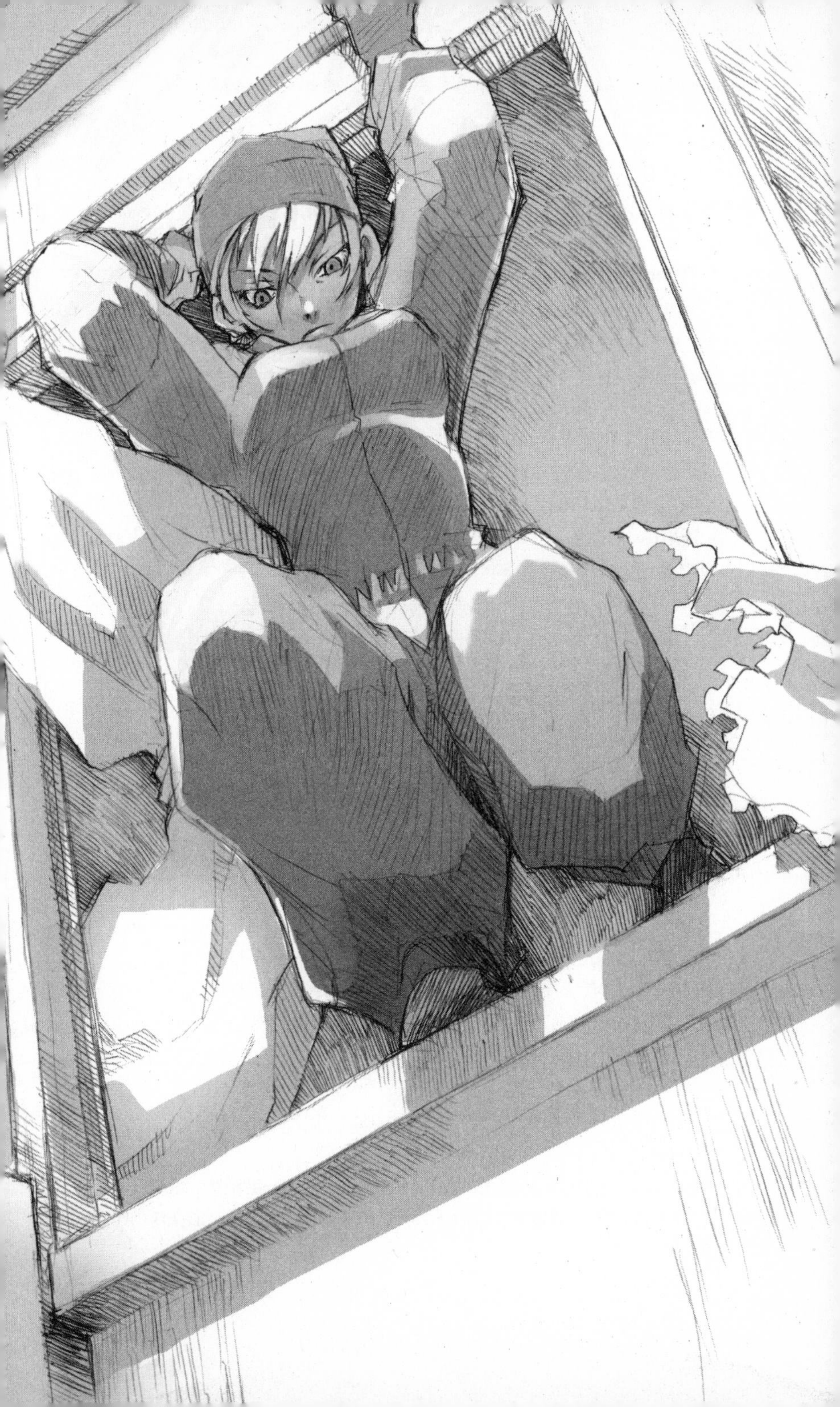

⟺

New York   Before dawn   Somewhere in Little Italy

"…Crap. I woke up too early."

Firo looked at the clock. It was only five in the morning. Outside the window, things were still deep black. In summer it might have been different, but now, when the days were short, the starry sky was still clearly visible.

"Well, I guess it's okay."

Rubbing sleepy eyes, Firo headed for the apartment's washroom.

"What's the matter? It's so early…"

Behind him, a young woman's voice spoke. The voice belonged to Ennis, Firo's roommate.

"Oh, sorry, sorry. Did I wake you?"

"No, it's fine. I was already awake."

"I see. That's good. I'm just impatient for noon today, I guess."

"Yes, I'm looking forward to seeing Isaac and Miria, too!"

As Ennis spoke happily, the corners of Firo's lips rose a little as well.

"Yeah, I'm looking forward to that, too. Besides, Claire's coming in on the same train."

"That's the childhood friend you mentioned last night, isn't it? What sort of person are they?"

The question had been asked out of curiosity. In response, Firo thought for a little while and chose several words.

"Mm… Well, personality will be obvious when you two meet, so… For starters, Claire's agile, with upper-body strength so good you'd never believe it from appearances."

"An amazing athlete, then."

"An athlete, hmm? No, Claire used to be in the circus, a long time back. If I had to say, *acrobat* fits better."

Remembering his old friend, Firo began to smile quietly.

"Right about now, that acrobat might be doing stunts on top of the train."

⟺

Just like an acrobat, the woman in the coveralls climbed up to the roof.

"All right, I'm going to lower a rope. Tie it around yourselves and hold on tight."

Doing as she was told, Mrs. Beriam tied the rope around her daughter first. While she was wondering where the object had come from, her daughter was pulled up onto the roof.

Tucking her skirt up and tying it tightly, Mrs. Beriam bound herself securely with the rope when it was lowered back down.

"*Ghk…*"

Partway up, they entered a curve, and her body thumped against the train.

However, she didn't let the chance slip past her: She set the soles of her feet against the side of the train and pulled the rope toward her with all her might.

Finally, after their short separation, the Beriams were reunited on the roof. In addition to the darkness, the soot and smoke were thick, and neither of them could make out the other's expression well. In the midst of this, mother and daughter embraced each other tightly.

"Come on. Save the celebrating until we're safely away from here."

Spurred on by the woman in the coveralls, the pair began to hurry over the roof.

"Be careful. A flat-out run is better than an unsteady walk."

"Right!"

The three of them ran to the very end of the car, then jumped, all in a rush. Mary almost lost her balance, but the woman in the coverall caught her hand, and she managed to recover.

It might actually have been fortunate that the darkness and smoke kept them from seeing the surrounding landscape. If they'd sensed the speed of the train and the height of the roof, they probably wouldn't even have been able to stand up properly.

After they'd kept running for a short while, a gunshot rang out, half-lost in the noise of the train.

The woman in the coveralls gave a short shout.

"Get to the dining car! Once you're past it, it's okay to get down from the roof!"

Then the woman in the coveralls stopped in her tracks.

When the Beriams looked back, wondering what had happened, the trousers of her coveralls were split at the thigh, and a red stain was spreading across the area. In spite of herself, Mrs. Beriam almost stopped. Anticipating this, the woman in the coveralls yelled loudly:

"It's fine! Just go!!"

Their eyes met. They illustrated the unspoken words between them with terrible clarity.

With a small, polite nod, Mrs. Beriam took her daughter's hand and broke into a run.

The girl tried to turn back, just for an instant, but her mother's hand pulled her along firmly, and she gave up struggling and followed.

After watching them go, the young woman turned on her heel. If possible, she would have liked to run away as well, but the wound on her leg seemed to be deeper than she'd thought. Realizing she'd be a sitting duck if she kept moving around, she decided to stand between the Beriams and the sniper.

The upper body of a sly-looking man was protruding from the gap between the cars they'd leaped over. A black sniper rifle had been set up in front of him.

Looking disappointed, Spike called out:

"Listen, do you think you could get out of the way? I can't aim for the kid's legs like this."

"Somebody go up to the roof and drag that woman down. Spike, keep your gun on her."

"Yeah, yeah. Hey, though, camping on the platform in this damn cold was worth it. I looked up right when they jumped over, so I had a great view of the young missus's panties."

They probably wouldn't be able to capture the mother and

daughter on the roof in time. Goose sounded sour, but Spike kept right on bantering without seeming to care.

"Watch your tongue."

"'Scuse me. Still, you know what they say: In this world, most stuff doesn't go according to plan."

He ignored Spike's words and put a question to him instead:

"By the way, was that man in the white suit really an even match for Chané?"

"I'd say yeah, probably."

"I see..."

After a short silence, Goose spoke gravely:

"We may have to keep withdrawal in mind as we act. However, before that, if nothing else, we will execute one more plan."

Then, lowering his voice, he gave Spike an order:

"If you see a solid opportunity, get rid of Chané."

⇔

Help me, help me.

Why, why, why did this happen?

At first, we were supposed to go as a group of five, so I felt safe, but then—I thought there was no such thing as monsters, but then—

We split into two groups by Room Three, and my group was supposed to go on to the conductors' room alone. At that point, I already had a bad feeling about this.

After that, when I saw our comrade's corpse in the freight room, I wanted to cut and run so bad I could barely stand it.

And then, right after that, that guy—that white devil appeared in the room. He slit my friend's throat before we knew what was happening!

My other friend got caught, too. I'm sure he's already dead.

I ran away on my own. So what?! I wasn't really on board with this plan to begin with.

Master Huey wouldn't take hostages, and he'd never even consider killing a little kid as an example. It looked like Miss Chané knew that, too, but she obeyed Goose because she had to, in order to save Master Huey.

Besides, I know: There's one crucial difference between Miss Chané and Goose. Miss Chané idolizes everything about Master Huey, but Goose only wants the "blessing" Master Huey talks about. Of course, most of the guys are probably like that; I'd like that blessing myself.

Nader's group, the ones that sold us out and got killed yesterday, didn't know about Master Huey's body, see. Their betrayal was pretty inevitable.

But I can't do it anymore, either. Master Huey's one thing, but I can't follow Goose.

To think he's planning to dispose of Miss Chané because she's in his way! Miss Chané, who was more devoted to Master Huey than anybody.

Dammit, dammit, dammit, I'll just keep going and make a break for it. I'll open the door in the conductors' room, and when we come to a big river or something, I'll jump.

I'll be killed; if I stay here, I'll be killed for sure.

Ah, this is the last freight car. Once I get through here, I'll be at the conductors' room.

Just as I passed by the door to the freight room, I realized that the door was standing half open.

By the time I saw a big, brown hand stretch out from it, it was too late. A huge palm covered my face.

Help me, help me. I don't want to die yet.

He dragged me into the freight room. It's all over. I'm gonna get killed by the big guy in front of me. This guy has to be that Rail Tracer monster.

I don't want to die, I don't want to die, please, please spare me——

"Relax, we won't kill you."

The man beside the monster spoke. He had a face like a devil's, with a tattoo on it, but he looked like an angel to me.

"In exchange, there are a few things we want you to tell us. That's all right, isn't it?"

⟺

In the first-class compartment that was serving as the Lemures' temporary headquarters, the woman in the coveralls lay beside Nice and Nick. Five or six black suits surrounded them, and Goose stood at their center.

"Well, now. Our second meeting has filled my heart with delight, young lady in coveralls."

Contrary to his words, a flame of fierce hatred blazed in Goose's eyes.

"I've heard rumors. They say there's a hitman called Vino who kills in excessively gruesome ways. When I heard about the condition of the corpses, I thought that might be the case, but... I never dreamed it'd be a woman."

With a small sigh, Goose stooped down and tilted his captive's chin up.

However, her soot-smeared face remained expressionless. Her only answer to Goose's question was silence.

"You've certainly done it now. Thanks to you and those white suits, our plan is on the brink of ruin. How many of my comrades have you killed? Why would you do a job that brings you no profit, Vino... Or should I say, Rail Tracer?"

Nice and Nick had watched the exchange silently until that point, but at those words, their eyes went wide.

However, when she heard that, the woman in the coveralls gave a muffled chuckle. Before long, the chuckle gradually grew in volume, until she was laughing loudly.

"And what...is so amusing, pray tell?"

"Ah-ha-ha-ha-ha-ha! How could this be anything but funny?! Ha-ha-ha-ha-ha-ha-ha-ha! Ha-ha...ha-ha-ha... No wonder I had no idea what you were talking about! You've got it wrong, pal, you've got it all wrong! That's a lethal mistake!"

"A mistake?"

Goose raised an eyebrow.

"You're mistaking me for that thing, aren't you? For that red monster! Too bad! It's not me! By now, that monster's probably eaten its way through all the white suits and black suits! No, if this keeps up, I bet we'll all get eaten, too! I mean, it even butchered that child!"

Goose started to say something, but his voice was drowned out by the noise of the door being wrenched open.

"Goose! There's a problem!"

"What is it?"

"W-well, our comrades who were in the dining car have vanished!"

"…Vanished? What do you mean?"

Clicking his tongue, Goose took his subordinates and left the room.

Afterward, the only ones left were the three bound hostages. Possibly they no longer had enough people for it, or possibly he'd simply forgotten to give the order, but he hadn't left a guard in the room.

The moment she'd confirmed this, the rope that had bound the hands of the coveralls-clad woman slipped off.

"Huh?"

As Nice's and Nick's eyes went round, she dexterously scraped her fingernail against the rope that bound her legs and severed that one, too.

Nick, whose eyesight was good, noticed something odd about the woman's nail. She'd grown the nail long, and it was sharpened like a blade. A portion of it had fine bumps and dents carved into it, like the teeth of a saw.

It was a nail that seemed to have been designed on the assumption that it would be used to cut ropes.

"All right, I'll untie your ropes, so hurry and run."

Even as she spoke, she was expertly undoing Nice's and Nick's bonds.

"Th-thank you very much!"

Nice thanked her and stood, but then she remembered something. She asked the woman a question:

"Excuse me… That child you mentioned…"

In response, the young woman looked uncomfortable. After hesitating just a moment, she confessed the truth to Nice:

"There was a kid joking around with you at the counter in the dining car, remember? It was that boy."

She'd half-expected that answer, but even so, Nice's vision seemed to dim.

More than anything, it hurt that she'd have to tell Jacuzzi about this.

Assuming they made it off the train alive, that is.

⟺

A few minutes earlier, an incident had occurred in the dining car.

"Change."

Two black suits had been guarding the hostages in the dining car when two of their black-suited companions appeared.

"Right. Take care of the rest."

Handing over their guns, the two who'd been on guard duty headed back to the first-class compartment.

They stepped out of the dining car onto the connecting platform, and just as they were about to open the door to the first-class cars...

From the dining car behind them, they heard what sounded like a passenger's scream.

"What's that?"

When the pair turned around, it was obvious at a glance that something was wrong. The lights in the dining car had gone out.

They immediately turned back, flinging open the door to the meal car. A little moonlight filtered in, but they couldn't make out the details of the situation inside. However, of the row of windows along the side, they could tell that the very farthest and the very closest were wide open.

"What happened?!"

However, there was no response from the comrades who should have been there.

As they broke out in cold sweat and kept a wary eye on their surroundings, before long, the incandescent lamps in the dining car lit up again.

There was nothing wrong with the bulbs. The car had probably suffered a temporary power outage.

However, that wasn't important.

The problem for the two black suits was that…

…the comrades who'd come to trade places with them were gone without a trace.

They felt the volume of their cold sweat double. The wind that blew in through the open door was rapidly cooling their sweat-soaked bodies.

"What is this?! What happened?!"

One grabbed the shirtfront of the passenger closest to the door and hauled him up.

The response that returned was incredibly simple and easy to understand, and everything about the shuddering man seemed to vouch that it was the truth.

"A reh—! A-a-a reh—reh! …A red monster just, mo-mo-mo, re-re-re-re, a red monster! A red monster! I-it leaped in through the window and dragged the two in black out of the windows!"

"A monster?! What did it look like?!"

"I-i-it was dark, so I don't know! I just, it was, I know real well that it—it was—bright red!"

The man had seen something terrible, and he seemed to be shaking so hard that the words wouldn't come out right.

With no help for it, he returned to the connecting platform and spoke to his waiting comrade:

"Hey, I'm going to go report this to Goose. You have a pistol, right? Use that and guard the lot in the dining car for a bit."

"With one pistol?"

"It's fine. They can't do a thing."

He turned back to the dining car, checking on the passengers through the window. Nobody seemed to have a weapon.

"There won't be a prob—"

The instant he turned around to tell him there wouldn't be a problem, he found himself faced with an extremely big problem.

There was no one there.

He didn't understand what had happened. However, he was sure that in the instant he turned, he'd seen something out of the corner of his eye.

Something dimly lit by the sky, which had begun to pale. A bright-red something.

In the space of a breath, he understood perfectly:

The passengers might be one thing, but against that red monster, a pistol would be no use whatsoever.

Before he knew it, he'd run back through the door of the first-class passenger carriage as if he was fleeing from something. As a matter of fact, he was.

⇔

Inside the dining car, an awkward silence reigned.

No black suits had come in since the uproar a moment ago. At this point, it would have been easy for them to just walk out.

However, what would happen if they left this place?

They didn't know what had happened to the white suits after that, and there was no telling where that red monster would appear. In that case, it might be better to stay here, where there were lots of people.

Besides… Of the people who'd left this place earlier—the weird gunman and the children—not a single one had come back. At that thought, they couldn't have moved even if they'd tried.

How many minutes had passed? Eventually, the uncomfortable silence in the car was broken by the sound of the door opening.

It was the door on the opposite side from the first-class carriages. Had the group of five black suits who'd passed through a little while ago come back, or was it someone else—?

The correct answer was the second one. In addition, of all the possibilities, it was one of the worst answers available.

"All right, nobody move!"

"If you move, we'll shoot, I swear!"

Two men with guns made this declaration the second they appeared in the doorway.

None of the passengers recognized the men's faces, but it was obvious at a glance that they were dangerous.

Aside from the fact that they had guns, both men were dressed all in white.

"Who'd have thought the black suits would just disappear for us? We sure got lucky."

"I guess hiding by the dining car this whole time was worth it."

"So, folks, let's have you hand over your money and valuables."

"Wait, you're sure we don't need to take 'em hostage?"

"It's fine, it's fine. The kidnapping's pretty much failed anyhow, and there was no way it was gonna work in the first place. I say we just take the money and make a break for it."

"Yeah. Ladd's disappeared somewhere, too."

Chatting away loudly, the white-suited men took one step into the car.

Clunk.

A dull sound, as if someone had struck a tree with an ax, echoed through the dining car.

"*Gyaaaah…*"

"*Ahg!* ……?"

With brief groans, the two white suits' eyes rolled back in their heads, and they fell to the floor.

When the passengers looked past the fallen white suits, a big man whose head practically brushed the ceiling was standing there. His enormous fists were clenched tightly, and they hovered in the area where the white suits' heads had been.

Was this a savior or a monster?

The passengers followed the big man's movements with tense gazes.

However, the first one to speak was a young guy who appeared from the former's shadow. His face sported a tattoo, so it was obvious that he wasn't a respectable individual. He held a Thompson machine gun at the ready, and there was a bright, childlike smile on his face.

A few of the passengers realized that he was the guy who'd been crying at the counter before the incident.

Jon and Fang were watching the situation develop with round eyes.

Then the words he spoke plunged the passengers back into despair.

"We've captured this train. If you don't want to die, please follow our orders!"

⇔

About that time, Spike was on the roof, leveling his sniper rifle. His body was flattened on the roof, and he was looking through the scope of the abnormally long barrel. He had two figures in his sights. They were a good distance from here, probably on top of the freight car.

However, that wouldn't be much of a problem. Now that the sky had begun to lighten, he could clearly see the difference between the two shapes.

One wore a black dress, and the other was an incredibly deep red.

When he'd first made out Chané's figure, he'd just assumed she was fighting the man in white, but apparently, she'd switched opponents at some point during the last several hours.

It's amazing she's still got strength left, after several hours of mortal combat.

Spike was impressed all over again at Chané's irrational strength, but the red shadow that had continued to fight her was something else as well.

It wasn't clear what they were doing now; both had stopped moving and seemed to be facing each other. Whatever the reason, the fact that Chané wasn't moving was all to the good.

"Is that the monster everyone keeps talking about? From here, it doesn't look like it's shaped much differently than a human..."

Feeling the train sway, he calculated the slope of the curve the car he was on had just passed through. Using those results, he estimated the trajectory of the bullet, then quickly pulled the trigger.

"Annnd kaboom."

A gunshot rang out, and a moment later, one of the figures fell.

It was Chané, the woman in the black dress. Even on top of a moving train, the bullet Spike had fired had found its target like a charm.

"Poor doll. Well, if we're going to take Huey's 'blessing' by force, you'd be in the way, see."

With a light whistle, Spike began to line the red shadow up in his sights.

"Okay, Mr. Monster, would you hurry and finish off Chané for me?"

Even seeing the monster at a distance, Spike felt no particular fear. From what he'd seen of it, it wasn't as if he'd be going up against a dinosaur. Spike didn't believe in superstitions of any kind, so he was convinced beyond a doubt that that red shadow was human.

And if it was human, there was nothing to fear.

He'd snipe its body before it got close, and when it stopped moving, he'd nail it in the head. That would be that.

As long as it didn't gauge the timing with which he'd pull the trigger, with Spike's skills, this would be easy.

However, the red shadow didn't move. Spike got the feeling that its face was turned toward him, glaring at him.

"C'mon, what's the matter? Hurry up and kill Chané…"

His words stopped, and his heart jumped.

The red shadow had moved. It was traveling at incredible speed. Over the roof, in a straight line, heading for Spike.

"What the hell?! What *is* that thing?! That's way too fast!"

Spike sounded flustered, but his eyes and fingers were still calm. The red shadow didn't even sway from side to side; it was simply running toward him in a straight line. It looked like a red cannonball skimming right above the roof.

He took aim, then pulled the trigger.

"Just die."

However, the instant he squeezed the trigger, the red shadow changed its course for the first time, slipping out of the crosshairs.

"What?! Aw, c'mon!"

He lined up the crosshairs and pulled the trigger again.

But, as before, just as he squeezed the trigger, it slipped out of the center of the sight.

He fired twice, three times, but it evaded every bullet.

"Can it see my finger or something?!"

With a stunned expression, he pulled the trigger, but all that emerged was a futile *click*.

Out of bullets. For the first time, Spike sensed that the red monster might not be human, and he felt fear.

"Dammit! What about this?!"

Pushing the rifle aside, he brought forward other equipment he'd had ready, just in case.

In contrast to his weapon of choice, it was a rough gun with a barrel that was fat the whole way down.

It was a Lewis light machine gun, a barrage piece designed by an American and adopted by the British army.

"If you're all red, then *act* red and turn into chopped meat!"

As Spike yelled, a barrage that easily surpassed five hundred rounds per minute erupted.

At that, as you'd expect, the red shadow stopped moving. It rolled sideways on the train roof, then fell right over the edge.

It was two cars behind the one where Spike was, probably just about the middle of the dining car.

Involuntarily, Spike whistled, or tried to; his jaw was shaking, and the sound didn't come out right.

It might climb back onto the roof. Keeping his guard up, Spike kept his aim fixed on the roof near where the red shadow had fallen.

However, it showed no sign of coming back up.

Finally giving a sigh of relief, Spike felt his heart begin to settle down. When he looked across the roof again, Chané was still sitting where he'd sniped her.

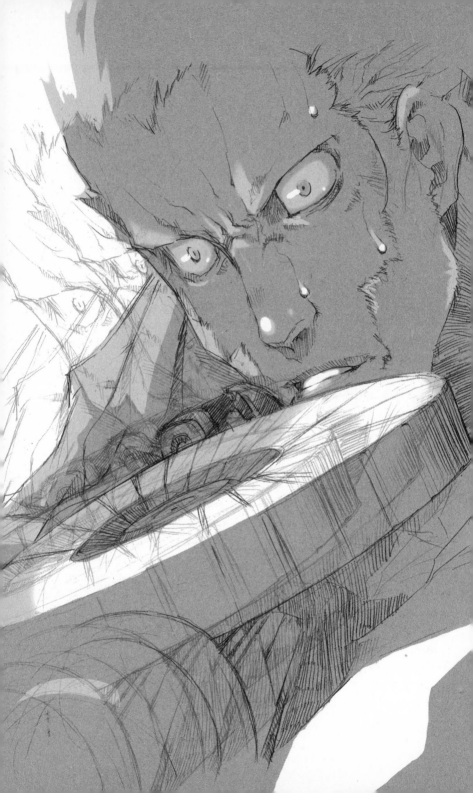

Apparently, he hadn't killed her.

"Stubborn lil' pup. She's trained way too well. That's the problem."

Spike took aim through the scope, intending to make a flower of blood bloom in her head.

However, naturally, the Lewis light machine gun was equipped with no such thing.

"Whoops. I guess I'm still feeling jumpy."

At that, he picked up the sniper rifle beside him.

"Right, I have to reload…"

He didn't see his ammunition case. Had he left it on the connecting platform?

When Spike climbed down to the platform, the ammunition case was indeed sitting there.

"Man oh man…"

He put out his right hand for the case, which was on the foothold by the coupling, and in that moment…

…a bright red arm reached out from under the train and latched onto Spike's right hand.

"_____!"

Tremendous strength pulled Spike's body down.

Before Spike even had time to scream, he was dragged under the coupling.

In the time before his body connected with the ground, Spike finally realized something:

No wonder nobody ever ran into that red shadow on the move.

He'd seen it. The surprisingly big space underneath the train, into which the wheels and all sorts of mechanical systems were packed. And the red shadow that clung dexterously to those metal fittings.

This thing, this monster, wasn't going over the roof or through the train. It went under—it was creeping around under the train!

Then a shock ran through Spike's head, and eternal darkness came.

⇔

Initially, the black-suited orchestra had had nearly thirty members. Now it had been reduced to the six who were gathered in Goose's room. There had been no further contact from the five who'd headed for the rear cars. Had they been killed by the Rail Tracer or the white suits, or had Chané finished off her would-be killers instead?

It had been a little while since the gunshots they'd assumed were Spike's had stopped. Goose had personally gone to check, but he hadn't seen Spike anywhere.

Goose was certain of two things. One was that Spike was probably no longer among the living. The other was that the conditions for winning this game were no longer to bring the train under control, but to escape from it alive.

When his thoughts had taken him that far, he realized once again that he really wasn't a military man. A soldier would never have compared the situation to a game.

It was possible that he hadn't been able to cope with the abnormal circumstances on this train because, not being a soldier, he'd harbored some sort of naïveté.

He didn't know how many of the white suits were left. He did know that his group was at a complete disadvantage in this game.

"There's no help for it. Let's abandon the mission and retreat. We'll cut the coupling to the freight cars and escape."

As he thought of his next words, he realized, yet again, that he was a terrorist, not a military man. There wasn't a shred of regret or repentance in that thought.

"We'll make sure no one remembers our faces. As per the original plan, dispose of all the passengers."

Just then, the door of the room opened slightly.

As everyone's eyes focused on it, something was thrown in through the gap.

It rolled, noisily; at the same time, it made a sort of popping, sparking sound, and it was smoking very slightly.

Realizing what the cylinder really was, Goose quickly picked it up.

As if he couldn't spare the time to open the window, he smashed the glass with the butt of his gun, then flung the object out through it.

A few beats later, a roar shook the train.

The cylinder—the dynamite—hadn't had as much force as he'd anticipated from its size, but it probably would have been more than enough to incapacitate the people in this room.

"The corridor! Eliminate the enemies in the corridor immediately!"

At Goose's order, a few men leaped into the hallway.

A new stick of dynamite lay there, hissing.

"Close the door!"

Hastily shutting the door, everyone hit the floor.

Immediately afterward, the door of the room blew off with a roar.

As he gazed at the wooden fragments, Goose bit his lip in hatred.

"I'd forgotten. Those hostages aren't easy to manage, either."

Goose smiled masochistically, then put a hand on the window frame behind him. That blast had shattered the glass to smithereens.

"I'll get rid of them. You get your equipment in order in the room behind this one, then wait."

$$\Longleftrightarrow$$

Naturally, the sound of the explosion had been audible in the dining car as well.

"Oh."

Jacuzzi stopped moving, then turned in the direction of the sound. Then he spoke to Fang and Jon, who were beside him.

"Sorry. Could you take care of the rest?"

"C'mon, man, where are you gonna go?"

"That sound just now…was that Nice?"

Fang had connected the explosion to the one-eyed girl with glasses. If he was right, there was only one place Jacuzzi would be going.

"Yeah, that explosion was probably Nice. I'm going to go help her."

"Are you nuts? Donny's already headed to the freight room. Why don't we go along and—?"

"No, that's no good. I'm leaving the dining car in your hands. The plan is what I just told you. I think it'll go better if Jon gives the orders instead of me."

"Yeah, you've got a point there. In situations like this, you just get in the way."

"That's harsh…"

Jacuzzi answered with unusual composure, and Jon questioned him, puzzled:

"Come to think of it, you're not crying, for once. Aren't you scared?"

"I'm scared."

The response was immediate.

"I'm so scared it feels like my legs are going to start shaking any second. There are probably still several black suits in the first-class rooms, and I bet they've all got guns."

"Then just skip it. You'd usually be crying and making a break for it right about now."

Jon tried to stop his friend from being reckless, but Jacuzzi smiled at him apologetically and spoke:

"I promised. I told her I'd absolutely come back alive. If Nice dies, I won't be able to go back to her, see? That means I have to go while she's alive."

Then, shouldering a single machine gun, the young, tattooed lad started for the door to the connecting platform.

"Besides, I decided that I wouldn't cry anymore. That I'd be ready for any kind of pain."

On hearing that, Jon and Fang immediately gave up on trying to stop him. As they watched his receding back, Fang muttered:

"He's not worried about Nick…?"

"Well, the guy's kind of forgettable, y'know."

⇔

"You okay, Miz Nice?"

When the man who was kind of forgettable spoke to her, Nice nodded happily.

"Yes, I'm fine. I'm enjoying myself, I'm having fun, I'm so incredibly happy to be able to use so much dynamite like this, one after another."

The eye he could see behind her glasses looked rapturous, and her mind seemed to be elsewhere.

"Yeah, you're not okay."

Nick sat down uneasily.

He'd known about her bomb mania, but to think the coolheaded Nice would turn into this…

Ordinarily, Jacuzzi scolded her right away, so he hadn't noticed it. If she was like this, forget "bomb fanatic"—she was a complete *mad bomber*. Still, he'd been startled by how she'd adjusted the amount of explosives right beforehand, lowering their force to something that wouldn't affect the train's walls or the way it was traveling. Privately, Nick genuinely admired her skill, thinking how impressive it was that she could do that much through rough estimates.

Two nights ago, she'd blown the mafiosi's corpses away, but from what he knew, she'd never blown up a live human being—except for herself, anyway.

"Let's beat it soon, all right? We should go meet up with Jacuzzi and the other guys."

"Yes. As reluctant as I am to leave, that would probably be best."

Taking out another of the sticks of dynamite she'd hidden under her clothes, Nice removed a moderate amount of explosive, then lit it.

The fuse smoked and sputtered. She opened the door and hurled it out into the corridor.

The sound of an explosion echoed, and the vibrations resonated in the pit of his stomach.

At the same time, Nick set his hands on the window frame. He had to get up to the roof first, then pull Nice up. Parenthetically, after releasing them, the woman in the coveralls had promptly exited through that same window.

Just as Nick looked up, about to set a hand on the ornamentation…

"Gyaah!"

A pair of boot toes swung down in an arc, kicking him back into the room.

"Wha...?"

The feet that had sent Nick flying belonged to a figure who'd come down off the roof. Nick was probably lucky he hadn't been kicked outside.

"You're—!"

The person who'd appeared in front of Nick and Nice was a man with sharp, dark eyes.

Goose had made it clear into the room. He held a gun in each hand and was pointing one at Nice and the other at Nick.

"Checkmate, scum."

Slowly, he walked toward the two.

"To think you had dynamite stowed under your clothes, young lady. Apparently, treating you with courtesy backfired."

Even as his lips smiled, his eyes glared at Nice's body with hatred.

"Let's have you remove all the remaining explosives, shall we?"

Nice glared back silently, but when she saw Goose's hand tense on the gun he was pointing at Nick, she hastily checked him.

"Wait! ...All right."

Looking down as if in frustration, she took all the remaining dynamite from her clothes and set it on the floor.

There were about twelve sticks.

"To think you had that much... I'm glad we didn't try to shoot you. It wouldn't have done to cause an explosion."

Without lowering his weapon, Goose walked over to Nice and decked her with the butt of the gun.

"*Ghk!*"

"Bastard!"

Seeing this, Nick flew into a rage and raised the knife he'd taken from an inside pocket.

Bang.

There was a dry sound, and blood spurted from Nick's raised arm.

"Uaaah...aaah!"

"Be quiet, oaf."

With zero hesitation, Goose took aim at Nick's head.

Then, just as he was about to squeeze the trigger, someone kicked the door in.

Immediately, he whipped his gaze and guns that way. A man with a leveled machine gun stood there. He had a tattoo on his face and the air of a devil about him.

Realizing that the guy's finger was on the trigger, Goose leaped sideways, squeezing his own as he did so.

The bullets launched from his hands grazed the youth's arm and side.

At the same time, the tattooed young man's machine gun spit fire.

"Uooooooooooooh!"

Yelling, Goose leaped even farther to the side. Hearing the sound of bullets striking closer and closer to his feet, he rolled behind the deluxe bed that was exclusive to the first-class passenger compartments.

Nick took that opportunity to help Nice up, and they slipped out behind Jacuzzi, evacuating into the hall.

Jacuzzi himself backed up, strafing the bed with the machine gun as he went, then shut the door with a bang.

When Goose crawled out from behind the bed, he had a warped smile on his face. It was as if he was enjoying the unexpected situations that kept cropping up one after another. However, the flames of hatred in his eyes were blazing even more fiercely.

"Interesting. Is this a trial? A trial, in order to become a being like Huey?! In that case, I really must not die here, nor must I run! As with Chané, I'll rip through all obstacles on this train!"

⇔

After Jacuzzi and the others had passed by, Goose's subordinates, who'd been on standby, poked their heads out into the hall. At first, they'd thought the gunshots were Goose's, but he hadn't taken a machine gun.

Then Goose came walking toward them from farther up the corridor. His eyes were bloodshot, and his expression seemed to say that, like Chané, he'd discarded his humanity—only in the opposite sense.

"Have you put the equipment in order?"

"Y-yes, sir!"

On seeing Goose's expression, his subordinates' voices tensed involuntarily as they responded. Goose passed his men, crossing to the equipment that was for his private use.

Goose shouldered that heavy weapon, and then, with an expression somewhere between anger and a smile, he started after Jacuzzi's group.

⇔

Meanwhile, on the connecting platform by the dining car, Jacuzzi was giving Nice and Nick their next instructions.

A look to the side showed that the train was about to cross a great river. They could see a vast body of water through the gaps in the iron bridge. Sunrise was already near, and the surface of the water reflected the pale light beautifully. Several boats, large and small, floated on it.

On seeing this, Nice realized that this was where they'd arranged to meet up with their companions.

In fact, she'd forgotten that they were technically here for a robbery.

That's right: They were going to drop the cargo in question into this river. That had been their plan. And Jacuzzi hadn't abandoned the plan; in fact, on top of that, he'd come to rescue Nice and Nick—with a recklessness that would have been unthinkable under normal circumstances. Nice was appalled, but at the same time she felt renewed confidence that Jacuzzi really was their leader.

In an ordinary organization, he probably wouldn't have been qualified to lead. However, in a way, Jacuzzi's actions suited their group better than they would have suited any other people.

The boss of an imperfect, thoroughly vague gang of delinquents began to speak; his tattoo was shivering.

"Donny's in the freight room right now, unloading! I told him to keep one box back, Nice, so you take that one!"

After yelling this, Jacuzzi set a hand on the connecting platform's ladder.

"I'll draw him away! You two run straight through the dining car! Just leave the ones who come through below to Fang and Jon!"

Jacuzzi nodded, his gaze steady and firm. There was no time for questions. All they could do now was believe in his confidence.

Nice pushed her glasses up to her forehead and peeled back the eye patch that covered her right eye.

With a practiced motion, she took out the thing she'd had in her eye socket, then pressed it into Jacuzzi's hand.

It was a black, round object the size of an eyeball, with a long fuse wrapped tightly around it.

"That's the last bomb I've got. It isn't very powerful, but take it, just in case."

At Nice's words, Jacuzzi nodded firmly and answered:

"Thank you, Nice. I'll think of it as you and detonate it carefully!"

"Don't be creepy."

Nice smiled. Jacuzzi listened until she'd finished speaking, then immediately began to climb the ladder.

"Miz Nice! They're here!"

Nick, who'd been looking through the window into the first-class carriages, raised his voice roughly. Nice nodded in response, and then she and Nick opened the door to the dining car and broke into a run.

⟺

When Goose opened the door, the tattooed guy had just stepped off the top of the ladder.

"I'll go after him! You men go underneath and circle around behind him!"

His expression might have been abnormal, but part of Goose was still calm. After issuing orders to his subordinates, he began to climb the ladder himself.

On the roof near the middle of the carriage, Jacuzzi was waiting for Goose and the others to come up.

He didn't know how many of them would come up, but he was pretty sure only one could climb the ladder at a time.

He didn't really want anybody to come up. Even now, killing people hurt. He'd seen corpses lots of times, and he'd seen his friends kill opposing mafiosi, when he himself had been the cause of it all. Talking to Isaac and Miria had softened the feeling of guilt somewhat, but killing people directly was still painful.

But I have to do it.

Swallowing hard, fighting to keep his balance on the swaying train, he waited.

Then a shadow appeared at the break in the roof.

He put his finger on the trigger, but something was very strange.

For a human head, it seemed really narrow. Almost as if it was some sort of nozzle—

As he was thinking this, said nozzle turned his way. It was caught on the corner of the roof and angled slightly upward, but it was definitely turned toward Jacuzzi.

I've got a bad feeling about this.

The moment he thought that, the premonition came true.

With abnormal force, the end of the nozzle spit fire.

"—Huh?"

As Jacuzzi stood, stunned by this unexpected situation, his face was brightly illuminated by red flames.

Because the nozzle had been tilted, the band of flames passed far over Jacuzzi's head. Even so, a wind so ferociously hot it nearly burned him struck his face.

"Wah, waaaaugh!"

In spite of himself, he fell on his butt right there, then hastily scooted backward.

He'd been surprised by the jet of flames, too, but what had surprised him more was the distance. Although he was sure the nozzle had been at the end of the car, the column of flame had clearly reached the opposite end of the roof. If it had that sort of range when shot at an angle, if fired horizontally, it would easily surpass the length of the car.

This distance was dangerous. Jacuzzi hastily got up, then began running full tilt, trying to widen the gap.

When he looked back, he saw the owner of that nozzle come up onto the roof. But the man didn't chase the fleeing Jacuzzi; he simply took aim from where he was.

When Jacuzzi leaped across the next coupling, the nozzle spit fire again.

As he staggered from his landing, a band of red flame passed by him. Jacuzzi had gained a certain distance, but the wave of heat that assailed him was no joke. He worried that his clothes might catch fire, but the skin on his face seemed likely to blaze up first.

Because the train had been heading into a curve, he'd managed to avoid a direct hit, but if the direction of the nozzle changed, he'd be barbecued.

As he'd feared, the trajectory of the flames began to move. Jacuzzi continued running desperately, finally sprinting clear of the flames' range.

He could tell the tip of the flames had cut behind him. The heat felt as though he'd been thrown into an oven. That wave of heat was probably more than enough to kill a person, even if they didn't directly catch fire.

Jacuzzi kept on running, then turned back when he thought the influence of the superhot wave had lessened.

"Please hit home…"

He took aim at the fire-man and pulled the trigger. At this distance, when the person firing was an inexperienced amateur, it was hopeless. Even so, all Jacuzzi could do now was shoot.

Click-click-click-click-click-click.

"Huh?"

The reality was beyond hopeless.

Never mind amateurs and those other things: The machine gun was already out of bullets.

The guy leveled the machine gun, but before long, he threw it away. Out of bullets, apparently. What a cretin.

"An imbecilic end for someone who gave me so much trouble. I'll take my time burning him to ash."

With a fiendish smile, Goose slowly began to walk toward the rear cars.

In his hand, he held a 1918-model flamethrower, made in Germany. In addition, it had been modified a bit to bring it in line with current technology. It was an antique, purchased through illegal channels, and he'd never expected it to be this useful. The weapon had originally been used by Master Huey, but he'd brought it just in case, and it had been the right move.

Still, it was a mistake not to wear fireproof clothing. If I fire this repeatedly, the heat may do me in.

As he pursued the fleeing man over the roof, Goose's head gradually regained its composure.

That aside, aren't the men who went through the car up here yet? Well, if that's the best my adversary has, I'm more than capable of handling him myself, but...

⟺

Goose's men had run through the dining car and reached the door to the coupling.

On seeing them, the passengers huddled into themselves like frightened rabbits.

Without sparing a glance for them, the black suits reached out to open the door to the platform.

Clunk.

However, the sliding door only shook dully, and it wouldn't open.

They tried several times to release the door. As they did so, all the subordinates piled up at the back of the car.

"Hey, hurry and open it."

"Hold on a minute. The door's stuck..."

Click.

At that sound, the black suits froze. The noise had sounded quite a lot like a hammer being cocked.

       *   *   *

Ka-chak.

The next thing they heard was the sort of sound a leveled machine gun made.

Click Ka-click   Taka   Clack   Chak   Click
*   Cha-chick   Tikki Taka Click   Clackka*
*   Clack   Tak*
Click Click Tikatik Ka-chak Ka-click Chak Takka Ka-chak
Ka-chak   Click Tikka Ka-chak Tik-a-chak Tikki Clackka
Ka-click Takka   Ka-chak

Sound summoned sound, and they began to guess what was happening behind them.

If they'd turned around when they heard that first click and strafed with their machine guns, they would have won.

However, because there had been no resistance from the passengers until now, they'd gotten careless. What had clinched it was that, compared to Goose and Spike, they were overwhelmingly short on experience.

Even if they pointed their guns behind them now, no doubt it would be far too late. All the black suits could do was turn their heads, slowly, to look back.

"If you'd throw your guns down before you turn around, it would really help us out."

Jon's voice rang out coldly.

"They're all amateurs, see. The only thing we taught them was how to pull the trigger. If you turn around holding guns, some coward's going to shoot for sure."

The black suits gave up, lowered their guns, and began to place them on the floor. They had no experience, and on top of that, they didn't have even half of Chané's faith in the organization.

This time, slowly, they did turn around, and saw the same dining car passengers who'd been there a moment before.

Just one thing was different: Every one of the passengers was armed with a gun, and they were pointing the barrels at them with fear in their eyes.

In ironic tones, Jon and Fang spoke to the men:

"Letting the train you hijacked get hijacked out from under you? That's pretty sad. Complete with your hostages and weapons, yet."

"That's no good, guys. You've got to take responsibility and watch your hostages all the way to the end, you know?"

A moment ago, Jacuzzi had captured one of the black suits and gotten a certain amount of information out of him. One of the things he'd heard had been that their plan included a siege strategy that would use the train as a fortress.

That meant they must have brought quite a lot of extra weapons, didn't it? Jacuzzi's guess had been right on the money: The freight room had held a veritable mountain of spare guns and ammunition.

Then, a little while ago, Jacuzzi had captured the dining car and asked the hostages for their help. Parenthetically, only Jon's and Fang's guns had been loaded with live rounds.

Even so, as a result, Jacuzzi had won the bet.

As Jon tied up the black suits with a torn-up tablecloth, he was mildly pensive.

They've always said people tend to develop trust relationships with criminals they spend a lot of time with, but... Man, Jacuzzi... He hijacked even that trust.

When he'd tied all of them up, he asked Fang a question:

"What was it they called this in the Far East?"

"The thing that gunman said at the counter? Nah, I'd never heard of it, but..."

The two of them fell silent for a little while, then slowly recalled Isaac's words.

"Uh, 'Maybe you did, but—'"

"'—I ate *you*.'"

⇔

Jacuzzi had finally been cornered.

Right now, he was at the very last coupling. Should he get down, or should he cross to the last car up top?

If he went down, though, the other guy would go down into the car, too. He could wait until the man got onto his car and then make his move, but if the range of the flamethrower was longer then the car, there was no point. Even if the other man never got onto this carriage, the flames could burn up everything in it.

Besides, if he got down and tried to hide, the man might burn the entire car along with him.

That's not even funny. Nice and the guys are in the freight room...

If he was going to get burned either way, he might as well just do all he could.

Jacuzzi drew a deep breath, then turned to face Goose.

"The fool. Has he grown desperate?"

Giving a small, satisfied smile with bloodshot eyes, Goose slowly closed the distance between himself and Jacuzzi.

First, he'd burn this man to death. After that, he'd burn up the woman with the eye patch and the others. The woman in the coveralls and the white suits and the hostages: He'd use these flames and burn them all to ash.

I am a bit concerned about fuel, though. We may have increased the capacity, but a full-power blast only lasts a bit over ten seconds. I have extra fuel on hand as well, but I'm rather uneasy.

Just to be on the safe side, he closed down the firing valve slightly. It would shorten the distance by half, but the fuel would probably last longer.

Carrying a load that weighed more than sixty pounds on his back, Goose decided to close the distance between himself and the tattooed man until he was certain he could incinerate him.

Little by little, the man was closing in. He'd gotten onto the roof of the first freight car.

He'd be within firing range soon. Taking a gamble, Jacuzzi took out the bomb Nice had given him.

The weird thing on that guy's back has to be filled with fuel. If I manage to ignite that...

However, at this point, he came face-to-face with his own stupidity.

I don't have anything to light it with!

It was hopeless. So what if he did have a bomb? If he couldn't light it, it was completely useless.

Well, no, there was fire around. The other man would probably give him tons of it for free, but it was likely that he'd either just burn to death, or that the explosive would catch directly and blow his arm off. The end result would probably be both of the above.

If this was how things stood, maybe he should just jump off the train. He might still have a chance that way.

However, Nice and the passengers would die for sure.

Stuck with no way out, Jacuzzi began to consider charging his opponent.

Ahh, would somebody who's fighting this guy show up? White suits or the Rail Tracer, I don't care which. If possible, it would be great if they'd take each other out...

Keeping this desire to rely on others clamped down inside him, Jacuzzi resolved to make a suicide run at his opponent.

In that instant, saviors arrived.

People he hadn't asked for appeared from a place he'd never even imagined.

"AAAAAAAAAAAAAAAAAH————!"

Suddenly, a nerve-shattering scream rang out. It came from below the train, at the side, right where Goose was standing.

"What's that?"

Foolishly, in an attempt to discover the source of the voice, he went closer to its point of origin.

Was it hubris, because he had an ultimate weapon? Was it

carelessness, because he was sure of his victory? Or was it his policy to investigate such abnormalities as a rule?

If only he hadn't approached the voice, he would have avoided disaster, and yet...

Leveling the flamethrower's nozzle, Goose carefully looked over toward the ground, and in that instant——

They came swinging up from underneath.

"WAAAaaaaaAAAaaAAAUUuugh!"

The instant Goose peered over, the scream abruptly got closer and louder. Then, suddenly, from behind Goose, a huge mass appeared.

A thick rope stretched from the side of the train. A big lump was clinging to the end of it, flying through space in a motion like an upside-down clock pendulum. It looked like an enormous yo-yo.

Jacuzzi, who was watching from a short distance away, picked up on the identity of the lump at the end of the taut rope.

It was the figure of a gunman, holding something in his arms, and a woman in a red dress, hanging onto his legs.

"I...Isaac?!"

At the sight of the sudden intruders, Jacuzzi's eyes went round.

"Why?! What are you doing here?!"

The next instant, a gust of wind reached Jacuzzi.

In order to bring him victory, the southeast wind had indeed blown.

"AAAAAAaaaAAAaaaAAaaaaaaaaaaaaaah!"

In the blink of an eye, the scream faded away on the other side of the train. Moving at a low-angle trajectory, like the winter sun, that gigantic human yo-yo had sketched a neat arc over the top of the train.

Goose's body had been located just inside that angled orbit. As Isaac and Miria fell down the opposite side of the train from him, the thick rope that stretched behind them scooped Goose's feet out from under him.

"What?!"

A powerful shock ran through Goose's Achilles tendon. The string of the enormous yo-yo had caught on his legs, and the black-suited figure took a magnificent tumble.

His back slammed into the roof. His spine was forcibly compressed, molding to the shape of the tank.

More than that, Goose was terrified that the impact might have broken the tank. However, it didn't seem as though fuel was leaking, and he couldn't hear the sound of escaping hydrogen gas. Apparently, it had come through unscathed.

"Damn it, what was that?"

Slowly, Goose got to his feet, then began walking toward the tattooed man again. The lump that had been at the end of the rope bothered him, but he'd burn that tattooed child first. Although it wasn't easy to jump with a sixty-pound weight on his back, if he took a bit of a run-up, he'd manage to leap across the coupling somehow.

So doing, Goose finally reached the last carriage, where the tattooed young man was waiting.

"All right, tattooed man. Are you prepared?—Though I suppose I should at least ask your name."

"No way."

When he'd closed the distance to half a car length, they spoke to each other for the first time.

"Oho? And why is that?"

"I'm planning to throw you off this train, and if you survive— You'll probably try to find me and take revenge. …So I'm not going to tell you my name. I don't want you figuring out my address."

Jacuzzi tried to keep an extremely cool head as he responded, but when he saw the other man's bloodshot eyes, no matter what he did, his answer came out distorted.

On hearing his opponent's words, Goose felt slightly deflated. He hadn't expected to get an answer that was this childish, and street-smart to boot.

Was this really the same guy who had fired that machine gun barrage a little while ago?

"I see. That's a shame. Are you prepared to die?"

"If possible, I really don't want to."

"Appeal rejected."

As he spoke, Goose studied his opponent's face.

I don't think I could ever get to like that face. He looks ready to burst into tears at any moment, yet his eyes seem somehow reasonable. … Still, if I burn him up here, it will all be over.

With a sneering grin, Goose yanked the nozzle's trigger.

The tattooed youth began to charge him, but he'd roast him whole, and that would be the end of it. *Go on and die.*

However…

"What?!"

It did spit fire, but the flames were nothing like what they'd been before. They stretched a few feet at most.

"That can't be!"

Had he tightened the valve too far? Hastily, he put a hand around behind his back, but the valve was bent oddly, and he couldn't move it from its position. The impact from his fall had done definite damage.

"Damn it!"

As if to say this was fine as well, he began to point the nozzle forward. However, by that time, he was already in Jacuzzi's space. Jacuzzi took a great leap forward, dodging past the flamethrower's nozzle.

Jacuzzi had neither strength nor technique. The attack method he chose after leaping into the other man's bosom was far too simple and direct: He ducked under Goose's chin, then shot up as far as his torso and legs would take him.

With his forward momentum layered over the attack, Jacuzzi's forehead crunched into Goose's nose, crushing it. When the man staggered involuntarily, he head-butted him again. Goose's front teeth broke, and his blood began to splatter Jacuzzi's face. However, even so, Jacuzzi didn't stop. With the nozzle of the flamethrower restrained, he rammed his forehead into his opponent's face twice, three times.

Splutch splutch splat pop bluch.

Little by little, the sensation when his forehead struck home was getting softer. At first he'd thought he'd crushed his own skull, but apparently, it was the bridge of the other man's nose that had broken.

I can do this!

Feeling a definite response, he pulled his upper body back one more time, and in that instant, a dry sound echoed in his ears.

Bang bang   Bang

"Huh?"

Sharp pain ran through his side and his legs. It felt as if someone had rammed the point of an umbrella into his stomach with all their might.

When he looked down, he saw his opponent's left fist. There was an odd device attached to the palm of the hand opposite the one with the flamethrower nozzle.

"It's a handheld firing mechanism. Huey made it himself."

At the end of the device on his hand, there was something like a miniature gun muzzle. White smoke was trickling out of the hole, only to be immediately snatched away by the wind.

"Convenient, isn't it? All you have to do to fire bullets is clench your fist and press it against your opponent."

With blood streaming from his mouth and nose, Goose grinned and began to explain his weapon. Ordinarily, it should only have been capable of firing one round, but this one, which Huey had made himself, seemed to be equipped with three rounds.

One of these rounds had grazed his side, while the remaining two had buried themselves in both his thighs.

"Now then, it appears the tables have tur*nyagh!*"

Jacuzzi had slammed his head into his mouth yet again.

"Wh-why you!"

Goose jammed the fingers of his left hand into Jacuzzi's wound. Unbelievably fierce pain ran through him, but even so, Jacuzzi didn't stop.

"Would you just give up?! Scream and cry from the pain!"

He couldn't do that.

He'd been prepared for pain on this level since the moment he'd made up his mind to defeat these guys. That meant he couldn't cry. No matter what, no matter what, no matter what.

⇔

A short while earlier.

"Jacuzzi is—"

As they walked down the freight car corridor, Nice murmured to Nick.

"As a rule, he's a crybaby, but when he's made his mind up about something, he won't cry, no matter what."

"Huh… Really?"

Nick's question sounded dubious. Smiling, Nice nodded.

"Yes. When he got that tattoo on his face, although I'm told it hurt terribly, he didn't complain even once."

"Then why is he usually such a crybaby?"

"I asked him about that as well. He said, 'It's natural for humans to cry.'"

A memory of Jacuzzi's face at the time rose in Nice's mind. Jacuzzi's face at fourteen, when there had still been something child-like about it. A face with an innocent smile and a brand-new tattoo.

"'But I think the times when people want to cry are the times when they need to work the hardest. So I decided that I'd cry all the time while things were normal, that I'd never try to pretend I was tough. I'd take all those tears from when I really wanted to cry, and I'd cry them out now. That way, when I really need to work hard, all my tears will be dried up and gone.'"

It was something he'd said five years ago, a kid's silly notion. Even for a fourteen-year-old, it had been childish, a grade schooler's belief. Jacuzzi had kept that foolish resolution all this time. Nice really loved him for that.

Just then, they heard three gunshots.

"Miz Nice! That was—!"

The sounds had seemed to come from a car farther back.

Before she knew it, Nice had broken into a run. …With several bombs hanging from her waist—ones courtesy of the box they had been after.

⇔

"Die!"

Having watched for an opening, Goose unleashed a kick that ripped Jacuzzi away from him. Jacuzzi lost his balance and hit hard on his butt.

"This is it, then. Any last words?!"

Spitting out blood and saliva together, Goose yelled triumphantly. He resettled the nozzle of the flamethrower, pointing its end at Jacuzzi.

His pain and anger had made him lose his cool. If he'd been calm, at this point, he would have burned his legs and made it so he truly couldn't move. As was evident from the incident with Nader, even when Goose was calm, he wasn't the type to kill quickly. He had a complex about having been unable to completely become a military man, but this may have been the decisive difference that separated him from the professionals.

For a moment, Jacuzzi prepared to die, but then he remembered the bomb from Nice in his pocket.

At this distance, he might be able to drag his opponent into the explosion. If he did, the tank on the man's back would probably ignite. He was sure it held fuel for the fire. If that happened, the man would go up in flames, and that would be that.

Although, of course, Jacuzzi would die, too.

He was out of options. Even if he rolled, fell off the train, and escaped, he'd die from the impact or from massive blood loss. If he was going to die anyway, no matter what, he wanted to take this guy—

Firming up his resolve, Jacuzzi reached into his pocket.

Deciding that he was planning to draw some sort of weapon, Goose's fingers tightened on the nozzle.

However, those fingers stopped moving.

"……?"

Jacuzzi watched him, puzzled. Goose's eyes were focused behind Jacuzzi, on what little was left of the train before the end.

He didn't really get it, but this was his chance. Sensing this, Jacuzzi tried to stand, struggling against the pain in his legs. Then he stopped moving as well.

"???"

Something was squirming at Jacuzzi's feet.

The thing that had poked its head out from the shadow of his leg was a red lump. It was a red, pulpy mass, as though ground meat had been kneaded with blood. That red matter was heading from Jacuzzi's feet toward Goose.

Jacuzzi hastily scooted backward. However, Goose was still looking behind him. Another red lump passed by on Jacuzzi's left.

At that point, for the first time, Jacuzzi turned around. Then, speechless, his eyes went wide.

There were dozens of the red lumps there, sliding and rolling, coming their way. They looked like a colony of bright-red army ants. When they bumped into each other, they fused, doubling in size, and began to move again.

Then Jacuzzi caught on: It had finally, finally, shown itself. At this worst of all possible times, a new enemy had appeared.

Quietly, he called the monster's name.

"The Rail Tracer—"

"What is it?! What is this ghastly monster?!"

Goose had a hunch regarding its true identity. A red monster. The monster that had had the hostages babbling about "the Rail Tracer," the one that had erased several of Goose's men.

"Die, die, die, die, burn, burn!"

Forgetting about Jacuzzi, Goose began burning away the fragments of meat that were closing in on his feet. A tremendously hot wind struck Jacuzzi, and he hastily retreated backward.

The red matter began to burn, but weirdly, no smoke rose. Then the outer layer—which had charred—cracked, and the red color reappeared from underneath.

As though nothing had happened, the meat fragments began their advance again. Screaming obscenities, Goose waved the nozzle around.

Some of the scattered fuel was on fire, a little ways in front of Jacuzzi. The roof itself was made of iron, so apparently, the train as a whole wouldn't burn.

Seeing this, Jacuzzi was struck by a sudden thought.

"—A fire starter!"

"Damn it! Stay back, stay *back*! Buuuuuuuuuurn!"

Goose swung the flamethrower around. If the blast volume hadn't been controlled, no doubt he would have run out of fuel long ago. ... Not that it was controlled because he'd wanted to control it...

"Burn, burn, bur...n?"

Tunk.

He felt as though something had sailed over his head and fallen. When, in spite of himself, he turned to look back, a sphere about the size of an eyeball was rolling around.

A sparking fuse was sucked into that black sphere.

The roar of an explosion, then an impact.

"Gwoooooooouh!"

The blast flew at Goose's back, shoving him toward the rear of the train. To be honest, the explosion hadn't been a big one, but the weight of the flamethrower increased his momentum. Add in the unstable element of the moving train, and he wasn't able to stop the way he wanted to.

In front of him, the tattooed young man barred his way.

"You fool! What do you plan to do this late in the game, unarmed?!"

Goose had let go of the nozzle, but even as the impact pushed him, he took a knife from an inside pocket and raised it high, aiming for the youth.

In response, Jacuzzi yelled at the top of his lungs.

The words of the world's greatest gunman, the man who'd given him courage.

"My gun——is in my heart!"

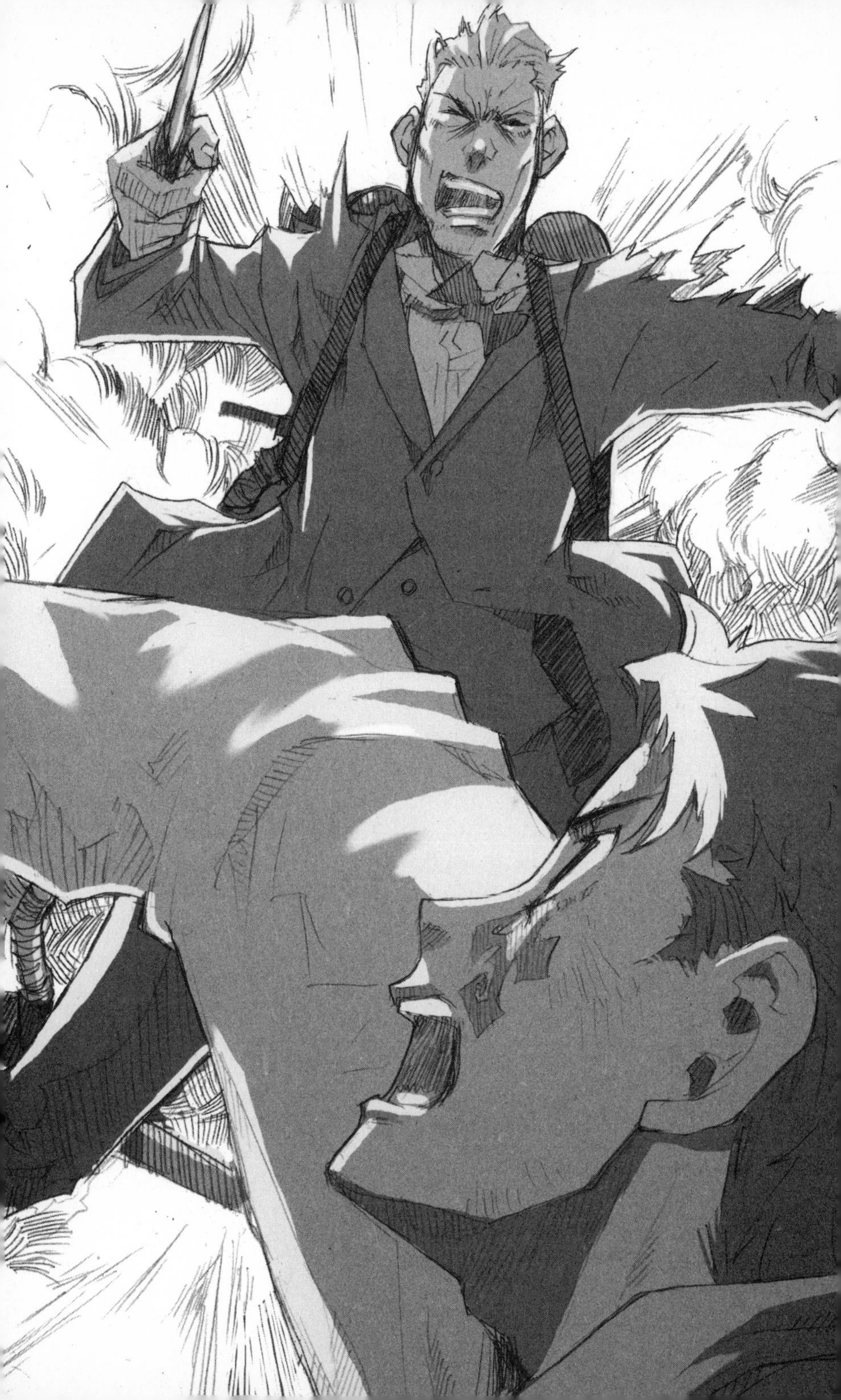

Goose's knife stabbed deep into his arm.

Jacuzzi didn't fight it. Instead, he *flopped down*, hard, right where he was.

"Whaaaaat?!"

Goose lost his balance. As he pitched forward, beginning to fall, Jacuzzi sent a mighty upward kick into his stomach.

He pushed the weight of the man's body, with the added weight of that sixty-pound flamethrower, up with all his might.

Searing pain ran through him, and blood spurted from his wounded thighs. Even so, Jacuzzi didn't lower his legs. That single moment's battle felt like a very long time for both men. And then—

Goose's body did a 180-degree flip in midair and was flung away behind Jacuzzi. The most unfortunate thing for Goose was that the roof of the train ran out at that point.

Immediately after he'd felt an abrupt falling sensation with his entire body, an impact that was beyond comparison with the one before it ran through his back.

Then he was entirely surrounded by red, blinding light.

Jacuzzi had fallen faceup, and a hot wind skimmed over him. When he lifted his head, red flames were climbing brightly through the dim landscape (which looked upside down to him).

Was it over? The sounds of the explosion, the train, and the wind all seemed hollow. In the midst of them, just one voice came to him clearly.

"Jacuzzi! Jacuzzi!"

At Nice's voice, he sat up. As he did, the pain in his side and thighs returned.

"Oh, Nice, you're okay… That's great."

"I'm fine! Never mind that. We need to stop that bleeding, fast…"

"Huh? Those clay things at your waist… Oh, they're bombs, aren't they? Fantastic; we got the treasure, too."

As Jacuzzi forced a smile, Nice pulled him into a tight hug.

However, he gently pushed her away.

"Jacuzzi?"

"Nice, listen."

Slowly, with a smile that seemed a bit lonely, he spoke to Nice:

"I think I might have done a little too much crying up until now."

"Huh?"

"So listen, I'm going to say that those extra tears I cried were yours."

At that point, Nice realized that Jacuzzi's eyes were focused on something. There was something up ahead, toward the front of the train.

The morning sun had begun to rise, and the train was traveling straight into it.

The "something" was standing in the center of the sunlight. As a result, Nice couldn't make it out clearly, but there was one thing she was sure of.

The figure was red from head to toe.

A red shadow with the sun at its back. The shadow had two eyes in the same place a human's would be. In the shadows cast by the light behind it, the eyes were filled with a deep darkness, a further singularity. Although they seemed like calm, black jewels, they also looked like portals to purgatory that absorbed and trapped all the surrounding light.

The color of those eyes seemed to link this world to the afterlife. A negative light that engulfed everything they saw.

Seeing this, Jacuzzi felt certain that the red shadow was the Rail Tracer. The red meat from earlier must have come together to form a human shape. That was what Jacuzzi had determined.

Looking at Nice, who'd frozen at the sight of the shadow, Jacuzzi quietly continued what he'd been saying:

"So, you see, since I cried enough for you, too, you keep on living, and even if painful stuff happens, don't cry. The only thing I can't handle is seeing you cry."

With that, before Nice could stop him, Jacuzzi broke into a run. At the same time, Nice realized that two of the grenades with the new explosive were missing from her waist.

"Jacuzzi!"

By the time Nice started to run after him, Jacuzzi's body had already slammed into the red shadow.

Then they both went over the side of the train.

Nice screamed. She screamed Jacuzzi's name so loudly it nearly shredded her throat.

Just as her scream ended, there was a flash of red light behind the train.

The tremendous explosion roared. A shock so powerful it was hard to believe it came from grenades welled upward, and the wind of the blast sent Nice's glasses flying. As her glasses fell further up the train with a clatter, she dropped to her knees.

The explosion echoed all through the train, but before long, as though nothing at all had happened, silence returned.

⟺

Nice was remembering something from her childhood.

It was the time when she'd badly injured herself with her own explosives. She'd lost her right eye and gained scars all over her body. The shrapnel had wounded her left eye as well, and she'd lost much of her eyesight.

She could only vaguely make out people's faces. She'd been afraid she'd have to spend her entire life this way, unable to see anyone's face, and she'd cried and cried, refusing to meet anyone.

One day, Jacuzzi had sneaked into her house and told her something. Half his face was covered with a tattoo so striking she could see it clearly even with blurred vision.

"See? Now you'll be able to tell which face is mine! Just stick with me all the time and you'll be fine."

Jacuzzi had laughed when he'd said it, and on hearing his voice, she'd cried tears of happiness. When he'd seen this, Jacuzzi had thought he'd made her cry; he'd started to feel anxious, and he had burst into tears, too.

Even as she remembered this, Nice kept on crying.

Her glasses had fallen, and her already blurry vision was soggy with tears. Now she'd never be able to tell people apart. At most, she'd be able to make out Donny's huge body. If she didn't think about pointless things like that, it felt as if she'd cry even harder. Remembering the last thing Jacuzzi had said, she tried desperately to stop crying, but it really wasn't possible.

However, she didn't sob, not even once. She fought to keep the sounds locked inside her throat. Just when she was worried she'd stop being able to breathe...

...a figure stood in front of her.

Was it Nick, or a surviving white suit or black suit? When she looked up, no longer caring what happened—

—she saw a blurred, black pattern over half its face.

"That's mean. I told you not to cry..."

The blurred tattoo was warping into a weird shape.

"When you cry, Nice, it makes me want to cry. So, look—please don't cry."

She gave up trying to stifle her cries and hugged Jacuzzi hard.

...Sobbing his name all the while.

Before long, Nick and Donny also climbed up onto the roof and stood around Jacuzzi and Nice, who were quietly leaning against each other.

By that time, Nice had stopped crying, and Jacuzzi was smiling cheerfully.

"By the way, Jacuzzi. How did you get rid of that red monster? I was sure you'd fallen off the train; how did you survive?"

"Umm, I'll tell you later. I don't really understand it myself yet. Only, that red monster is—"

Just then, Jacuzzi finally noticed Nick and Donny, and he greeted them, still smiling.

"H-hey, great timing."

His voice was trembling slightly.

"Sorry, but D-Donny? Do you think you could carry me to Room Three in the second-class cars? A-apparently, there's a doctor in there."

Abruptly delivering information he seemed to have heard from someone else, he began looking more and more as if he was about to cry.

"My side and my arm and my thighs really, really hurt. There's lots of blood, and I think I'm gonna…cry…"

Immediately after he said this, he looked at his own blood, shrieked, and passed out.

The regular Jacuzzi was back. As they scrambled to carry him away, Nice and the others knew the incident that had occurred on this train had come to an end.

The morning sun gradually rose higher, shining down on the endless rails.

It seemed to be quietly wishing them well as they headed for New York.

Local—The End

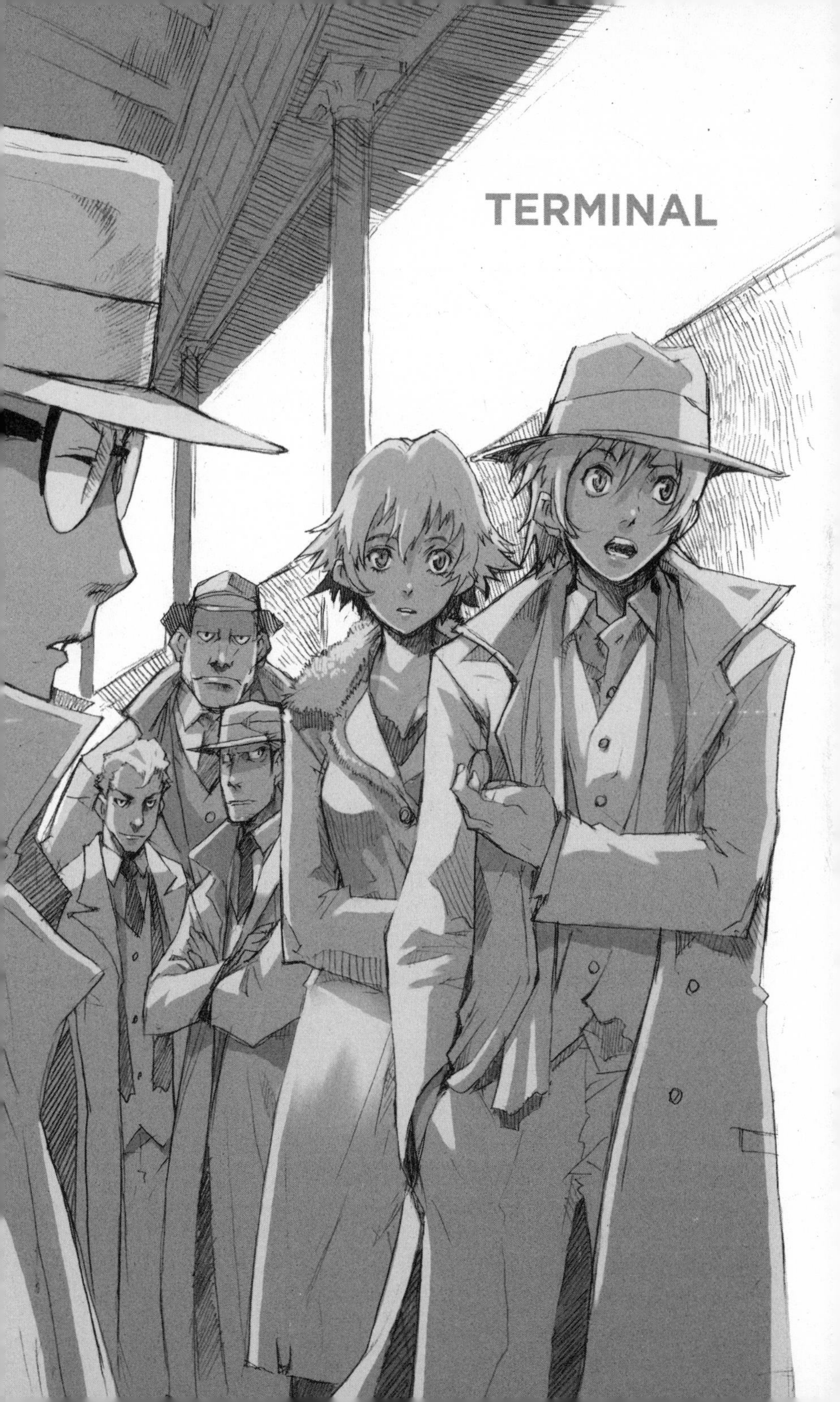
TERMINAL

December 31, 2:00 PM   New York, Pennsylvania Station

"Man, it's *late*."

The three brothers who were the acting bosses of the Gandor Family stood in the lobby. The *Flying Pussyfoot* had been scheduled to arrive at noon, but that had been two hours ago, and it still wasn't here. The middle brother, Berga Gandor, raised his voice in irritation.

"Calm down, Berga. Long-distance trains arrive a few hours late all the time."

"..."

Luck, the youngest, reprimanded his older brother, while Keith, the oldest, remained silent.

Right beside them, another group was waiting for their friends. It was the party that was there to meet Isaac and Miria and the fellow alchemist. In specific terms, this was Firo Prochainezo, a Martillo Family executive; his rent-free lodger, Ennis; and Maiza Avaro, the Martillo *contaiuolo*. Of the group, Maiza was an alchemist from two centuries ago, and one of the immortals.

Firo looked over at Keith and the others, asking them a question in a voice that wouldn't be overheard by the people around them.

"Are you guys sure? Having all three bosses in a place like this... You're squaring off with the Runoratas, right?"

"We're able to relax and go out *because* it's us, Firo."

"Yeah, I guess that's true."

Firo was convinced. Like Isaac and Miria, during a certain incident a year ago, they had also become immortal. ...Although not even the Bureau of Investigation knew this yet.

"By the way, what sort of person is this alchemist, Maiza?"

The man with glasses and a gentle face answered Luck's question:

"Let's see... He's the type who tries to shoulder everything himself, even though he gets lonely easily."

"The type who can't live a long life, then. ...If he were an ordinary person, I mean."

Luck spoke pragmatically. As if picking up the conversation, Berga began talking about the person they were waiting for.

"Claire's kinda like that, only the other way around. The kid's ego is way too big. Cheerful personality, so it could be worse, but y'know."

Ennis, who was watching them, decided to ask about this person she didn't know.

"Then Miss Claire is a wonderful woman, cheerful and lively, with a self-assured core, isn't she?"

At that question, Firo and Luck looked at each other.

"Firo, didn't you tell her? That's rather important..."

"Actually, I guess I forgot. I mean, we talked about personality and things, but..."

"Hmm?"

As question marks appeared above Ennis's head, there was an announcement that the train had arrived.

"Okay, let's go. Ennis, once you two meet, you'll see."

Then they started toward the train, which was still exhilarated after its long journey, to meet the people they were waiting for.

"Huh? Something seems kinda off."

The train that had arrived wasn't the *Flying Pussyfoot*. It was a perfectly ordinary train, completely different from the luxury train they all knew.

"From what I hear, there was trouble of some sort and they replaced the carriages."

Satisfied by Maiza's words, everyone waited for the doors to open.

"Come to think of it... Huey Laforet, wasn't it? They nabbed him, didn't they, Maiza?"

At Firo's words, Maiza's expression clouded slightly, and he nodded. Seeing this, Keith gazed at Maiza wordlessly.

"Oh, we should tell Keith and the others, too, shouldn't we?"

Maiza smiled as if to say there was no help for it. Then his expression tensed again, and he began to speak.

"Huey Laforet, the self-styled revolutionary who was arrested a short while ago..."

Everyone listened intently to Maiza's words.

"...he's an immortal as well."

Just then, the doors opened, and the passengers began to pour out. For some reason, there were many whose expressions tended toward extremes, from faces that were flooded with relief to those that seemed strangely fatigued.

Then, after the flood of disembarking passengers' feet had subsided and a little time had passed, a woman in coveralls appeared. She had a very vigilant air about her, and when Ennis saw her, she thought she might be Claire.

However, the woman passed right by Keith and the others. She seemed to have an injured leg; her left leg had a bandage wound around it, and she dragged it a little as she walked.

Next, a man who looked like a magician appeared. From the look of him, he could have been nothing else: He was entirely enveloped in gray cloth. The Gandors' eyes opened wide; they thought that this weird guy had to be an alchemist for sure… But Firo's group was also muttering, "That's a strange outfit."

The gray magician was followed by a man who seemed to be his assistant and was carrying his luggage. Behind him, a young man's pitiful, tearful voice echoed through the area.

⇐⇒

Even as he cried from the pain in his legs, inside his head, Jacuzzi kept worrying.

Where had that Ladd Russo guy disappeared to, anyway?

And why had Isaac and Miria turned into that…yo-yo-like thing?

What had happened to Czes? When he'd asked Nice, she'd only said she didn't know and looked away.

Speaking of Nice, even though they'd detonated all those bombs, the train hadn't stopped. Why not?

…And most of all, the red monster… No, the *person in red clothes*… Who had that been?

What in the world had happened on that train, in the places they hadn't seen? He knew worrying wouldn't solve anything, but he couldn't help thinking about it. He would have liked to have seen Isaac and Miria, but with his legs this way, he hadn't been able to go around looking for them.

I'll ask at one of the local information brokers. They say there's an information broker in this town that knows absolutely everything.

Oh, but his legs did hurt. If he didn't let these wounds heal up first, he'd get nowhere…

Jacuzzi took a break from worrying for the time being and began whimpering about the pain again.

⇐⇒

"I-i-it hurts, it hurts! Wa, wait a second! Go a little slower!"

A guy with bandages wound all around his body was crying and wailing. He had an impressive tattoo on his face. After him, others descended from the train: a girl who wore glasses over an eye patch, a man with a bandaged face, then a man who might as well not have been there, and finally a brown-skinned giant who was over six feet tall.

"Do you think they're a circus or something?"

Firo and the others watched the odd group go, then continued waiting for their friends to arrive.

The disembarking figures grew few and far between, and a forlorn atmosphere began to envelop the platform.

Even so, they didn't have the slightest doubt that the people they were waiting for would arrive.

When the station workers had begun to close the carriage doors. The very last ones to emerge from the train were——

To be continued

AFTERWORD

First, a big thank-you to everyone who read this book, even though it has nothing to do with the main story.

This story does have the "Baccano!" title on it, but the characters from the previous volume...do not tear up the pages in a new incident (with the exception of one couple). The world in which they're set is the same, but the intent was to keep each incident separate. Most of the characters have been switched up, too. However, it's still America during the same time period, so please assume that the characters from the last volume are still there, living somewhere offstage.

I'm terribly worried that if I write a huge, sweeping, epic series, it will get axed right in the middle, or I'll set up tons and tons of foreshadowing and the story won't go anywhere, or I'll run out of ideas at the climax and pull a "Catch the rest in the next volume!" and then never publish another volume. I do want to get good enough to write a long series like that someday, but...

Partly as a consequence of that thought, for this *Baccano!* series, I'd planned to keep each volume as self-contained as possible, but—

—as you can see from the "To be continued" there at the end, we've got a split volume right off the bat.

Although it does say "To be continued," the "Express Run" volume that comes next doesn't start right after the end of this one. It's actually going to be a story written about the same incident and set during the same time frame as this "Local" volume, but told from different perspectives.

This volume rivals the previous one as far as the number of characters is concerned, and as before, it would be great if you'd think of your favorite character as the protagonist... Or that's how it should have been, but as you probably noticed, there are a few characters that just disappear partway through the story. I'll be writing about those characters' movements and endings in the Express Run, so I'd be terribly thrilled if you'd read that volume as well.

This one turned into an irregular split volume, but I'll do my best to create stories that live up to your expectations, so please keep an eye out for me in the future as well.

Movies, plays, novels, manga, and more: Trains make frequent appearances as an archetypal set in most genres. I chose a transcontinental railway for the setting this time around because, among other things, I like watching stories like that.

In all sorts of stories, trains appear as more than simple sets. Sometimes they're props, sometimes they're important keywords, and sometimes they become the main character and add color to the story. I love that sort of atmosphere, but... Even now, after I've finished writing it, I'm not sure how I handled the train in this story. As I was putting the plot together, I imagined a train rolling with ferocious speed over an intricate web of rails, but all the way to the end, as I wrote, I was afraid the story might suffer a derailment.

...Well. This is the first time I've been published in half a year, and I'm not quite sure what to write here.

I managed to graduate safely, and aside from writing books, I'm living a terribly laid-back life.

I got a late start due to my graduation thesis, and I'll psych myself up and make up for that lost time: I plan to challenge myself to see just how much I can write in the year after this book is released. Of course, in this first year of my new life, I want to do my absolute best to polish my writing and story-creation skills, so that the day never comes when my editor smiles and tells me, "You're boring. Don't write anymore." That's my current goal, at any rate. I hope you'll be patient and bear with me.

 * Like last time, note that everything past this point is thank-yous.

To Chief Editor Suzuki and the good people of the sales and PR departments, who really helped me out—or rather, for whom I caused nothing but trouble—thanks again with this release.

To Mine, who isn't my supervising editor, but who told me a certain something that put pressure on me and made me shape up, and to everyone in the Dengeki Bunko editorial department.

To the proofreaders, who caught the typos and dropped characters in my inexperienced writing, as they did for the previous book.

To my family, friends, and acquaintances, particularly everyone in S City, who helped me out in all sorts of ways.

To Katsumi Enami, who captured the individuality of all these diverse characters and added a dashing liveliness to the story, even though he was very busy.

And to those readers who picked up this book as well, or who've picked up one of my books for the first time.

Thank you very much. I want to hang on to this feeling of gratitude without letting it fade and devote myself daily to producing better results next time and into the future. I hope we'll meet again then.

Until next time...

May 2003, at my place
Playing the last five minutes of *DEAD OR ALIVE* (directed by Takashi Miike) on repeat.

Ryohgo Narita

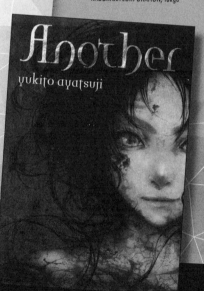

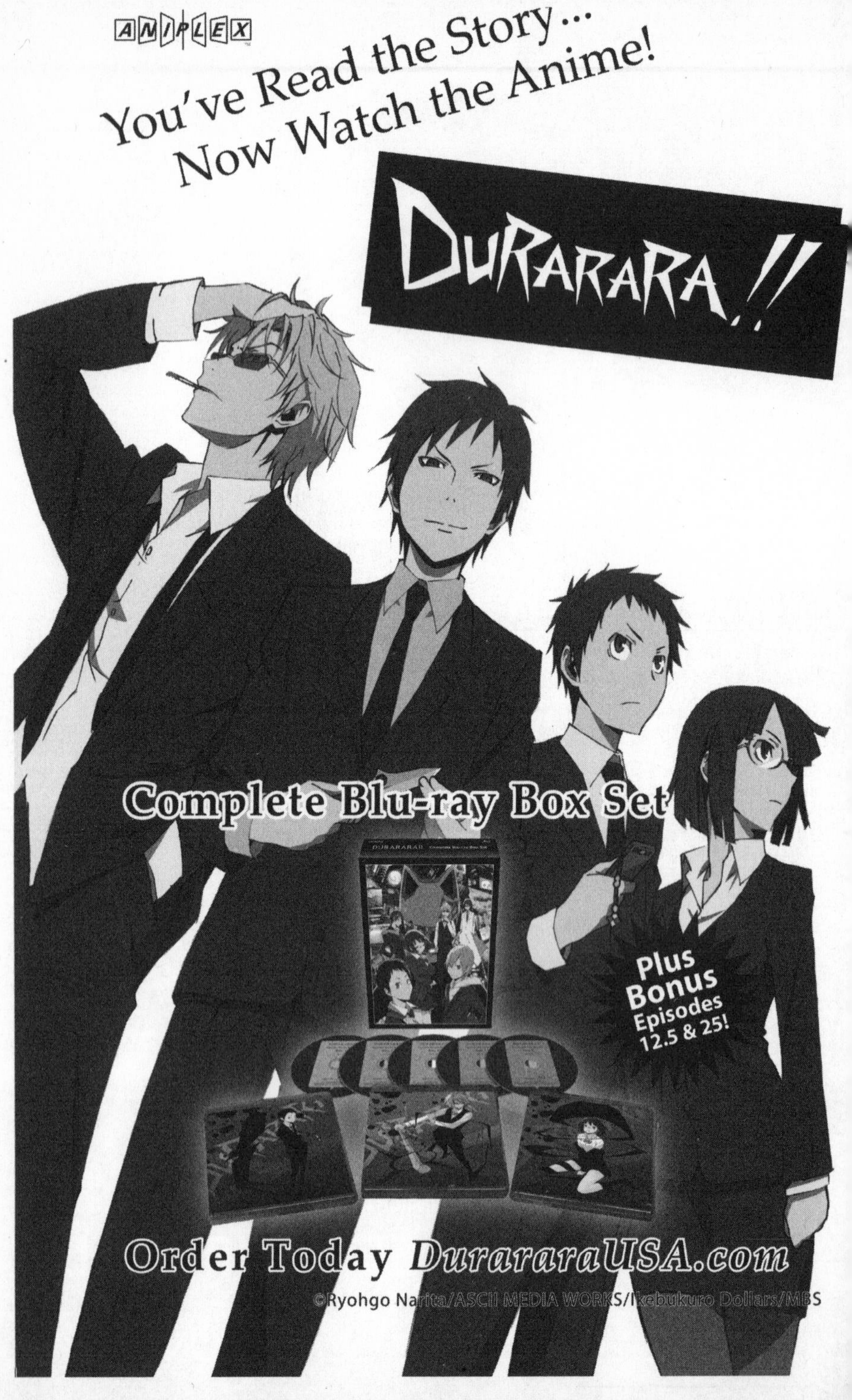
ANIPLEX
You've Read the Story...
Now Watch the Anime!
DURARARA!!
Complete Blu-ray Box Set
Plus Bonus Episodes 12.5 & 25!
Order Today DurararaUSA.com
©Ryohgo Narita/ASCII MEDIA WORKS/Ikebukuro Dollars/MBS

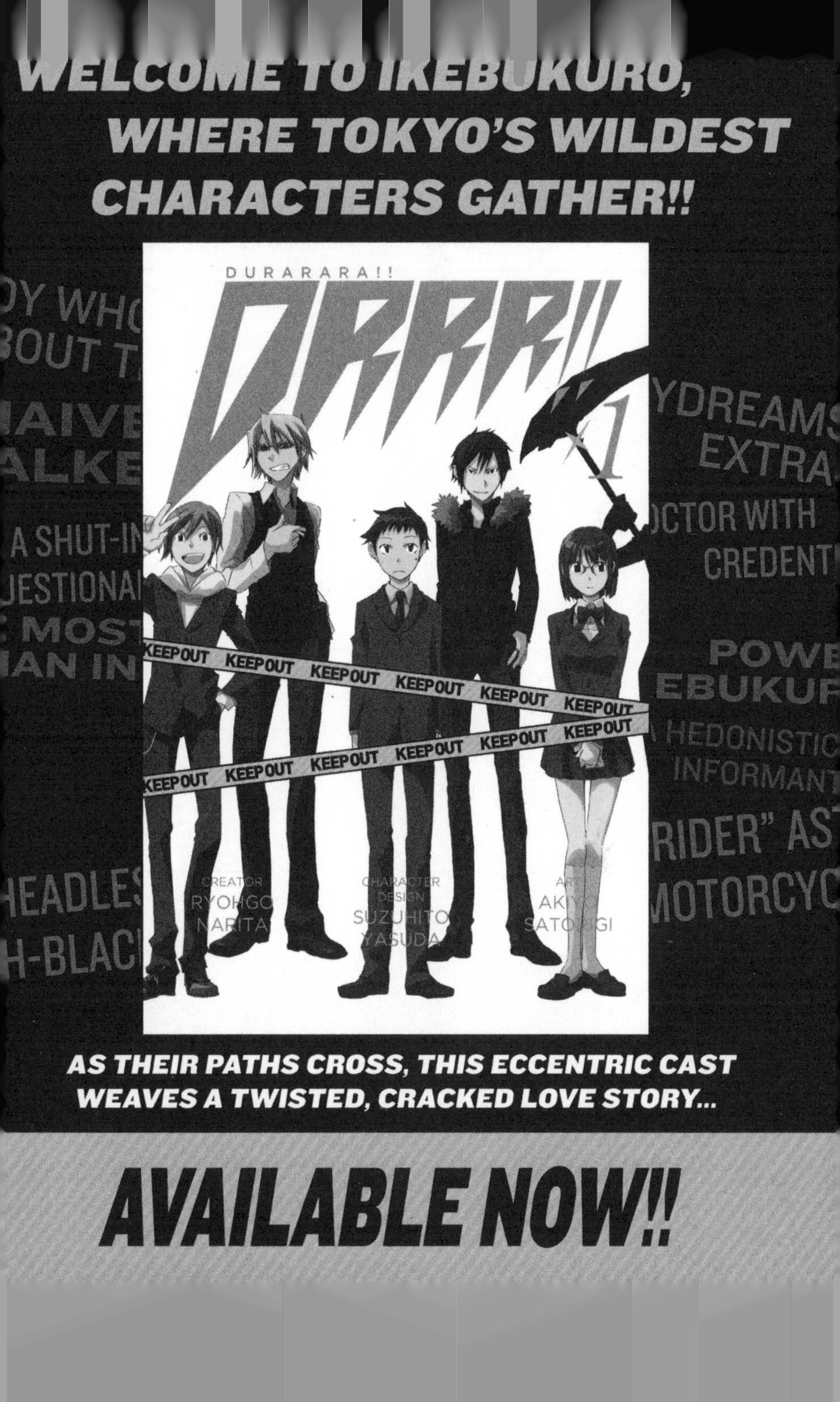
DURARARA!!
DRRR!!
1
KEEPOUT
CREATOR
RYOHGO
NARITA
CHARACTER
DESIGN
SUZUHITO
YASUDA
ART